SUMMER CYCLONE

SUMMER CYCLONE

MAGIC AT MYERS BEACH™ BOOK FOUR

ALAN B. GIBSON

DON'T MISS OUR NEW RELEASES

Join the Florid Romance email list to be notified of new releases and special promotions (which happen often) by following this link:

https://floridromance.lmbpn.com/about/sign-up-for-our-newsletter/

This book is a work of fiction. All of the characters, organizations, and events portrayed in this novel are either products of the author's imagination or are used fictitiously. Sometimes both.

Published by Florid Romance
an imprint of LMBPN Publishing
PMB 196, 2540 South Maryland Pkwy
Las Vegas, NV 89109

Version 1.00, August 2023
eBook ISBN: 979-8-88541-755-6
Print ISBN: 979-8-88878-614-7

THE SUMMER CYCLONE TEAM

Thanks to Jan Hunnicutt

Editor
The SkyFyre Editing Team

To Ken Wilson, one of the most generous and fascinating people I'll ever know. We met as liveaboard yacht neighbors and quickly became best friends. We traveled the world, shared a love of fresh, straight-out-of-the-oven Parisian croissants and Campari spritzes. He introduced me to the Amazon jungle and shared his secret to making flawless scrambled eggs. I will never forget how he kept me glued together after Scott died, nor will I forget watching him take his last breath during the writing of this book.

CHAPTER ONE

Theos

How do you say goodbye to the place you've called home for over a thousand years? This was my challenge as Lily and I prepared to lead our fairy subjects on a modern-day exodus from our home country to a new beginning on a California beach.

We didn't leave because we wanted to. I saw no other alternative. Since the fairy dust contamination, we had hung on as long as we could, but after today our reserves here were depleted. As king, I decided it was best that we roll the dice and take our chances by moving them all to Myers Beach to be with the rest of our fairies.

I say roll the dice because the move won't necessarily guarantee our safety or survival. Zsa Zsa Hajdu, the human who has tried to destroy us twice before, still threatens, and she could attack us anytime. Defending ourselves against her here without ample fairy dust would be foolish.

I was hedging my bets that we would have a new supply of dust in time to protect us. My brother Alias has not let up on the task, but without the final ingredient, he's taken the project about as far as he can. As soon as we arrive, I and the other kings will work doubly hard to locate it. Since we found the other elements in Myers Beach, we feel confident that the Yano we seek is hiding there, too.

The good news is that his most recent version is already improving the lifestyle of the fairies. After being dusted with it, they're seeing increased pep and vitality, and many find that they can once again do some basic magic. Sadly, in the long run, it lacks the power to keep us alive.

Since all of us were evacuating, King Zsombor and I decided to reach out to the Outliers, the fairies that don't claim allegiance to any of the three kingdoms. Neither Zsombor nor I had ever met any because they'd always kept their identities and whereabouts a secret, but we were sure they had to be out there. So when we sent the message that described our dire situation to our own fairies and announced the mandatory relocation, we used fairy telepathy to ensure we reached everyone with the same information. We encouraged them to join our exodus in the interest of their safety, and apparently we struck a chord. We weren't able to tell exactly how many showed up, but our guesstimate put the number in the thousands.

Before we left, Lily and I divided the remaining bit of pure fairy dust equally among all the fairies to give them extra energy for the flight and a bit more as a boost for the initial month of survival in their new world. Zsombor and Greta did the same for their subjects.

Then I and every man, woman, and child fairy took a position along the perimeter of our land. Queen Lily flew overhead, and when she gave the signal we focused our collective magic to erect an invisible protective dome over our entire kingdom. That way we'll have a home to return to, should our stay in Myers Beach be temporary.

We gathered together in front of our palace one final time, and despite the fear of doom that dug at my heart, watching our subjects push out their wings for the first time in many months brought tears to our eyes.

And I was never so proud as when, under the cover of night, several thousand brave six-inch fairies took to the air and fell into formation behind their majestic queens and flew off to an uncertain future.

CHAPTER TWO

The basketball-sized crystal orb that floated above the patient's bed spun slowly and noiselessly. It would glow periodically or sometimes emit subtle pulses of light in different colors as it monitored Princess Zoë's vital signs. At that hour, the signals were indicating a trend—a trend of no change in her condition.

Since they'd brought her to the clinic, that spinning ball had produced an identical full-body hologram every fifteen minutes. When Stefán noticed the latest one to emerge looked exactly like the previous one, he felt he could lean back in his chair and close his eyes.

He'd meant to rest for only a few moments, but the fatigue of remaining awake at her side day and night had finally gotten the best of him, and he fell asleep. When he heard Christophe shushing Julie in the doorway, he jerked to attention.

"Sorry, Your Royal Highness. I haven't been sleeping long, really."

"Please, Stefán, sit back down. And for goodness' sake,

after all we've been through, call me Christophe. I mean you risked your life for me by playing my stand-in in the battle against Zsa Zsa. I'm the one who should give *you* a title."

"Thanks for the offer, but I'm really not the title-type. Anyway, you know I was just doing my part and was glad to help."

"So how's my sister?" asked Christophe.

"No change, I'm afraid."

"Nothing at all?"

Stefán rolled his head in circles and massaged the back of his neck. "A few hours ago we thought her eyelids wanted to open, but… Still, I'm counting that as progress." His eyes lit up when he saw Christophe's takeout cup. "Is that one of those Queen Greta's Fairy Frappuccinos from Joe's?"

Christophe nodded. "Gosh, I didn't realize you liked them. I would have brought you one."

"I think I might. It's chai, after all, isn't it?" Stefán asked.

Christophe passed him his paper cup. "Yes. Here. Have a taste."

Stefán put up his hand. "Oh, no. I would never dream of drinking from a king's cup. Are you sure?"

Christophe shook his head and then rattled the ice cubes. "Don't be ridiculous."

Stefán held it to his nose to enjoy the aroma.

"The inmates here have been begging us to put it on our menu in the tearoom, but I didn't want Joe to think we were competing with him, so I never followed through." He took a taste before he handed it back. "Mmm. Dee-lish. Maybe it's time for me to rethink things."

"I'll get him one," called a woman's voice from outside in the hallway. "I was going to pick up one for myself, anyway."

"Who was that?" Stefán asked. He and Julie didn't really know each other. He'd only met her once, and that was briefly when she'd been a guest at the glitzy gala opening of The Fairy Kingdom Teahouse where at the time he'd been the manager.

It was common knowledge that he and Greta had been at odds for some time before her store burned and she married King Zsombor and became a fairy queen. He'd often grumbled that the Saturday morning noise from the rowdy skit she staged next door on the boardwalk for the tourists made it difficult for his customers to carry on conversations and that it disrupted the teahouse ambiance.

She'd countered that her weekly play was responsible for attracting dozens of tourists to the businesses on both sides of her store—customers who might not have thought to pay them a visit, otherwise.

His biggest objection was to her fog machine and the thick blankets of pea soup that discouraged customers from sitting in the outdoor dining area. She claimed that she'd been using the machine for years, long before the teahouse began serving customers outside, and that The Fairy Kingdom should have taken that into consideration when they added their patio seating.

The impasse continued until he'd saved her life in a daring rescue from the blazing fire that was consuming her building. Prior to the fire, Julie had been working closely with Greta, albeit from home, and therefore because of her loyalty, she and Stefán rarely crossed paths. By the time he and Greta had reconciled, Julie had left the country for the skating competition, so they'd had few opportunities to get acquainted.

"Gee, she didn't have to make a trip to Joe's just for me," said Stefán. "But it was awfully nice, considering that I hardly know her."

"Oh, I'm sorry," said Christophe. "I assumed you did. I would have introduced you."

"No worries. I mean, I know she was best friends with Lily and Greta, but I don't think we ever met formally."

"Well, you can add me to that list. She's one of my best friends, too. You probably didn't know that we knocked around Europe together for several months. And we both are fairly decent on skateboards."

"Decent? No way. I heard you are a champion. I've always wanted to learn."

"Then we should all go to the skatepark sometime. You probably don't know that Julie had a hand in getting it funded and set up, either. So, do you play any sports?"

Stefán tried to suppress a yawn. "Yeah, when I lived in Europe, I played underwater rugby."

"Does Alias know that? I haven't heard him mention that he played, but it sounds like it would be up his alley. Anyway, I'm sure he'd help organize a team." He took a big slug of the frappuccino. "By the way, you look terrible. When was the last time you got any sleep?"

"It's been a while. I've been watching your sister twenty-four seven. Then, of course, Theos and Lily recently arrived with several thousand new fairies, which I helped get settled." He yawned again. "And tonight, Zsombor and Greta are due in with theirs."

Christophe sympathized with Stefán's workload, and for the next twenty minutes or so he shared heart-warming stories about growing up with his sister. When Julie came back with a frappuccino in each hand, Stefán stood and extended his hand.

"I realize that we kind of know each other, but to formally introduce myself, I'm Stefán."

She juggled the cups so that he got one and she was left with a free hand, and they both giggled when they finally shook hands. She gestured to herself. "Yeah. So…Julie, obviously."

When he'd first seen her at The Fairy Kingdom's opening night gala, he remembered thinking she looked the epitome of glamour. Her long, wavy blonde hair with sun-bleached lighter streaks had shone golden under the warm lighting.

Now she'd dyed her hair a brilliant platinum and cut it drastically into an inverted bob, with feathery bangs that contrasted well with the pixie undercut at the back of her head. And those eyes he'd once thought a simple brown turned out to be vividly hazel, with flecks of gold and green that glittered under the white lights of the sickbay.

In contrast to the simple black she'd worn to the gala, that morning his eyes went to the blue Converse sneakers with little white daisies on them and the knee-length light yellow V-neck dress with an empire waist. Her dark jean jacket was covered in patches depicting unfamiliar logos, and by rolling the sleeves to her elbows, she'd made the outfit a curious mix of traditionally feminine with an arresting edge that intrigued him. Just being near her lifted his spirits.

He knew from Greta and Lily that she was fiercely loyal, kind, and overall a bright, cheerful spirit, but her sly little crooked smile told him that she was shrewd, and maybe a fan of the spontaneous, the surprising. Perhaps even the dangerous.

The dichotomy between her sense of style and what he'd heard about her fascinated him, and he hoped he'd have the privilege of bumping into her now that she was back in town.

To distract himself he fished in his pocket and pulled out a ten-dollar bill. As he handed it to her, his throat went dry.

"Will this cover it?" he squeaked. "I think that's what Joe was charging the other day when I stopped in for something else. But he raises his prices all the time, so—"

"I know. Crazy, right?" She waved away his offer of money, but she accepted the chair he pulled over for her. She looked around the room at the few other empty hospital beds and scrunched her face. "Even crazier is that I just figured out that this sickbay is in about the same spot as where Greta's office used to be."

"Yeah, this place has been redone quite a bit, just since I've been here." He looked over at Zoë again and up at the orb. "I heard you'd been gone for quite a while. How do you like being back?"

"It's weird. A lot has changed around here, not just this building. I'd planned to stay with my folks for a long time, but when Alias told me that Lily and Theos were back, I came running.

"I hadn't seen them in ages, and for the first couple nights, I stayed with them up at their compound. God, we had so much fun. I felt like we were in one of those movies where a bunch of best friends get together in a fabulous beach house." She took a long swig of her drink. "But last night I moved back to my old apartment."

"And how is it living above your new, um, tenants?"

Her face tensed and she jerked her head toward Christophe. "Does Stefán know that I know about…you know?" He nodded, and she relaxed and answered his question.

"I was going to rent out the middle floors, anyway, and since the Third Kingdom was looking for space, well, the timing couldn't have been better. And since Christophe added soundproofing to the entire building, I can't even tell anyone else is there."

"Well, your loft is huge. I can't imagine having so much space," said Stefán.

She lowered her cup. "Wait. You've been there?"

"Stefán helped with the renovations," explained Christophe. "Along with a few others."

A look of relief fell over her face. "Oh. Well, thank you. In that case, your frappuccinos will be on the house from now on." She held up her cup and they touched their paper cups together in a mock toast. "Truth is, I don't really need the whole place. I basically run my business from my phone, so honestly, I can live anywhere. But you guys really did a great job. It's beautiful."

Stefán shifted in his chair. "So I was wondering. Did you notice anything in particular that makes it special?" When he winked at Christophe she caught the exchange.

"Okay, guys. What's the private joke?"

Christophe laughed. "It's a surprise. Trust me. You'll

know when you hear it. But I'll give you a hint. Stefán helped Alias install it."

"Now you've got me worried." She took a sip of her drink and became silent for a moment. Then she turned to Stefán. "Oh, so, then, I guess you're one of them, too?"

He nodded. "Guilty."

He stood and motioned to Christophe to swap chairs. He gave up his chair next to Zoë so Christophe could be closer to his sister, and he moved to the other side of the bed where Julie was sitting. From that new perspective he could see both Christophe's and Zoë's faces, and he couldn't help noticing the striking resemblance of the siblings.

Though at the moment her condition made her look pallid, he could tell that Zoë's bronze skin would match Christophe's. She had his same sharp, slightly upturned nose, high cheekbones, almond-shaped eyes, and full lips, too.

The only difference Stefán could see came with their hair. Zoë's curly hair was cropped into a messy undercut with the top curled in well-defined medium-sized corkscrews. If she hadn't spent so long in a coma, unable to control the frizz and style, it would be an edgy, bold, and on-trend look. If Christophe's hair was any shorter, they'd look almost like twins.

Even while lying in her hospital bed, Zoë was tragically beautiful. Serene, as if she'd just fallen asleep. Free from any worries or anxiety, her delicate features looked as though she might break apart like glass if Stefán breathed the wrong way.

It was that feeling that tugged at his heart. Hoping that

he'd eventually see the day when she opened her eyelids made him determined to get her back to full health. He cleared his throat and forced himself to look away from the unresponsive patient.

"So, Christophe, how do you like being the Third King?" he asked.

"So far, so good. It's finally sunk in that it's official. I suppose by now you've heard how my homophobic aunt banished me from my family and my kingdom. And how she screwed with my mind to make me forget who I was and where I came from."

Stefán nodded. "Alias told me that she did the same thing to him. How did he put it? Something about letting you remember that you'd fallen head over heels for each other, but that she made it so you couldn't remember who the other person was? Man, that had to suck."

"Yeah. She was a cruel one, that's for sure. Before I got reunited with Alias, I'd been carrying that heartache around with me. On top of it, I had no inkling that I was a king. All that time I'd thought of myself as a normal fairy. Looking back, I can think of a million times that king magic might have come in handy.

"It's funny how I managed to do some pretty phenomenal stuff, though. The extent of my magic sometimes shocked Alias, but I think I was even more surprised, because things just kind of happened by accident. Since neither one of us had any idea who I really was, and with all our memory gaps, we both chalked it up to someone teaching me some 'advanced magic' somewhere along the line."

Stefán leaned against the side of Julie's chair. "I've often wondered what it would be like partnering with someone from, you know, a different station. Was it tricky with Alias being royal and you not, or at least thinking you weren't?"

"Not really. Honestly, we were attracted to each other from the get-go, and we had so much in common that our backgrounds never entered into the equation. I was never one of those social climbers. We'd already been living together for several months before I learned he was a prince.

"He didn't care where I came from, either. Come to think of it, he never asked, not that I would have been able to tell him, so it all worked out well."

Julie placed a gentle hand over Stefán's. He hadn't even realized he'd rested his own on her shoulder. "I can vouch as to how crazy these guys are for each other. They couldn't stand to be apart for one day."

"Well, I'm impressed. I should be so lucky."

"You and me, both," she said.

"Look. There were some awkward times, for sure," Christophe continued. "We have the usual tiffs most couples have, and I admit that I did go through a period of feeling inferior. That was all on me, though. He never made me feel that way.

"Here I've been rambling on and all you asked was if I liked being king. Well, I do. Alias gets a kick out of the fact that I have a real job now. We still have coffee together at the pool every morning, and then I'm off and at the palace by seven."

Stefán laughed. "So, the king commutes."

"Yep, just like people do. Not that I have to take the

subway or anything. I do fly. And we started taking turns. Sometimes he and I sleep at my palace, and he's the one who has to do the traveling."

Stefán cocked his head. "Speaking of royals, what's it like sharing a house with another king, and a queen, if I might ask?"

"Again, so far, so good. Technically the house belongs to Theos and Lily, of course, but the guest house is huge, as you know, so about the only thing we share is the pool. Lily's son Jamie is away at boarding school, so it's just been the four of us, and Theos and I have always been very close. "

Julie bent forward to look at the patient. Then she looked up at Christophe.

"It's hard to believe that after all our time together, I never learned your sister's name."

Christophe's eyes watered. "Zoë. A name that's been in the family for centuries."

Stefán adjusted Zoë's blanket and put a finger on her cheek. He and Alias were in constant communication about her condition. Alias had even shared a private fear that she might not make it, and that if she did wake up, there was the possibility that she could be seriously disabled.

As Zoë's king, Christophe should have had sufficient power to bring her out of her coma and restore her body. But after he made several unsuccessful attempts, they concluded that Zsa Zsa had occupied her body for too long and had absorbed so much of her fairy-ness that she was beyond his help.

"Christophe, if you need to go, I've got this," said Stefán.

"I was planning to stay with her anyway, at least until she comes out of it."

After Christophe left, the room became quiet again, and for some time Stefán and Julie sat without speaking.

Finally, he turned and looked into Julie's sparkling eyes. "You don't have to stay either."

"But I don't mind," she answered. She took a book from her bag, and when she started to read, Stefán got up and consulted the orb. Discouraged at the lack of progress, he sat back down and leaned into the chair. In a few moments, he nodded off.

He jerked his head awake briefly and smiled when he felt the blanket Julie was draping over him. She gave him a sweet smile, and he fell back asleep.

CHAPTER THREE

The next day Stefán stared at the mirror, not recognizing the man with the huge dark bags under his eyes looking back. He'd spent another all-nighter getting Greta and Zsombor's fairies situated, and it hadn't been easy. When they'd onboarded the previous groups, they'd known how many and whom to expect, and they'd had time to prepare appropriate accommodations.

The sudden and hasty back-to-back emigration of thousands of fairies from two kingdoms made it impossible to give his ground operation an accurate count in advance, and it was not until after they arrived that Stefán learned how far off their estimates had been.

The discrepancy was in large part due to the unknowable number of Outlier fairies who joined in the mass exodus at the last minute. After receiving the message from the kings, they'd swarmed in from all corners of the globe and fallen immediately into formation with the others.

While the orderly assimilation of fairies had always been a hallmark of The Fairy Kingdom, the sheer quantity of unanticipated migrants created unpreventable logistical nightmares and snafus in the check-in procedure. Exhausted newcomers found themselves waiting to be assigned rooms in endless lines which gave the impression that they had arrived at a refugee camp and not an oasis that promised a better life in a new and safer home.

Care needed to be taken not to split families and couples, and while many fairies insisted on being placed with their own kind, keeping kingdoms separate wasn't always possible. Stefán managed to squeeze in a few more rooms, but there was only so much magic he could do.

He was off the hook at least as far as Theos and Lily were concerned. Fortunately, their own luxurious compound lay waiting for them. Queen Greta and King Zsombor were a different matter. They were moving back into The Fairy Kingdom, which meant that Stefán had to vacate the royal suite that he'd been enjoying as manager in their absence.

Because he'd been up all night taking care of everyone else, he'd forgotten his own needs and ended up shoehorned into a tiny room off the kitchen next to the sick bay. The bed was too small and his legs had hung over the end, so when he finally called it a night, he didn't sleep well.

He woke up early. The day ahead would also be long and tedious, settling unfinished business and complaints from the night before. To give some fairies a place to sleep, he'd had to force them to double up temporarily, and those would be the first issues he'd have to sort out.

The day would require a serious caffeine fix, but before he dragged himself to Joe's, he stopped by the clinic to check in on Zoë. Through the doorway he could see the back of the head of the attendant on duty, so he raced next door and picked up a couple of high-test coffees and a frappuccino to go. When he got back to her room, Zoë was lying on her side and the attendant was asleep.

A quick consultation with the orb showed him that fifteen minutes earlier she had rolled over on her own. It did not, however, indicate that she had regained consciousness, so he assumed that her steady breathing was a reflection of continued deep sleep. In the meantime, he rousted the attendant and sent him to his room with a reprimand and a personal vow that Zoë was never to be left unattended again.

He wasn't sure if it was the double espresso or her condition's startling improvement that perked him up, but he was glad to be wide awake. It was still early in the morning by fairy standards, and given the late hour that they'd turned in, he didn't expect to hear complaints from the newcomers for several hours. He called for a new assistant.

The assignment was to not take their eyes off Zoë while he was in the shower. The second she made the slightest movement they were to contact him. His new broom closet of a room did not have a private bath, so he used the communal showers of the spa. As he expected, nobody was up and he had the facilities to himself. He was getting dressed when he got the message that Julie had arrived and relieved the assistant, and he changed his mind. Instead of what he'd chosen he put on a simple white button-down and black slacks.

"I thought you might need to take a breather," she said

from her position at the side of Zoë's bed. "I can fill in for you all day if you'd like. You looked so tired yesterday."

"Thanks," he said from the doorway. "Still am, and if you thought I looked horrible then, I better stay over here. The bags under my eyes are epic."

"Don't be ridiculous. And I didn't say you looked horrible. I said you looked tired."

He walked over and handed her the frappuccino. She was right. He was exhausted and had bought it for himself as a caffeine fix. But he liked her kind eyes and appreciated her down-to-earth honesty, so he wanted her to have it. He'd used magic to perk himself up instead.

"I just picked this up a few minutes ago from Joe's. Help yourself. I know you like them." She looked at his face as he approached, and he felt that she was studying his features. "I see you staring. I was right about those bags, wasn't I?"

Julie smiled and kept staring. "Yeah, they're good sized, all right, but I wasn't paying attention to them. It's that you are so much younger than I expected. Greta always talked about how competent you were at running things in the teahouse. I think she used the term 'prim and proper,' so I assumed you were older."

He blushed and was about to make a self-deprecating remark when they heard Zoë moan. He spun around and consulted the orb, but he didn't need to delve into the promising new data it was spitting out. Zoë had lost her lifeless pallor and was looking refreshed.

Her lips quivered, and when he and Julie leaned in to listen, their heads touched. Zoë rolled back over on her back and her eyelids fluttered. Then slowly they opened.

The strong reddish-brown burnt umber stared up at

him, and Stefán couldn't help but notice her eyes matched her brother's perfectly. With them finally opened, he noticed that she was even prettier now.

"You," she uttered at him. "You're still here."

"Of course, I am," he said.

"No, I mean, you've been with me the whole time. I know you have, because I've heard you talking."

Stefán's eyes watered, and though he knew it was completely inappropriate, he pressed his lips on her cheek.

"I'm sorry for this indiscretion, Princess," he said. "I'm just so grateful to see you back with us."

When he looked over at Julie, he saw her hazel eyes flash with something like understanding. Then she turned away and busied herself with pulling out another book from her leather messenger bag.

CHAPTER FOUR

Zoë squeezed Stefán's hand and blinked. Then she saw Julie sitting in the chair behind him.

"Who are you? You don't look like a fairy."

"This is Julie," Stefán explained. "And no, she's a human. She's your brother's best friend, and she's been sitting here with me waiting for you to wake up."

Julie swallowed. "Good morning, Highness." She looked at Stefán and mouthed her question, "Is that what I should call her?" He nodded.

"Hello, Julie. Thank you for using my title, but listen. Please call me Zoë. I don't come from a culture of first names, so it's fun to hear people use mine."

"What do you mean? Your brother has always gone by his."

Zoë tilted her head. "My brother doesn't have a first name."

The bewilderment on Julie's face would have been hard to miss. Stefán was equally puzzled, because he'd only known her brother by the name Christophe. He wondered if Zoë was the one who was truly confused.

Since she'd fallen into a coma, he'd been studying up on that medical emergency. He learned that while people waking up from one can often start out confused, they generally came around, though often gradually. He hoped that she would be like one of those and recover completely and quickly. Still, he'd read too much not to be realistic. Others didn't recover so nicely, and there was a distinct possibility that Zoë could suffer from disabilities caused by the damage to her brain.

Her case was more complicated, of course. A witch had taken up residence in her body, after all, though how long she'd controlled Zoë was unknowable, as was the extent of the havoc to her brain and other organs.

On top of that, she was missing a lot of information about her brother. She'd lost track of him from the moment their aunt had banished him, and it would take some time to bring them both up to speed on the enormous life changes they'd both gone through during those blank years. Stefán took a breath, resigned to expecting the unexpected for a while.

"Sure he does," said Julie. "His name is Christophe."

Zoë looked out into the room. "Hmm. It sounds like we're talking about different people. See, in our lineage the first-born child of the king is not given a name, only the title, 'Third King.' In his case, we called him the 'young Third King' to differentiate him from our father, who was still alive."

"But they gave you a first name."

"Yes." She grimaced. "Our kingdom always gives one to the spare."

Julie scratched her head. "But you at least share the same family name, right? DuBois?"

Zoë sat up in her bed. "He told you that? That's weird. Our family doesn't have a last name, and DuBois is not a name I recognize from anywhere in our family tree. I know, because I've done a lot of reading about us." She turned to Stefán. "I wonder why he needed to pick names, anyway. Do you have any idea?"

He laughed. "I do, and it's a funny story. He tells it better than I do, but the gist is that, after your aunt banished him in the cyclone funnel, he literally ended up on the grass in the Bois de Boulogne in Paris.

"As an extra part of her punishment, she'd wiped out any memory of his family, so when someone asked his name, he needed an answer quickly, and he improvised. Apparently, at that precise moment, a bus rumbled by with an advertisement on the side for a Café Christophe. Then he looked behind him, and the trees in the park gave him the inspiration for DuBois as his new surname."

"Hmm. That sounds like him. But it doesn't explain why he needed them in the first place." She put her hand on her throat. "I'm so thirsty. I think I'm going to conjure some tea. Shall I get three cups?" She clapped her hands. Then she snapped her fingers. She clapped again and then snapped a few more times. When no tea appeared, Stefán saw the fear in her eyes. He hoped she hadn't seen the same in his.

Julie passed Zoë her frappuccino. "Here. While we're

waiting for the tea, why don't you try this? I promise that I haven't touched it."

Zoë's hand trembled and the ice rattled as she brought it to her lips.

"Mmm!" she said. "As Alias would say all the time back in the palace, 'Dee-lish!'" While she took another swallow, Stefán dropped his hand to his side, and after he noiselessly snapped his fingers, a silver tray with tea for three instantly appeared on Zoë's lap.

"Finally!" she said. "I was afraid I'd lost my touch." She handed the frappuccino back to Julie and licked her lips. "Yum. Thank you."

Stefán faked a laugh and poured tea. "Better late than never. I'm sure you are just out of practice." She took a sip of tea and scrunched her face.

"Gosh. How long was I in the coma?"

"A good while," said Stefán. "Why?"

"Because you're right. I clearly am out of practice. I conjured jasmine, but this tastes like Earl Grey."

It was obvious to Stefán that Zoë had lost at least some of her magic powers, but he'd manifested the tea to keep that fact from her. He feared that during her delicate recovery, discovering her loss of magic might send her into serious depression. Maybe into something worse. What she really needed was time to recuperate. Besides, the loss of magic might be temporary. Either way, she'd confront that issue on her own soon enough.

He sent messages of her emergence from the coma to the three kings, who decided as a group that Christophe and Alias should visit first so as not to overwhelm her. The two rushed over, and Stefán intercepted them in the hallway before they went into her room.

"Zoë is wide awake and alert. I haven't checked the monitors, but from what I've seen in the last few minutes, she's in excellent physical condition, especially considering what she's been through. But—" Christophe stepped forward toward the door.

Stefán wasn't through briefing them, and he took a deep breath before he blocked the door to the kings. He touched Christophe's arm instead. "I fear that she's lost her magic…at least at the moment." He stepped to the side and let them pass.

"Hey, good morning, Zoë." Christophe set a vase of yellow tulips on her bedside table. "Welcome back to the living!"

Stefán and Julie relinquished their chairs, and Zoë's face brightened at seeing her brother and Alias at her side.

Alias let Christophe catch up, and while they were chatting, he placed his hands on the orb to download her recent medical and neurological findings. The startling report indicated that Zsa Zsa had not only absorbed Zoë's magic, but she'd also stolen her wings. He hoped Zoë would have a chance to recuperate more before she discovered that second, equally tragic loss.

"They tell me you're going by Christophe these days." Zoë's eyebrows scrunched in confusion as she gripped her brother's hand. "Stefán told me."

"Yes, I am. But even Stefán doesn't know the whole story. The funnel cloud that took me away from the palace that day dumped me in Paris. Our aunt's spell erased all family memories, so I had no idea who I was, and I needed a name. I knew that I was a fairy, of course, but I only recently learned that I had been the real Third King all along." He squeezed Alias' bicep. "Thanks to this guy."

Alias sat back next to Zoë. "Do you feel like talking about what happened? I mean, none of us can imagine the horrors of someone invading your body."

"Gosh. I hardly know where to begin."

"You can start by telling us how she got in. Do you remember?"

She started at the beginning, at her brother's horrible eighteenth birthday party when the boys' pompous tutor, Györfi, revealed to their aunt that Christophe and Alias were gay. The aunt excommunicated Christophe from the family and tossed Alias and Györfi out, too.

"I never could figure out how you could stand that man," she said. "Thank goodness, I didn't have to study with him. Anyway, things happened very quickly. At the same time she sent Mister Györfi off in one of her funnel clouds, she dropped dead from a heart attack."

"So, that's what happened to her," said Christophe. "I wish I could say something nice about her, but I can't."

"Nobody liked her, including me," said Zoë. "And I was not unhappy that she was out of my life, but her death left me in a very uncomfortable position."

As the eldest child, Christophe automatically became the Third King when his father died. He couldn't officially take charge until he turned eighteen, however, so until then their aunt had been serving as Regent.

"But see, a few seconds before she died, the clock struck twelve, which made you king and things got really complicated. With you banished, and our aunt dead, the crown fell to me."

Though she'd been a naive child when that happened, she'd done her best to follow the advice of her advisers to enact the new laws and treaties she and her brother had talked about fixing when they were young. So while she mourned the absence of her brother, at least their kingdom thrived.

"The thing was, I inherited the crown but didn't get the true king power. That, of course, meant that you had it, which also meant that you were still alive. I sent our senior fairies to search for you, and now I know why they came up empty-handed. You'd given yourself a new name. Then the dust poisoning happened and everything in the fairy world came to a crashing halt.

"I had no idea what I was doing." She gripped Christophe's hand. "I mean, everyone believed I was king. But I knew I was only pretending, because you were out there somewhere.

"It was during those uncertain days that Zsa Zsa Hadju showed up. One day she just appeared in the solarium where I was sitting. It would have been impossible for a normal person to get past the guards, so I assumed she'd been cleared."

Christophe turned to Alias. "Well, we now know that someone showed her how to access the tunnel and the secret passage to the solarium."

"That's right," added Alias. "She escaped the same way. What do you bet that Györfi was responsible for telling her? It couldn't have been anyone else. I can't imagine how the two of them found each other, but now it makes sense that he was in on it with her."

Zoë continued, "She told me she was the Fortune Teller to the Crowned Heads, or something like that, and that she'd been sent by a friend to read my palms. I told her I wanted nothing to do with that and asked her to leave. But she had this very convincing way of making me do what she wanted, like she was hypnotizing me. Before I knew it, she'd talked me into putting this red pendant around my neck, and from then on I was under her spell."

"I know that pendant," said Alias.

"Yeah." Zoë's voice started to go dry, and she took a sip of tea. "I'm getting a chill just remembering that look of pure evil in her eyes. And that icky voice. It dripped with contempt.

"I saw her rub the red stone and then I felt her press against me. That was it. The second she possessed me, I felt heavy and nauseous. I mean, don't forget suddenly there were two of us inside my body.

"I could tell by the eyes of the palace staff that they wondered why I, the girl who'd always been a tomboy, was suddenly paying so much attention to my clothes. They seemed shocked that I started wearing makeup, too.

"I felt silly with the long fingernails and hated her ridiculous outfits. Other little things drove me crazy, too, like Zsa Zsa's obsession with wearing perfume, which gave me constant headaches.

"Still, I know there were courtiers in the palace who liked my new look. I even heard some of them say that it was high time the princess ditched her jeans and stepped up to look the part of the Third King.

"Of course, I couldn't speak or do anything to resist. Zsa Zsa was in complete control of my body. I felt weaker and weaker and could just tell she was draining more life out of me every day."

"That's exactly how Zsombor felt," said Alias. "She didn't possess him like you, but she used the same pendant to transfer his spirit to her." He swallowed. "She almost sucked his whole life out of him."

Christophe patted him on the shoulder. "Thank goodness you and Greta were able to sever it before it was too late."

"She used it again, this time on Christophe, when she realized he was the one with the king power," said Stefán. "But of course, since I was pretending to be him, she was really siphoning out my spirit, not his, so believe me, I know the feeling. I felt weak, too. That witch is really powerful. Believe me, I was glad when that little skit of ours was over and I got my energy back."

"What do you mean by 'your little skit?'" Zoë was trembling so much she needed both hands to steady her teacup.

"Allow me to tell you what went down," came a voice from the doorway. "Because I choreographed it."

Zoë gave the newcomer an inquiring look, and Alias introduced her to Dame Gabor, the award-winning former actress and grandam of the fairies.

"Your Highness." Dame Gabor gave a respectful bow before approaching the bed. "I prefer calling the skit a sting operation. The ruse had two parts, and it needed to be complicated, because we needed to trap Zsa Zsa yet keep her alive so we could rescue you. Since she'd taken over your body, extracting you was going to be delicate, to say the least, and we had to be extremely careful."

She began to pantomime the action as she described how Stefán had pretended to be Zoë's brother, and how she herself had transformed herself to play the role of Alias.

"We both played the characters so convincingly, if I do say so myself, that Zsa Zsa fell for it. Eventually, when the real Christophe and the real Alias appeared, they disarmed her with their magic long enough to split you out of her before it was too late.

"You collapsed to the floor, and while we were attending to you, that damned Zsa Zsa got away. Unfortunately, by then she'd absorbed enough magic from you that it was easy." Dame Gabor paused and held an outstretched arm to her audience. "She still roams the planet with your princess power and is going to remain a threat until we finally put an end to her and her wicked ways."

Zoë reached out her hand. "You know, listening to you relate that story, I felt as though somehow I knew you."

Dame Gabor turned to Alias and chuckled. "Well, then at least we know she's gotten her memory back. I played at her palace several times back when she was a child."

"I can't thank you enough, Dame Gabor," Zoë said. "It must have been a nightmare for all of you. Please stay and have tea. I'll get us another cup." She snapped her fingers. Stefán thought fast and snapped his at the same time, and a cup appeared.

Worried that continuing to relive their shared horrific ordeal would do more harm to Zoë than good, Alias changed the subject.

"Why don't we try to focus on the positives?" He pulled the orb to him and clicked around for a second before pulling back. "It's predicting that you should be able to walk in a day or two, so I'll set you up with a physical therapist who will help you relearn how to be in control of your own body." He stood. "And I suggest we move her to your palace, Christophe. What do you think?"

Stefán frowned. "Of course, having her stay there will make it more difficult for me to look after her."

"I realize that, and I'm sorry," said Alias. "I'm only thinking of her security."

"I can take over," Julie offered. "After all, I live just upstairs."

"Then it's settled," said Christophe. "Now, I think we should go, so we don't overexert her."

They said their goodbyes, and after they left, Zoë sniffled. Her eyes were glassy with tears Stefán thought she'd been holding in. Julie handed her a tissue, and as Zoë plucked it from her hand, she saw the book in Julie's lap.

"What're you reading?" she asked.

"*Legends and Lattes*," Julie answered. She grinned and held the book out so Zoë could see the cover, which depicted two women, one with bright pink skin and horns protruding from her forehead, and one with bright green skin and tusks coming out of her smiling mouth. "It's about Viv, an orc barbarian, who opens the first coffee shop the city of Thune has ever seen."

Julie blushed when she realized that Stefán was still in the room, but he thought it was cute the way the bright red bleached into her cheeks and down her neck. And as she pulled the book back to her chest, Stefán found her momentary self-consciousness endearing, especially since he'd only known her as carefree. "I—I'm kinda obsessed with romances. Specifically romances with fantasy elements."

Zoë's bronze eyes grew wide. "Where can you find books like that here? We don't have anything like that in the palace library, and I've read almost everything in there."

Julie lit up. "Are you ever in luck. It just so happens that there's an amazing indie bookshop on the ground level of the building that houses your palace. It's actually my building. Your New Third Kingdom rents the middle floors, and I live on the top floor."

She placed her book in Zoë's lap face down, so she could read the summary. "You can have it. I've read it a few times. The store has all kinds of hidden gems, like this. And, if there's a book you want that they don't have, they'll order it for you. I love that store so much!"

Zoë fingered the worn spine of the novel. "I miss reading so much."

"Before you dig into that, though," Stefán said, "we should probably get you moved and settled. And Alias is right. It'll be more comfortable for you there."

"Right," Zoë said. "Let's go." She clapped her hands and snapped her fingers.

Stefán bit his lip before he interceded again, but he silently snapped his fingers and transported all three to Julie's building at the other end of the boardwalk. Zoë's rooms were on the palace floor, which was human-sized and a lucky break for Julie.

"Whoa," Julie said as she fell into an oversized chair. "Trippy."

CHAPTER FIVE

"One Queen Greta's Fairy Frappuccino and a blueberry scone, please, Derek." Stefán had learned the name of the young boy behind the counter at Joe's Java Joint from Alias. He'd also informed him that Derek was Joe's gay grandson and the catalyst behind Joe's new appreciation for being a good gay ally. His conversion was the only reason Alias and Christophe had decided to patronize the café again after their boycott. "For here, if you don't mind."

"Stefán, right?" Derek asked as he fiddled with the espresso machine behind the counter. "That's the third time you've been in this week. Don't tell me we're running The Fairy Kingdom out of business."

Stefán smiled at the joke and shook his head. "No. I just happen to like shots of espresso with my tea, and we don't offer that kind of thing yet." When Derek handed over the scone, Stefán added, "Also, I'm meeting some people here."

"Well, if you're here for the PFLAG meeting, you're early." He looked at the wall clock. "It's not for a few more hours." He handed over the finished drink. "You know what that is, don't you?"

Stefán nodded. "Yes, but I don't have kids...yet. I'm meeting friends." He tapped his credit card on the reader and placed a few bills in the tip jar.

"You know that you don't have to be a parent. You can also be a friend. The group could use some more people who are, y'know, actually with the times." Derek shook his head. "Now that my grandpa is on board, I really wish my parents would come. At least give it a try."

"Wishes are powerful things," Stefán said. He leaned into the theatrics he'd seen Greta use so many times and wiggled his fingers at Derek to lighten the mood. Then he touched the young man's forehead. "Poof!"

Derek's eyes were bright with contained laughter.

"Does this mean that you're now my cool fairy godfather? I'd like that."

Stefán shrugged. "Why not? Anyway, try asking your folks again tonight. I have a sneaking suspicion that they'll be closer to going to one of those meetings than you think." Derek's hold on his laughter finally broke, and he waved Stefán off with an extra scone for his trouble.

Like every fairy who had been getting by with less during the fairy dust shortage, Stefán hadn't granted a wish in ages. While Alias' newest dust concoction fell short of extending fairies' lives, it had restored that particular power, and Stefán felt deeply satisfied from actually granting one.

"I'll be in tomorrow morning. Let me know how it went, okay?" He waited for Derek to promise before he made his way to the back of the café where two men and a woman were waiting at a table for four.

He'd met Magda the day before in the bookstore when he stopped in to special order a cookbook. It was his first time inside the store, and to his knowledge, he had never laid eyes on her before.

He'd watched as she walked toward him from across the floor to ask if she could help him. It wasn't her blonde hair and the slight Eastern European accent that set off his internal alarm—it was that only fairies moved with as much grace as she did. He'd picked up a few other even more subtle indicators, too, things that he would never be able to describe. It was his "fae-dar," as he called it. His knack to recognize a fairy anywhere.

As a test, he had casually dropped a single word of standard fairy speak into their conversation. She smiled and led him to a corner of the store, where she whispered a response in the same dialect.

"Magda," she said, extending her hand.

"Stefán," he responded.

"I know," she said. She startled him further when she admitted that she'd always wanted to meet him. "Today was my lucky day, I guess," she'd said. "As the owner, I only work odd hours, but I came in this afternoon because we were light-staffed. Humans, you know. They always seem to get sick."

He laughed along, but quickly got serious. "How do you know who I am, and why would you want to meet me?"

"Okay, I'll tell you. You're probably going to think this is a bit creepy, but my friends and I have been interested in you since you started working at The Fairy Kingdom Teahouse."

Stefán jerked his head back. "You've been spying on me? What did I do?"

"No, no. Nothing like that. Again, please don't take it the wrong way." She lowered her voice. "It's just that we've been the only fairies in Myers Beach for a century and a half or so. Since the town began. And then Theos came, and well, then you."

Stefán swallowed. "What brought you here?"

"I can explain all that at another time. How about tomorrow at Joe's? I know you go there, so we won't look suspicious. I'll bring the other two, and we'll be at a table in the back. Oh, and obviously we need to keep this little relationship *entre nous*."

He was flabbergasted that secret fairies not only lived in Myers Beach but also owned a business on the boardwalk only steps away from The Fairy Kingdom. It blew his mind, too, that they knew he frequented Joe's Java Joint.

He found himself a little tongue-tied, so instead of speaking, he held out both hands, palms facing up. He hadn't used that body language in ages, and he was surprised that the gesture came automatically.

She responded by hovering her palms over his. When they got close enough for him to sense her warmth he closed his eyes and mumbled an archaic phrase that also suddenly came back to him from his youth.

After a few seconds, she drummed her fingers on his palms and clapped her hands. When she lifted them away, he was holding the cookbook he'd ordered, and when she opened hers flat again, they held an imported chocolate bar.

"My favorite," she whispered.

They both laughed, and after she turned to help another customer, he left the store and walked back to The Fairy Kingdom. He spent the remainder of the day in a daze, followed by a sleepless night during which he replayed the remarkable event several times.

The redhead in a nurse's uniform who flagged him over to her table threw him for a loop. He was there to meet with Magda, and he expected to see the blonde-haired beauty he'd met the day before, so he approached her with caution.

When she greeted him in the same manner as Magda had the day before, using the palms of her hands, he knew it was her, and he smiled and relaxed. She introduced him to the two men at the table with her, and after he sat down, he launched into how happy he was to meet them. The men nodded back, but when they didn't offer their names, Stefán worried that perhaps he'd come across as too forward, or maybe too eager, too American.

"So glad to meet you. I work just down the boardwalk, at The Fairy Kingdom." He was about to elaborate on his responsibilities at the teahouse when they cut him off.

"We know," said the man on his left with the eye patch. "We've probably seen you outside in front of the place a million times."

"Really. Then I'm surprised that you never stopped in, you know, out of curiosity if for no other reason."

"Oh, we have, many times," said the other man with short, cropped hair. "It's safe to say that we're regulars."

Stefán threw back his head. "Gosh. I've always had excellent recall for faces, especially for customers, so I'm surprised that I don't recognize either of you. You either, Magda."

She and the men broke into big smiles and gave each other high-fives.

"That's the idea. You weren't supposed to," said Cropped Hair Guy. He must have seen Stefán's perplexed expression because he added clarification. "We assume new bodies every time we go out."

"Been doing it every day for over a hundred years. Since we came here." Eye Patch Man took Magda's wrist. "Do you remember the first time?"

"I do," she said. "You were most convincing as a grizzly old prospector, and I went as a prim schoolmarm, as I recall. What do you have planned for tomorrow?"

He pointed to his eye patch and snickered. "Obviously, I'll ditch this, though, I'm really digging it and will probably bring it back again sometime. Tomorrow, expect to see me as a waitress, with big…you know…knockers."

Stefán relaxed at their playfulness. "So, getting back to when you stopped by. Why didn't you introduce yourselves? I mean, we're all fairies, after all."

The three looked at each other as though they would reach an unspoken agreement on which one would respond. Magda took the lead.

"The truth? We didn't know that we could trust you.

When you first arrived, we weren't even sure you were a fairy."

"Well, many, many thanks for that. It's the best confirmation ever that I've been doing a decent job of blending in with the humans. That's been the number one goal for all of us at The Fairy Kingdom."

Cropped Hair Guy gave Stefán a friendly jab. "Don't let her comment go to your head. I was ninety percent sure you were."

Stefán raised his frappuccino in a salute and then asked them how they'd ended up in Myers Beach. As the longest fairy resident, Magda started.

"I'll make it short," she said. "I basically escaped from an unpleasant political climate back home when I was in my early twenties. I traveled the world for a decade or so in search of the perfect spot to make my new home. As we all know, the world is full of beauty, and I fell in love with many locations.

"But I'd always dreamed of living on a beach, and Myers Beach had something the others didn't. Perhaps you know that I'm referring to the air and water here. Both are so rejuvenating, magical really. I felt it immediately and that's why I ended up staying."

"Hear, hear," said the two men.

"Oh, I feel it, too. I know Theos did when he first came here on the kitesurfing tour. I remember him describing how much more powerful he felt flying through the air around here. He smelled the magic in the water, too."

"Ah, yes. Theos the King," said Cropped Hair Guy as he scratched his scrawny beard. "You're close to him?"

"Yes. Very. His father took in my family, so my allegiance has always been with him. He's the one who sent me here to help out at The Fairy Kingdom."

"So he's a good man?" asked Magda. "A good king like his father? We weren't sure, but we were hoping so."

"Absolutely! Better, even," Stefán said. When their anxious faces relaxed in front of him, he knew he'd struck a chord, and he was glad he'd established a connection with the strangers he hoped would become friends.

"But I'm eager for you to get back to your story. So which of our three kingdoms did you belong to that you found so disagreeable?"

"None of them," she said.

A revelation like that might have taken him by surprise had he not just taken care of several thousand other kingdom-less fairies. He'd heard rumors all his life that they were out there, but the ones who arrived with Theos' group were the first he'd ever met. He was dying to know more about her experience and was hoping she'd continue when she countered with a question of her own.

"What about you? Which is yours?"

He stared at his drink. "Tough question…because honestly, I'm not sure. I've always felt adopted. I mean I had real parents, of course, but I lost them when I was five, and so obviously I don't really remember much about them. And I never knew them."

Eye Patch Man leaned back in his chair and ran his good eye up and down Stefán's body. "Are we looking at the real you, or are you playing games with your looks like we are?"

Stefán laughed. "Yep. This is all me. Pretty much the same body I've had all my life."

"Then I hope you don't mind my saying that, aside from your bluish eyes you look nothing like the fairies of Theos' kingdom."

Stefán turned up the corner of his mouth. "I'm well aware that I'm not one of them, but I'm loyal to him just the same. I don't really know anything more about myself to tell you, but please go on, Magda. You said 'none of them.' What did you mean by that?"

Magda looked to the others for encouragement. "There was another kingdom once," she said.

She explained that her ancestors had participated in the overthrow of their own ruler, whom she described as a horrible man with dictatorial inclinations that ran counter to the traditional fairy live-and-let-live lifestyle. Following the dissolution of the monarchy, her family and many others chose to live outside the fairy kingdom structure and had ever since.

She hooked a thumb at her friends. "These guys arrived in Myers Beach a bit later. It took a while for us to come out to each other, as they say. We spent a great deal of time watching and learning, as we did with you, but when we finally figured out that we were all fairies and from the same place, we became good friends."

"We bought up property. Back then, the boardwalk was only one short block with a hotel and a small café. But we picked the land on both sides, and when the town eventually expanded the strip, we not only made a lot of money, we negotiated prime locations on the new boardwalk."

Stefán's jaw dropped when he heard how many properties they owned—buildings he walked by nearly every day and businesses that he patronized since he'd arrived. The deli, the newsstand, the Sandpiper Hotel, and even The Sea Catch restaurant belonged to one or more of them.

"Call me naive, but how were you able to buy anything? You weren't exactly citizens, or humans running around with IDs. I mean I don't even have one."

"Oh come on, now," said Cropped Hair Guy. "Didn't you just tell us you were a fairy?" He looked around the room, and when he was sure nobody was looking, he hovered his palms over the table. When he pulled them away, a zippered wallet appeared in front of him, and he slid it to Stefán. "There you go. Now you can buy property, too. How hard was that?"

Inside was everything Stefán would need to prove he was an American citizen, a birth certificate, passport, and social security number.

"I hope you don't mind that I anglicized your first name and made up a last one. And I took a guess at your birthday." He winked and waved his hand in the air. "But you can always change those with a little magic of your own."

As Stefán was putting the cards back in, he held up the driver's license. "Good choice on my last name. *Lord*. I rather like it. Thanks. But what about that supposed unspoken rule that keeps property ownership among the current residents?"

Magda laughed. "Take another look at your birth certificate. I guess you must have forgotten that you were born here. You could buy a house tomorrow, which will be easy with that line of credit he gave you. It's tucked inside along with a credit card. Neat, huh?"

Cropped Hair Guy tapped his hand on the table. "Besides, who do you think came up with that residency requirement, anyway?" He winked and pretended to buff his nails on his lapel.

"And let's face it, with the way prices have gone up, I have to admit that it was genius," added Eye Patch Man.

Stefán shifted in his chair. "I'd like to go off-topic for a moment if you don't mind. How have you managed to stay alive without fairy dust? Or do you have your own supply? I mean, I assume you heard about the pandemic."

"Like I said. It's this place," said Magda. "There's literally something in the air and water here that sustains us."

"For centuries our people had limited access to fairy dust anyway," added Cropped Hair Guy. "So we've gotten used to doing without it. Not sure how your fairies will manage, though. It must suck."

"Geez, guys. My head is spinning from all this. But now I've got to ask why you didn't want to trust the fairies with your secret."

"Let's be clear, Stefán. We still don't trust them," Magda said. "We singled you out because we could tell you were different. And really, it all goes back to politics and the reasons we left so long ago. We don't want Theos or Zsombor or even the new Third King to know that we exist and get crazy ideas about making us their subjects."

Magda sighed and leaned her folded arms on the tabletop. "It was kind of all three kings to provide them protection, though, and we're glad they came," she said. "Because from what I understand, there are wicked people out there who want to eradicate all of us."

"That's another reason why we change our identities all the time," said Eye Patch Man. "We want to live under the radar and in peace. I suspect you'll find that the Outliers who you said arrived the other night will feel the same way we do."

"Yeah," said Cropped Hair Guy. "We don't know much about the fairies in the other kingdoms, but we do know the mindset of an Outlier fairy, and I suspect it won't take long being cooped up with others before they start getting twitchy."

Stefán sighed. "They already have."

CHAPTER SIX

"They said I could find you here," said Julie.

She knew she'd surprised Stefán when she unexpect-edly showed up in the kitchen of The Fairy Kingdom the next day. He'd been bent over a tall-walled coffee mug and sprinkling a mixture of sugar and cinnamon over perfectly swirled whipped cream and caramel. He straightened up when he heard her voice, and the sharp movement threw a few of his carefully styled blond curls onto his face.

His determined look was something better suited for an intense battle, rather than a frothy and adorned frappuc-cino, and Julie internally laughed at how at odds it was with the cute blue-and-white striped apron he'd tied around his neck and waist.

"I've never been down in the kitchen before," she said. She hopped up to sit on the butcher block countertop next to him and gave the room a once-over.

It was homier than she was expecting. Instead of the standard stainless steel and metal, there were lots of warm yellow lights and wooden countertops. Pans and utensils hung from black iron hooks on walls and from the ceiling. The many blends of tea leaves were displayed on one whole wall near the back. They were contained in potion-like bottles with little cork stoppers and identified with spidery handwritten labels.

Fresh vegetables for the small salads that the tea house offered were resting on a butcher block counter, drying from what looked like a fresh rinse. Julie wondered if they got them from the town farmers' market every Sunday. Next to the vegetables was a large, industrial fridge with a glass door, which allowed her to see through to its contents. Little tarts and cakes and chocolates were displayed there, but since they were packed in restaurant-grade, sealable Tupperware, Julie had to assume that The Fairy Kingdom had made them from scratch and had put them in the fridge to sell later that day. A few kitchen workers milled quietly about, getting the store ready for the afternoon, but they left Julie and Stefán alone in the small corner they'd commandeered.

Julie glanced back at Stefán and noticed his eyes for the first time. Under the bright overhead light they appeared to be a pale blue, not at all like the striking cobalt blue of Theos' or Alias', or those of other fairies from their kingdom.

Until he cleared his throat, she didn't realize she was staring, and fighting the blush that wanted to paint her cheeks a bright, noticeable red, she jumped off the counter to move closer to the mug he'd been working on.

"I didn't know you *also* made the tea. They must work you like a dog around here."

"Uh, no." He stood to his full height, and Julie had to crane her neck to look up at him. "I don't. Not usually, anyway. Sometimes I like to help make some of the desserts, but it's not often."

She gestured to the mug. "Can I try it?"

His mouth ticked up into a crooked smile. "Don't you want to know what it is, first?"

"Nah. I like to live life on the edge." Then she smiled. "Unless, of course, it's going to make me sleep for a hundred years." When he didn't seem to understand her reference, she clarified. "Oh, it's from an old fairy tale. Bad joke, I guess. Sorry."

He held the mug to her mouth, and she leaned in for a taste. "Go for it," he said. She took a swallow, and then another. His eyes were glued to her reaction, and when she licked her lips, his face broke into a grin.

"Holy moly, this is amazing!" she said. "It's like a Queen Greta's Fairy Frappuccino…only ten times better! I didn't think it was possible."

She caught the light blush that crossed his pale cheeks and couldn't help but stare in fascination. She was used to classically handsome men, being surrounded by the likes of Theos, Alias, and Christophe. But Stefán was more than that. With his sharp jawline, luscious lips, and symmetrical nose and bone structure, he had a youthful, overarching beauty about him.

His soulful eyes and the light dusting of stubble across his chin evoked a kind of introverted depth. A dream-like quality. It was the kind of handsome that came with a remoteness that was pretty to look at but often made the person inaccessible. But something smoldered beneath her skin when she looked at him, that begged her to learn more. She was drawn to him, and even if she found herself burned, she wasn't sure she'd care.

Stefán cleared his throat, breaking her out of her assessment of him, and it was her turn to blush as she looked away.

"There's really not much to the one Joe makes, so it really wasn't that hard to deconstruct. I think people assume his drinks are complicated and difficult to make because he charges so much for them. Anyway, I've always been crazy for caramel, so I added a touch to the mug at the beginning."

"That was genius," she said. "It really adds that level of sophistication that his doesn't have."

He beamed. "Well, I think that might be an exaggeration, but I'm glad you like it."

"You're being too modest." She looked up at him for permission to keep drinking, and he nodded.

"Yeah, please, finish it." He handed her the cup. "I've been sampling them all morning, and I'm already high as a kite from the caffeine. By the way, you said you were looking for me. What did you need?"

"Oh, I was planning to stop by Zoë's and I wondered if you had an update you could share with me?"

"Probably nothing you don't already know. I was planning to see her this evening, so maybe I'll check with you before I go so *you* can update *me*."

"Sure," she said. She took another drink and leaned back against the counter. "Seriously, if you offered these here, you could put Joe out of business."

"Well, I don't want to do that, of course, but the fairies

have been after me to make them, so maybe I will. Of course, if I put a frappuccino on the menu here, I'd have to make a slightly different version. Queen Greta lives here now, and it wouldn't do to offer a competing beverage when Joe makes her namesake drink next door."

"Well, I really love this one. Seriously, now that I've tasted it, I don't want to drink anything else."

He looked at his shoes. "That's good. Because I made this one just for you. It was kind of a little passion project of mine." She looked up at him over the rim of the mug as he stammered on. "I know you're not Joe's biggest fan, so… um, I just thought—well, maybe if you liked this one, and it sounds like you do, that I'd make them for you and save you a trip."

Julie set down the cup and gave him a small hug. "Aww. That's honestly so sweet. Nobody's ever made anything special like this for me before. Thank you."

She held the mug to his lips and made him finish it. She couldn't help but track the whipped cream that clung to his plush top lip. "You have some…" Without thinking, she leaned in and wiped the cream from his mouth with her own thumb. The moment they touched, she realized what she was doing and pulled her hand away. "Sorry. Wasn't thinking."

"S'okay," Stefán said, his eyes wide. He looked away and ran a hand through his hair. "Anyway, I can make them for you anytime. I figured the less you have to be around Joe, the better."

"I'd love that, actually," she said. Then she grinned and held up a finger. "On one condition."

Stefán crossed his arms. "And that would be?"

"Whenever you make one for me, you have to keep me company and drink one, too."

CHAPTER SEVEN

The next day he dropped off Julie's first morning frappuccino at her loft. After making him promise to stay and drink one with her she felt bad that she had to cancel already. But she couldn't spend the time she wanted to with him, because she was leaving early to spend the morning helping Zoë with her rehab.

The physical therapist had encouraged the princess to take increasingly longer walks to build up her endurance, and Julie volunteered to accompany her those first few crucial days to keep her accountable.

She'd had plenty of experience years ago getting her older brother back up to speed after he'd broken his leg in a football accident, so she knew how important it was to keep a patient motivated. She also remembered how easy it was for him to want to skip a day.

Zoë complained that her legs were unsteady and suggested walking the halls of the palace. Since it was an exact replica of her childhood home, walking the familiar halls would give her confidence. Furthermore, the Palace

Level was the only floor of the New Third Kingdom that remained at human scale after Christophe's renovation, so it made sense to meet Julie there.

Julie's initial visit to the Palace Level had been brief. Christophe had been proud to be able to duplicate at least that one aspect of their homeland, and he'd wanted to show it off. She remembered vividly how two things boggled her mind.

The first was the jaw-dropping opulence. It wasn't only the gold everywhere, and the filigree, and the crystal chandeliers, and the artwork, and the thick carpets, and elegant everything. What astonished her most was the sharp contrast between that elaborate and detailed ornamentation and the otherwise simple, devil-may-care attitude of Christophe, the guy that had been her constant companion for many months and she thought she knew.

Not that he didn't have style. He did. He exuded it in spades, just like Alias. Their shared impeccable taste and uncanny sense of picking the exact right colors for everything was one of the reasons why the guys made such a perfect couple. Whether out and about in the perfect brand of bathing suits or sportswear or even in the occasional evening wear, they always gave the impression that they'd put it all together with no effort at all, a skill that didn't come naturally to her.

But neither one had ever shown an interest in anything as super fancy and over-the-top as the palace decor.

Christophe had taken one look at her face and had laughed. "I can see from your eyes that you're confused. Considering the starkness and simplicity of our house at the compound, you're probably wondering how or why I built all this."

"Yes. I mean, it's stunning. It's gorgeous, but it doesn't look like you. I feel like we're back in Europe visiting one of those grand old palaces."

"Well, that's because you kind of are. We're standing in a replica of our actual palace back home, which is very much like those places. It's just off the beaten path, so to speak, so not in the tourist brochures. I built this here partly because I'm a sentimental guy. As the Third King, it's up to me to continue traditions, and I'm really happy with that."

The second thing that struck her about the palace had nothing to do with decor. It had to do with physics. No matter how hard she tried, she couldn't fathom how the endless corridors and giant reception rooms with tall ceilings fit into the normal-sized second floor of her building.

"Yeah. I forgot to warn you," he'd said. "It's an illusion. Magic. You'll have to suspend your sense of logic, but I promise that once that gets untangled you'll feel quite at home."

Walking those hallways slowly and purposely with Zoë gave her another chance at suspending her logic, and though she found it nearly impossible to "untangle" as Christophe put it, at least she had plenty of time to drink in the grandeur. And Zoë made an excellent tour guide.

Julie had always found it easier to make friends with people older than she was, because more mature folks didn't expect her to be anything other than herself. Developing a friendship with a woman close to her own age, though, was turning out to be fun. While she and the fairy princess couldn't have been more different in obvious ways, she learned that they shared a love for rock music, television shows, and of all things—nerdy board games.

Despite growing up a tomboy who enjoyed extreme sports, Zoë also had an equal passion for reading, and she described for Julie the astonishing breadth of subject matter in the palace library's vast collection. To avoid becoming distracted, they agreed that they shouldn't go near it until Zoë had clocked enough steps.

So with only conversation to keep them occupied, Julie asked Zoë to talk about growing up in the palace with her brother. Julie learned that she'd always been the yin to Christophe's yang, the black to his white. Where they'd both been into sports, she'd spent much of her free time exploring the palace's many passageways, finding new and interesting places to hunker down with a good book.

He'd liked talking to people and making long-lasting connections, and she'd preferred to stick to the sidelines, making worlds up in her own head. It had served her well that he'd been born a few years before her. Because he was older and next in line, he'd always taken the brunt of the schooling. She, on the other hand, could afford to spend lazy afternoons hiding from her tutors.

It was no secret that their kingdom had a long history of being more traditional than the other two. Their parents, however, were progressive, and throughout their reign they'd righted the wrongs of eons of prejudice and hateful, archaic ideology. Unfortunately, their end had come too soon.

With the fatal accident and their parents' death, their aunt's rule and her firm belief in the old ways changed the dynamic dramatically. While they continued to live happy and lavish lives, during the ensuing years, they watched her undo much of their parents' work. Her brother had always felt his aunt hated him. The feeling was mutual, and he couldn't wait to become eighteen so he could demote her and set things right.

In the meantime, he worried that she would find a way to eliminate him so she could hang on to her control. So he made Zoë agree that should anything happen to him, she would transform herself into his lookalike and take up the mantle of Third King.

Her brother had always looked out for her in that way and doted on her the way only an older brother can.

"I remember when I was eight, I got in trouble for staying out all night catching fireflies. Our aunt sent me to bed without supper, but he snuck into my room with cakes he'd stolen from the kitchens."

She saw her brother a lot less when he and Alias began their tutelage together. Their aunt refused to let her join in on their lessons, because she said that princesses weren't allowed to study the same things as princes. Somehow, though, he made time to visit with her in the evenings and teach her as much as he could from what he remembered during his own lessons.

The night before his eighteenth birthday, they'd gone over a long list of changes he planned to enact on day one of his reign—changes that would allow the Third Kingdom to step out of its sixteenth-century mindset and into the future where the old ideals were no longer useful.

"But you know the rest. I was left to pick up the pieces

and rule the kingdom." She gestured to her legs. "Until this happened."

Julie nodded. She was slowly starting to learn the ins and outs of fairy culture and she couldn't help but think about all that Zoë had lost. "So, I guess the Doc finally told you, huh?"

Zoë took in a sharp breath, taking a moment to lean against the wall.

"Yeah." She crossed her arms and Julie thought it made her look so much smaller than the version of her, who'd been showing her around the palace, just a few minutes ago. She wiggled her fingers at Julie. "No magic." Sighing, she rolled her shoulders back, and Julie winced at the heartbreak that flashed across Zoë's face. "No wings." She collapsed back against the wall. "I'm barely a fairy at all."

To try and lighten the mood, Julie said, "Well, we humans don't have any of those things, and we get by just fine."

It was not the right thing to say, based on the look Zoë shot her.

"Sure. On wobbly feet that can't take you anywhere fast." She wiped a hand down her face and pushed off the wall. "But I'd rather be alive and in control of my own body, then the alternative."

"That's the spirit," Julie encouraged, threading her arm through Zoë's and marching them forward.

As a way to take the younger woman's mind off the situation, Julie began to share some of her own escapades with Christophe. She talked about how they first met, how they'd modeled for photo shoots together, and their escapades across Europe. And it seemed to work. Zoë was enthralled by the stories and shared even more of her own.

They ended their rehab obligation in the library, but Zoë didn't stop walking. She took Julie by the hand and walked the perimeter, pointing out the sections on science, history, and literature. She stopped at the shelves of books on fairy history, which she admitted was her favorite subject, and that while in her lifetime she'd read all the other books at least once, she was eager to reread the stories of her ancestors.

Julie gazed at a section of particularly dusty books. "Gosh, the only books I've read about fairies were the ones we sold in Lily's store, and they were written by people who I'm sure had no idea what they were talking about. Now that I'm surrounded by real fairies, I'd like to read something authentic. Can you suggest one to start with?"

Zoë ran her fingers across several volumes and stopped at a section where the bindings looked similar. "Our library has the largest collection of fairy histories. The originals were written in fairy, of course, but my father translated these right here. Look around, and if you find any of those interesting, I would be happy to translate them into English for you."

"I wouldn't want to put you through all that. It looks like there's plenty here." She pointed to the thickest volume. "What's this?"

"Ah. This is the most comprehensive of all. It's also the easiest to understand and has lots of color photos and illustrations. It covers all the kingdoms in depth."

It took both of them to lug the massive book to a table,

and Julie could hardly wait to crack it open. She drew her finger down the Table of Contents and stopped.

"It says there's a section on a Fourth Kingdom. Nobody ever mentioned that to me, though, now that I think about it, I don't see why they would have. Did you know about it?"

"Yes, of course," said Zoë. "They say the Fourth Kingdom flourished for thousands of years as the center for fairy art and literature. Then it apparently just disappeared. I'm trying to remember how exactly. Nobody talks about it much."

"Sounds fascinating. I'd love to dig into it. Would you mind?"

"Of course. Stop by anytime. I can't let you borrow this book, first of all, because it's way too big to move." Julie flipped to the chapters on the Fourth Kingdom as she listened. "There's another reason: it can't leave the palace. The book itself is magic, and it's going to blow your mind when I tell you why."

Julie looked up. "Why?"

"Because it constantly updates itself...on its own. That's why it's so big."

"No way!" Julie skimmed through the pages. Suddenly she stopped at a full-page portrait. "Zoë, look at this guy. He's the spitting image of Stefán."

CHAPTER EIGHT

When her physical therapist announced a week later that Zoë was back to full strength and gave her the all-clear, Stefán and Julie thought they'd introduce her to the board-walk and some fresh air. They agreed that she looked healthier, no doubt due to a combination of Alias' fairy dust therapy and Zoë's naturally fast healing properties.

The color had returned to her cheeks, and she dressed casually for the occasion in a deep red plaid shirt that hung open to reveal a well-worn graphic T-shirt and jeans with rips across her thighs and knees. The outfit was a refreshing change from her hospital gown and a startling difference from the clothes she'd worn while Zsa Zsa possessed her. Stefán couldn't help but notice how much more relaxed and sure of herself she looked in her own clothes.

"Spending a couple of hours watching humans sounds like a lot of fun," Zoë said. They hadn't walked ten feet before she stopped at a shop with surfboards on either side of the door. The exposed wood and warm tones of the exterior gave the impression that inside might be another summer tiki bar with a surfing theme, and the little potted palm trees outside drew her in.

The inside, though, was more akin to a bubbly eclectic person's playground. One long wall was covered with colorful surfboards in several makes and models. The wall across from it displayed an equal number of snowboards, and skateboards filled the racks on the floor in the center.

Any wall space not home to displays of gear and merchandise was home to local punk art for sale, and a large Naugahyde couch stretched opposite the register, adding a homey feel to the otherwise indie atmosphere.

"I didn't know you were into boarding," Julie said. "That's amazing, because so am I!"

Zoë nodded and pointed to a surfboard painted with an underwater scene of an eel swishing out the mouth of a giant skull. "I haven't surfed in a while, but I used to love it when I went to the beach with my brother and Alias." She turned and flashed Julie and Stefán a grin. "But since our palace was on a mountain top, I used to snowboard more often." She ran a finger along the smooth surface of a snowboard with a similar design to a surfboard she'd just admired.

"Those are apparently done by a local artist," Stefán said, pointing to a small tent card.

"They're neat," Zoë said. "But I'm surprised they sell them here. When do you ever get snow?"

"California isn't all sunny beaches and warm weather," said Julie. "We're home to some of the best snowboarding destinations in the world. I've always wanted to learn, so if I'm around this winter we should take a trip to Soda Springs."

They wandered to the center of the store, where Julie picked up a skateboard and scanned the information on the card next to it. "This is my real passion. Do you skateboard, too?"

Zoë nodded. "Yeah, snowboards, surfboards, skateboards. I'm a full triple threat."

"We could start a gang!" Julie turned to Stefán with hopeful eyes. "Please tell me you board too?"

Stefán laughed and rubbed the back of his neck. "I'm decent on boards, but my sport is underwater rugby. The problem is that I haven't found anyone else around here that plays. Back home, there were always teams." He blushed. "I hope this doesn't sound too nerdy, but to be honest I rather enjoy cooking. I consider it an art form."

Julie moved closer to Stefán. "I always think it's cool when people are able to make three-course meals out of random things they find in their refrigerators. I can barely cook eggs."

"I could show you how to cook a few simple things, sometime," he murmured back. "How about this Friday?"

"It's a date!" Julie said before turning to examine a few stickers that had been displayed on a nearby counter.

Stefán noticed Zoë testing the weight of the snowboard, and he pointed to another tent card. "This says that you can order a skateboard from the same artist that did the other boards. A triple set, for a triple threat."

They left the surf shop and only got a few feet further

down the boardwalk when Zoë stopped again, this time at The Belly Deli to try beach food for the first time.

They took a table at the front and gave her the seat that faced the window. When the full-figured waitress approached to take their order, she winked at Stefán. Her golden eyes looked full of mischief and humor, and it dawned on him that she was Eye Patch Man, the Outlier he'd met the day before. Stefán winked back.

Zoë noticed, and with a grin that was both sharp and playful, she predicted that the waitress would give him her phone number. Julie caught the gesture, too, but as a former server, she suggested that the woman was probably only working hard for a tip.

They ordered fried shrimp and onion rings, and Zoë asked Julie to talk about her childhood. Julie agreed and launched into a story about racing dirt bikes with her brother in the empty lot behind her parents' house and showed them the nasty scar on her leg she'd gotten when they'd accidentally crashed into each other. Zoë brought up playing tag-hide-and-seek in the palace and how she always managed to fool the palace staff but never her brother or Alias.

Stefán shook his head. "I have to admit that I'm a little jealous. Being an only child, I never had fun like that growing up. Theos and Alias are the closest things to relatives that I have."

"Interesting you say that," Julie said. "Zoë showed me a book in the palace library, and we ran across a picture of a man who I swore looked just like you. Maybe you have more relatives than you think."

He turned to Zoë. "I'd like to see that sometime, but

honestly, I don't know much about my family, and what I do know is a bit depressing." After he spoke he wondered if he should have opened up this can of worms. He hadn't shared anything personal with anyone for as long as he could remember, but when he cautioned them that his story was not exactly standard, they insisted he tell them, anyway. Looking at the sincerity on their faces, he took the plunge.

When he was very young, Theos' father, who was king at the time, had taken in Stefán and his family. The circumstances were still vague in his head as to why they needed the king's protection, but he distinctly remembered them fleeing from somewhere.

"I remembered people using the term 'asylum' whenever they referred to my parents. At the time, of course, I had no idea what the word meant.

"I suspected we were not one of your ordinary run-of-the-mill families, because the king set us up in our own home. It was a large one, too, with servants. I became certain we were special when I witnessed them killed one afternoon by someone who people later called a paid assassin, another vocabulary word I'd never forget."

From then on the king made certain that Stefán received the finest education, and he invited him to the palace frequently, which was where Stefán had learned upper-class manners.

"That must've been hard." Julie slipped her hand into his and squeezed lightly.

"Well, we all have each other now." Zoë patted him on the thigh where it pressed against hers. "And since you couldn't act like a goofball as a child, you can always play one with us."

"Double the trouble," Julie said with a wink. "And I know just the thing." She checked her watch. "Since there's a few hours before we meet everyone for dinner, we should totally play a game of beach volleyball!"

Stefán creased his brow. "Do you think that's a good idea? Zoë just got cleared."

"It'll be fun," Zoë retorted, and Julie gave her a high-five. "Besides, I grew up watching movies like *Top Gun*, and I've always wanted to do that."

After the first game, which the girls barely won, Stefán took off his sweaty shirt. He figured it wouldn't hurt to start working on a tan, and he didn't mind the way Julie's eyes lingered over his abs. He laughed when Zoë wolf-whistled.

During the third round, they switched teams so that Julie and Stefán played against Zoë. They were working well together and were leading when Zoë spiked the ball straight into the space between them. They dove for it at the same time, and when they collided and fell to the sand, Julie ended up on top of him. Stefán made no attempt to move her off until Zoë started teasing them.

By the time they left the beach to meet up with the others, they were all loose-limbed and warm, sporting grins and teasing each other like children. Stefán couldn't help but watch fondly, as Julie pulled Zoë into her shoulder, forcing the younger woman to skip down the rest of the sidewalk in a tangle of legs and giggles. If nothing else, he was glad he was becoming good friends with both of them.

When Zsa Zsa took over Zoë's body, she had thrown out all of Zoë's old clothes and replaced them with sexy outfits that Zoë found entirely uncomfortable. Christophe had used his magic to manifest a few new things that matched her vibe more while she was recuperating, but when Stefán stopped by to check on her, she complained about being in desperate need of a whole new wardrobe.

So, the next day Stefán suggested that he take her shopping.

"That sounds great, but see, I have this dilemma. I've got the money to buy anything I want, but I prefer the wear and tear of secondhand things. It's a vibe I can't really describe but it's something you can't get from new clothing."

"There's a neat consignment shop here on the board-walk. It's pretty popular, though, so the good things move fast. But if you get there on the right day, you can find everything you need. Maybe today you'll be lucky."

Zoë found lots of things she wanted to try on. To make it fun, she suggested they do a mock runway, and she forced Stefán to sit on the loveseat outside the fitting rooms for the better part of an hour so she could show off her outfits and get his opinion. Once he got into it he had a great time playing judge, and the longer they were in the store, the sillier they got.

He was catcalling her latest outfit when, out of the corner of his eye, he noticed that Julie had come in and was standing off to the side. He wondered how long she'd been watching them goof off and why she looked so unhappy. Zoë saw her too and waved her over.

"Stefán was helping me pick out some stuff. Wanna help?"

Julie stared at the floor. "Um. Sorry." She looked at her watch. "I'm actually late for something."

CHAPTER NINE

"Do you have a reservation?" asked the Tiki Hut host, who Julie hadn't seen before.

"Uh, yeah." She looked around to see if she could spot Greta and Lily. "No, not really. I'm meeting some people. Two women, more than likely dressed fabulously. They used to own stores on the boardwalk?" When she was met with a blank stare, she tried again. "Lily? Greta? No? Well, we used to be frequent fliers here, not that long ago."

Julie heard their shrieks from across the room, and she turned to see Lily and Greta shouting her name from the familiar table in the central palapa that the three women had dominated for so many years. They were sitting in the same enormous wicker throne-like chairs with backs that fanned out like peacock feathers.

She threw her hands in the air and matched their screams with one of her own. After leaning over to exchange long hugs, she plopped down in the middle chair they'd saved for her. She remembered joking about how sitting there made them feel like queens. It didn't escape her that she was now the only one who wasn't one.

"I'm sorry I'm a little late." She looked at the glasses on the table in front of them. "How many rum punches have you guys had while you've been waiting?"

Lily lifted her glass of water. "None," she said. "But we ordered you one."

"Thanks." She looked at Lily and then Greta. "Gosh. You two haven't changed a bit. I don't know what I expected." She lowered her voice. "I mean now that you're fairies and all." Without waiting for a reply, she raised an eyebrow. "Wait a minute. You haven't given up alcohol, have you?"

Greta pointed to her identical water glass and answered the unspoken question. "It's not good for the babies."

Julie looked down at their large bumps and put her hands to her cheeks. "How wonderful. How far along are you?"

Lily patted her tummy, her blue eyes bright with happiness. "Two months. So we actually have changed a bit. Isn't it fantastic? Greta and I are at the same stage, so our babies will be best friends just like us!"

Greta leaned across the table. "And so we thought, who better than our other best friend to be our kids' godmother."

Happy tears sprung to Julie's eyes, and she was drying them with her napkin when their old server, Eric, showed up at the table with menus.

"Wow! It's good to see you three queens back together again. Nobody looks as good as you do on those thrones," he joked.

"And it's good to see a familiar face working here, too," said Julie. "I've been gone for months, but I was surprised that I didn't recognize anybody when I came in."

"Yeah, the place hasn't been the same since you left. Lots of changes." He rattled off the list of specials and left to give them time to decide.

"Speaking of changes," said Julie. "Holy moly, have we got a lot to catch up on. And look, I don't want to spoil the vibe here, but I'm going to start by saying that I'm still mad at you... both."

"I know what you're going to say," said Lily. "And I don't blame you. We were inseparable, and then I went off and got married and left you alone. And then you never heard from me."

"Yeah. And you'd disconnected your cell, so I couldn't even contact you." Her eyes watered and she lowered her voice. "That was bad enough, but then I didn't even learn until like a few weeks ago that Theos was a fairy and a king, and that you've been one ever since with magic and everything. And a frigging queen."

Lily took Julie's hand. "How could I tell you? You really think you would have believed me?"

"I don't know. Probably not. But you could have tried at least."

"There wasn't time. We needed to get to his kingdom right away. Theos had suddenly been made king, and then there was the fairy dust pandemic, none of which I could have possibly explained, either."

Lily wiped her eyes. "Anyway, I'm really sorry. You didn't deserve that. I hoped that by leaving you the foundry and the business and the money you'd at least know how much I loved you and how much I valued our friendship."

"You're right. I probably wouldn't have understood. But I want you to know how unbearable it was going from being best friends to nothing." She tilted her head toward Greta. "Thank god this one came into my life and we became best friends."

Greta looked down at the table and shook her head. "And then the same thing happened."

"Sort of, but not exactly," said Julie. "I did leave first, remember? I went to Europe with Christophe. But you were flying high, and I expected you to be here when I got back." She lowered her voice again. "Okay. Now that I got that out of my system, I want to know everything."

"My gosh. Where do we even start?" asked Lily. She and Greta promised to spend as much time with her as it took to give her the full story, and the next few hours were punctuated by tears and squeals of joy and concerned looks from people at other tables of the busy restaurant as they covered the high points.

"Think about it, Lil. After all those years of struggling to sell your fairy figurines, you ended up as one. And Greta! You were such a convincing witch. It's hard for me to think of you as a fairy." She looked back and forth between them. "My two best friends becoming fairies. What are the odds?"

"Better than you'd think," replied Greta. "Turns out Myers Beach itself is quite magical. Theos discovered several elements in the air and water that make it special when he first came to town. That's why after the fairy dust got contaminated, he and Zsombor wanted to relocate all the fairies here."

Lily touched Julie's wrist. "What blows my mind is how our old store, The Fairy Kingdom, today has become an actual one."

"Yeah. About that. I haven't seen the other fairies yet. And how do they all fit into one building?"

"Good question," said Lily. "First of all, thanks to the addition of Greta's space next door, we've got twice as much room as before. The ground floor is still the teahouse, but the upstairs is completely different now. You'd never recognize it." She turned to Greta. "What do we have now, twenty-some floors?"

Julie threw her head back. "Did you say twenty? I'm having a hard time picturing how that would work. I mean each floor would have to be like a foot high, wouldn't they?"

"That's exactly right," said Greta. "When the fairies are inside, they have to shrink to their actual height, which is about six inches."

"There are tiny houses and apartments, parks, sidewalks, and trees. I wish you could see it," said Lily. "Maybe Greta and I can figure out a way to make you small one day so we can bring you in for a visit."

"Guys, it sounds so magical, my head is spinning. But I still don't see how there's enough room. I heard there are thousands of fairies in there."

Greta smiled and patted her belly. "Well, we've got enough space for now, but not for long. Lily and I aren't the only ones expecting. During the quarantine, they didn't have a lot to do, so now we're dealing with a baby boom."

"That's putting it mildly," said Lily. "Let's call it a population explosion. And we're going to need more space...soon."

"Gee. Alias, Christophe, and Stefán turned out to be fairies. Now Zoë's here. No offense, but I'm the only one in my circle of friends around here that's a human. I suddenly feel like I'm the alien."

"Stop it!" said Lily. "I understand what you mean, but what's happened to us doesn't change our feelings for you. Now, we've done all the talking. Tell us about you."

Over the next few hours, Julie's rum punch turned into a few mocktails to stay in solidarity with her pregnant friends. She brought Lily up to date on the figurine business and reported that sales were better than ever for both it and the foundry. Then she filled them in on her skateboarding adventure in Europe with Christophe and how, while she was there, she'd fallen in love with Mr. Right, who turned out to be Mr. Wrong.

"Anyway. I don't know how long I'm going to stay in Myers Beach. I really wanted to come back, but everyone is matched up now and living glamorous lives, and in addition to being the alien, I do kind of feel like the odd girl out."

Greta raised a finger in the air. "I've got an idea. How about Joe? You always had a thing for him."

All three burst out laughing. "I see the queen didn't lose her sarcasm," said Julie. "Man, Joe. What can I say? At least after he found out his grandson was gay, he's no longer homophobic. He's still nuttier than ever, though."

I haven't been by yet, but I probably should, considering our long history," said Greta. "But I'm afraid I wouldn't be able to resist my old double foam lattes he used to make me, and they're not good for the baby. By the way, someone told me that the frappuccino he named after me is a big hit."

Lily gave Julie a poke. "Especially with you. I know neither you nor I could stomach Joe, so it must kill you to have to put up with him to get one."

Julie blushed and looked away, pulling her hand out of Greta's grasp. "To be honest, I found another source, and that's why I was a little late."

"Hmm. At The Fairy Kingdom, by any chance?" asked Greta.

"Yeah, sort of." Julie rubbed the back of her neck and saw Lily eye Greta.

"I'm getting the sense that our friend Julie is keeping something from us," said Lily. "What do you think?"

Julie threw up her hands. "Okay. Okay. Stefán is making them for me. They taste better than Joe's, too. A lot better." When her friends said nothing she looked up and saw their blank faces. "What?"

"So…Stefán, huh?" Lily smirked.

Julie laughed. "It's not like that."

"I disagree," said Greta. "Seeing how frappuccinos are definitely an off-menu item at The Fairy Kingdom, I'd say he's making them just for you."

Julie rolled her eyes. "Yeah, but this is different. We're friends. And I prefer going there to Joe's Java Joint. That's all."

"Sure," said Greta. "That's what I told you when I was

sneaking coffee dates with Zsombor." She snickered. "How long have you been 'preferring his company,' as you call it?"

"We had a few dates, and to be honest, I'll admit that I like what I'm seeing." She took a drink. "But look. I can tell that he has the hots for Zoë, okay?"

"I wish I had a nickel for every time you tried to convince me that Zsombor was into me. I didn't believe you, either."

Julie held up her hand to stop the snarkiness. "Look. As you know, I haven't had the best luck picking guys, so whoever the next one is, I want to take my time and be cautious."

Lily nodded. "Fair enough." Then she quickly changed the subject. "But speaking of Joe and his frappuccinos, Dame Gabor told me the other day that he was taking on a new business partner."

"Oh, not this again." Greta sighed and ripped a bread stick into small pieces. "I'm almost afraid to ask. Who is it?"

"Apparently some woman, surprise surprise, who just moved here. That was all she knew, I guess."

"I'd love to find out more," said Greta. "As goofy as he is, I miss stopping by in the mornings. He passed on the best gossip."

"And I've missed this," Lily said. "The three of us, together like old times."

Greta agreed. "Yeah, it's nice to just have a moment to get away and talk, you know, what with all the problems going on."

"What do you mean? Sounds like your lives are glamorous from top to bottom." Julie asked.

Greta stole a piece of bread from Lily's plate. "Pregnancies aren't the only result of the lockdown. Between feeling cooped up and now the overcrowding, tempers are flaring. It seems like every day we're witnessing more and more fairy outbursts."

Lily leaned her head against her fist and sighed. "And it's only going to get worse. Unfortunately, we only have a couple months to find new space before the births start."

Julie raised an eyebrow. "I thought you said you were only in month two."

"We are, but fairies only need five," said Lily.

"Well, as their godmother, just let me know what I can do to help." She put her glass down and asked about their husbands.

Lily sighed. "Theos and Dos are spending every waking moment searching for the last element Alias needs to make proper fairy dust. They're confident that it's around Myers Beach somewhere, because they've found all the others here." She swallowed. "And the clock's still ticking away."

"What do you mean?" asked Julie.

Lily waved her hand as though to sweep away a bad thought. "Oh, let's save that discussion for another time."

Greta's hand clenched into a fist. "And as soon as they locate the element, everybody is going to focus on destroying that witch Zsa Zsa, who's at the bottom of all this."

Julie shook her head and sighed. "Yeah. Somehow I missed running into her. Alias told me about the fight at the lighthouse and about how you, Greta, threw her off. Man, I would like to have been there to see it."

"No, you wouldn't. She's a dangerous and powerful

psycho. The worst combination. But when we finally lock her up, our fairies can go back to their homelands."

Julie cleared her throat. "So, besides carrying my godchildren, how do you spend your days?"

Lily leaned an elbow on the table so she could pillow her cheek against her fist. "We're essentially running things at The Fairy Kingdom."

Julie scrunched her face. "I thought that was Stefán's job."

Greta nodded. "It is, slash was, but as queens, we're taking over most of it. Things have changed and there's far too many fairies for one person to manage." She sighed. "Your guy is a superman. I don't know how he handled everything."

"And there's another thing we didn't anticipate," said Lily. "We've got Outlier fairies living with us now, and they haven't been used to being accountable to anyone. We've heard that many of them are getting out and flying around and causing mischief.

"Of course, leaving the building at all is strictly forbidden, and the other fairies who are abiding by the rules are upset that they have to stay indoors."

"And we hear rumors and complaints that the Outliers are getting all kinds of other special treatment, too, because they don't have a king or queen to answer to," Lily added. "We know that's simply not true, but what happens is that they feed into other suspicions about them and we end up with all kinds of conspiracy theories."

Julie sat back in her seat and crossed her arms. "Like, what exactly?"

"That the Outliers are spying on us, for one." Greta swirled the ice in her glass.

Lily shook her head and made an exaggerated eye roll. "It's funny. We're having to settle squabbles over the dumbest things. Sometimes I feel more like a Dean of Students, than their queen."

CHAPTER TEN

Zsa Zsa sank her shoulders against her couch with a heavy sigh. She'd returned to her apartment to regroup from her revenge campaign against the fairies, and she needed to take a breather to assess her considerable wins and equally devastating losses.

The big win, of course, was phase one, the fairy dust contamination and the widespread death and destruction it had brought to the fairies of the largest kingdom. Györfi's brainchild to poison the dust at its source had been brilliant, and he credited her success to following his plan exactly as he'd specified.

Phase two of their master plan had been for Zsa Zsa to acquire fairy king power. He'd cautioned that it might take a little longer than the contamination, but had insisted that it would only require half the effort. Such power would make her ultimate goal of taking control of the remainder of the fairies a breeze, an even more rewarding outcome. Again, all she'd needed to do was follow his plan step by step.

He'd explained that the new Third King was young, naive, and therefore vulnerable. With Zsa Zsa's exceptional talent for mind control, she could easily infiltrate the king's body. He'd already told her how simple it would be to enter the palace using the tunnel and secret passages he had sketched out for her in a detailed map.

But she let her giddiness over her victory go to her head. Compared to how quickly and easily she destroyed the fairy dust, the elements of stealth and surprise necessary for this second scheme sounded risky. Worse yet, it sounded time-consuming. And as the Third Kingdom was the smallest of the three, she considered the prize small potatoes. So against Györfi's advice, she went off script and set her sights on a more prestigious target that she determined had a potentially more valuable payoff.

She learned that Prince Zsombor's father was critically ill and that the handsome young man was only months away from becoming the ruler of a kingdom twice the size of the Third Kingdom. Given the right access, she felt confident that she could seduce him and then use that same mind-control skill to coerce him into choosing her to be his bride and queen. And in her mind, queen power was just as good.

That plan, as opposed to Györfi's, seemed less risky to her because it drew on her natural sex appeal, which had never failed to turn heads. Her mistake had been not understanding that, unlike the young Third King, whom Györfi had insisted was vulnerable and isolated, Zsombor was strong and surrounded by powerful allies.

Still, she'd nearly succeeded. She'd absorbed much of his magic and was only minutes away from finishing him off when the combined forces of Alias, Zsombor, and Greta overpowered her and reversed the flow of magic back to Zsombor. When they hurled her off Hersey Lighthouse into Retribution Shoals, the fall nearly killed her.

After surviving the same treacherous waters for a second time, Zsa Zsa immediately regrouped. Without wasting time, she reverted to Plan A and entered the palace as effortlessly as Györfi had described. Using mind control to enter Zoë's body had been easy, too, but the end result hadn't gone as well as he promised, which she blamed on a flaw in Györfi's understanding of royal succession and power.

He'd watched the true Third King banished, and while he was right to deduce that his sister, Zoë, would ascend the throne, he was wrong to assume she would acquire king power. The sister did take on the role of king, but the magic power of the king remained with her brother.

While falling short of her goal, Zsa Zsa's mission could hardly be considered a failure. By the time Alias and Christophe were able to stop her and drive her out of their lives again, she'd absorbed fairy princess magic which made her very powerful. She'd even grown wings.

As she gazed around at the priceless antique furnishings that she'd acquired over the centuries when they were new, she was grateful they'd remained untouched in her absence, and she patted herself on the back for having the foresight to place an invisible protective dome around her apartment before she left.

She'd used a different strategy to keep her popular lounge, Gabriella's, from falling into ruin while she was gone—Györfi. After she'd gotten what she wanted from him that night, she was about to dispose of him, but he'd somehow talked her into letting him stick around for a nightcap. One led to many, and by the wee hours, he'd drunk himself into quite a stupor.

That's when she let down her guard. While she was passing him one last martini, he reached across the table and ripped the pendant from her neck. He kept a tight grip on the chain and giggled at his good fortune. The stone would protect him from her attempts at mind control and prevent her from retaliating.

"What do you think, now, you stupid bitch?" he said. "The tables have turned, and I'm calling the shots from now on. You're not the only one who's wanted fairy power, and after I take a well-deserved pee, I'm going to walk out of here and get just that."

He struggled to his feet and staggered toward the powder room, and while Zsa Zsa could no longer call on the power of her pendant, she had the presence of mind to give her Moroccan ottoman a kick. It slid across the floor and tripped him, and as he opened his hand to catch his fall, he dropped the pendant.

With the stone securely back around her neck she walked the inebriated Györfi to Gabriella's, where she used a spell her adoptive mother taught her which prevented him from leaving the premises. It also clouded his mind into thinking he wouldn't want to leave. Since then, as far as she knew, he lived as a prisoner in the upstairs apartment and waited tables in her club until she returned years later.

Zsa Zsa shook her head from reminiscing and walked the few blocks to the nightclub to check on how he'd fared in her absence. She barged into his bedroom and after rousing him from a deep sleep, she dragged him downstairs into the club. Then she flipped on the footlights and took a seat on the stool in the center of the stage where she'd sung for so many years.

"It's a pity," she said, as she pulled out an emery board to reshape the nails that had been damaged in the scuffle with Alias and his posse a day earlier. "I quite liked singing here. Mister Györfi. Why don't you tell them that I'm back and that I'll sing tomorrow night?"

"Fine," he said from his seat at a front-row table. "Then will you finally release me? You got what you wanted, and I'm really getting tired of this mindless life as a waiter."

She crossed her arms and smirked. "You know, I was going to let bygones be bygones and leave the fairies alone, but I recently learned that one of them assassinated my brother, probably the same one that separated me from the rest of the family. So now, I'm back on the warpath. In the meantime, I have a major bone to pick with you."

She joined him at the small table, and with a smile and a finger flick she lit a small votive to create ambiance. Then she railed at him for twenty minutes straight about how dead wrong he'd been about the Third King and how he wasted years of her valuable life.

Györfi remained without expression until she'd finished her rant. Then he smacked his lips.

"Are you quite done? If you'd stuck to my plan, you'd have had king power when you went after Zsombor. It could have been such a slam dunk as they say. But you had to do it your way. Now look where you are."

"Still a smartass know-it-all, I see," she smirked. "That's why I paid you so much to wait on my tables. Anyway, let's put aside that pettiness for the moment. Since I haven't been successful in either taking over a king's body or marrying one, no thanks to you, I've decided to take a different approach."

She stood, and he rolled his eyes as he watched her pace. "I want to make the kings turn on each other."

Györfi perked up. "Ooh. Nice. And watch them kill each other?"

"Yes, and since you find it amusing, I want you to listen to my plan and give it your own diabolical spin. You know, like we did before."

He looked away. "You're crazy if you think I'd be interested in destroying any more fairies. Don't you remember that my dream is to be one of them? I want their magic. I want to fly like they do."

Zsa Zsa waved her hands in the air. "Yeah, yeah. I found out what you really want. You're still gaga for Alias. In a way, I don't blame you. He's one handsome fairy dude." She let her eyes run up and down Györfi's body. "I see that you've been working out. You think that's going to win him over? My god, he's so far out of your league."

He rubbed his hands together. "You're wrong. Once I'm a fairy, I can make myself as hot looking as he is. He won't be able to resist me."

"In your dreams," she said. "Let's get back to an idea that can work. Now that I'm at least a partial fairy, I can do things I could never do before." She tossed her head back and let out a loud cackle. "I can even hear all the little communications they send out to the others."

Györfi shifted his weight. "And?"

"Theos, who seems to be the big shot among them, sent out a call. It seems he's scared of me, and he brought the whole lot of them to Myers Beach. And I mean every last one. Can you imagine? I've been there. It's a small town, and I'll bet they're already getting on each other's nerves."

Györfi wiggled his eyebrows. "Do you think Alias is there, too?"

"Of course, you idiot. I just told you that all of them were there now. Anyway, I'm still wearing the pendant my mother gave me." She threw her head back and roared in laughter. "Oh, that's right. You're familiar with it. You tried to steal it from me."

She pulled it out and fondled the stone. "And I thought mind control was so great. That's peanuts compared to what this baby can do. When I rub it, I can go directly inside people, without going through all those other steps. Eat your heart out, sucker."

He stared at the candle flame and yawned. "Nice. Anything else?"

"Yes, and you're going to die of jealousy. Watch this." She rolled her shoulders and squeezed out enormous red wings.

Györfi sat up and wagged his tongue. "Finally! Something I can work with."

"Wait until you see these beauties from the back." She spun around and ran her fingers along the tips that resembled black lace. Then she took her show-and-tell a step further. She looked him in the eye and wet her lips. Then she winked and fluttered her wings.

He leaned back in his chair and whistled. "Yeah, baby! Now that's what I call seductive. Now, do your runway thing." She turned back around, and as she strutted toward him like she had in her modeling days, he kept cheering. "Yeah, baby. Rock those wings."

"Soon, I'll be the most powerful fairy in the world!" She screamed when she got close.

"For sure!" he yelled back. "You're the greatest."

She started to reverse directions, and as she gave the mandatory model head toss, Györfi picked up the votive and splattered her face with hot candle wax. She screeched, and as she smacked her hands at her burning cheeks, Györfi ripped the pendant from her neck again. This time he made sure to clasp it around his own. Then he stood up and laughed in her face.

"For the longest time, I admired how clever and successful you were. Envied you, really. But now standing here looking at your pathetic stupid self, I wonder how the hell you managed to live so long."

Possession of the pendant broke her spell, finally allowing him to leave, so while she was picking wax off her artificial eyelashes, he strode into her dressing room and emptied the safe of all her cash. He grabbed the throw from her sofa and spread it out on the floor. Then he emptied a chest full of *Arbara* rocks on top of it and twisted the corners together to make a bag which he flung over his shoulder. On his way out he snagged the large bag of Spanish doubloons.

Zsa Zsa was still bent over in agony, and she spit on

him when he passed her on the way to the door. That's when he realized that even with her wings and all her fairy princess magic, she was powerless against him. He set down his bags and took a breath. He had unfinished business of his own.

CHAPTER ELEVEN

Györfi had never been to the West Coast. For that matter, he'd never flown First Class or hired a limousine before. Armed with his new fortune, the first thing he did was buy a cell phone. Then he acquired a platinum credit card and, after making a few calls, he did all three and made the trip in the style to which he had been accustomed in the palace of the Third King.

After retrieving his suitcases from the baggage carousel he elbowed his way toward the exit through the crowd of uniformed limousine drivers. While he searched for the one whom he'd been assured would be looking for him, he became distracted by a slim, good-looking fifty-ish gentleman with graying temples. Though he was wearing the same type of chauffeur's cap as the other, his Italian-cut dark charcoal sport coat and skinny white jeans made him stand out.

When the stylish man turned toward him, Györfi was thrilled to see his name on the card the man was holding, *Lord Birnam-Wood*. He hadn't used that alias since he'd tried to impress Zsa Zsa at her bar in New York City. While she saw through it right away, he still liked the ring of it, and with his elevated tastes and newfound wealth, he felt he could pull it off and the name was worth recycling.

"My name is Chet. Please let me take those," the driver said. Györfi released his grip on the handle of his roller bag slowly to enjoy the fleeting thrill when the driver's hand brushed against his. Chet wheeled away Györfi's luggage and led him on the short walk to the special parking area where his stretch limo was waiting.

Chet opened the door and after helping Györfi settle in, he pointed out the shaker of cold martinis, the Beluga caviar, the champagne, and the silk robe that Györfi had requested for his long ride.

"Should you need anything, you can speak to me by pressing the button here. Your wish is my command." The driver clicked his heels and laughed at his own gesture.

For the sake of privacy, Györfi waited until they reached the Interstate before stripping down to his briefs and slipping on the robe and slippers. He understood California traffic was unpredictable. The company was not willing to give him a definitive arrival time at Myers Beach, but they informed him that it would take several hours at a minimum. Györfi was unconcerned. He would be happy to enjoy his refreshments and the view of Chet's Hollywood handsome face in the rearview mirror for as long as it took.

After about an hour, Györfi was sufficiently drunk that he sought company, and he pressed the button. Chet lowered the glass panel, and during the long conversation that followed, he revealed that he was not only the driver but that he was also the owner of the one-man limo service, and that as a single man with no family, he enjoyed living vicariously through his clients.

Györfi was more than willing to provide entertainment, and in a slurred and rambling narrative, he regaled his driver with outlandish and fictional tales of his many exploits as a member of the aristocracy. Then he asked Chet to talk a little about himself.

"You have to be the single-most fascinating client I've ever had," said Chet. "I feel foolish. My life is so boring by comparison. When I'm not driving, I spend my time at the gym."

When he announced that they were about thirty minutes from the Sandpiper Hotel at Myers Beach, Györfi buzzed him back to inform him that there was a problem with the air conditioning, and he asked that they immediately pull over at the strip mall ahead to fix it. Chet stopped the car and got in the back with Györfi, and while he was leaning over to examine the vents, Györfi rubbed his ruby and became absorbed into Chet's body.

Moments later, after admiring himself in the car's side mirror, Györfi removed his suitcases from the trunk, walked to the other end of the mall, and called an Uber to take him the rest of the way.

"This is Lord Birnam-Wood in room number twenty-four," he said to the person at the front desk. "No. *Lord* is not my first name, it's my title." He let out an exaggerated sigh. "Yes. I'm a real lord. My goodness, you Americans have such difficulty understanding the aristocracy. Listen carefully, the room you gave me is completely unsuitable and therefore unacceptable. I will be staying for several days, possibly weeks or months, so please upgrade me immediately to your largest and finest suite. To give you time, I will leave the hotel and return in several hours."

With time to kill, Györfi decided to stretch his legs—Chet's legs, actually—and take a stroll along the famous boardwalk. He flung his new sport coat over one shoulder and headed toward the door, but the moment he stepped out of the hotel his pupils contracted and his eyes watered, and he had to shield them against the bright midday sun. He was about to purchase sunglasses from the souvenir shop that was only steps away when he remembered that Chet had been wearing a pair at the airport. He patted down his jacket and found them in the breast pocket. Armani. Perfect.

Györfi's stroll became more jaunty as he continued down the boardwalk. For the first time in his life, he felt confident in his body image and his style, and he slowed at every storefront window to reaffirm how suave he looked. While his looks rated a ten, he was still a bit tipsy from the tremendous quantity of alcohol he'd consumed during the long ride, and passing by Joe's Java Joint gave him the idea of stopping for a hit of caffeine. After studying the menu on the wall for a few seconds, his eyes reached *Queen Greta's Fairy Frappuccino*. The two trigger words *Queen* and *Fairy* sent a shiver down his spine.

"What the heck is that?" he said, pointing to the menu.

"What do you mean?" asked the young barista. "Who's Queen Greta, or what's a frappuccino?"

"Of course, I know what a frappuccino is," he replied. "It's the Queen Greta Fairy part I don't get."

"Sorry I can't help you," said the boy. "My grandfather is one of the owners, and he said that he named the drink after a friend. I don't know who the lady was, though. My name is Derek, by the way. Want one?"

"Not on your life," said Györfi. "I'll take a large coffee. Black. To go."

Derek poised a magic marker against the cup. "Name, please?" He'd already started to mangle the spelling of Birnam-Wood when Györfi made the addition. "Lord."

The kid crossed off what he'd written and took the pen away from the cup. He tilted his head. "So is Birmingham your first name, or is it Lord?"

"Neither, and it's Birnam-Wood, not Birmingham. And Lord is my title." He sighed. "Would it be too much trouble for you to use my whole name?"

The boy groaned. "Never mind. I've got it."

On his way to the door with coffee in hand, Györfi passed a man sitting in front by the window, and to acknowledge his presence, Györfi raised his cup and nodded to him. When the man snickered, Györfi stopped and glared back.

"What's so funny," he sneered.

The man pointed to his cup, and when Györfi turned it around and read the word *JERK* written in large block letters, he gave Derek the finger. As he walked out of the shop, he saw the man turn to Derek, break into a huge grin, and give him a thumbs up.

Györfi took a seat on a bench that faced the ocean, though the view he focused on was the vigorous game of volleyball directly in front of him, played by the young shirtless men who reminded him of Alias. When the guys ended their game and the two teams of women took over, there was no need to stick around, and he decided to return to his hotel to inspect his new digs.

He got up and tossed the cup into a trash can, but his mind was still on the men, and he headed down the boardwalk in the wrong direction. That's when he noticed the sandwich board sign in front of The Fairy Kingdom Teahouse.

Tonight Live!

Dame Gabor sings your piano bar favorites.

He stopped, not believing his luck. The personal allure of a piano bar notwithstanding, he reminded himself that he was in Myers Beach on a mission with two goals. First, to fulfill his dream of acquiring the kinds of magic powers he'd watched the fairies use when he was the tutor at the palace of the Third King. Second, to find and seduce Alias, a task that would likely require achieving his first goal to accomplish.

Infiltrating a fairy's body would be simple enough. Zsa Zsa's powerful red pendant stone, which he had made into a ring, would make that possible. He'd already been successful using it on a human. The trick would be finding the right fairy to worm his way into.

According to Zsa Zsa, Myers Beach was crawling with them, and a joint with the name The Fairy Kingdom seemed like a good place to find one. He made a mental note to come back later and, excited by his evening plans, continued walking until he found himself at the end of the boardwalk. Confused, he ducked into the bookstore to ask for directions.

"The Sandpiper? You passed it," said a woman with green hair who identified herself as the owner. "It's all the way at the other end."

CHAPTER TWELVE

Stefán found Theos in the lab conference room huddled around a map with Alias, Christophe, and Zsombor. He knew they were down to the wire in the desperate hunt for *Yano*, and he caught the tail end of the discussion on where they planned to search next and how they would divide up the effort.

On his way downstairs, he had stopped briefly on the landing of the level where the fairy dust was being manufactured. Even through the closed door, he could hear the hum and feel the vibrations of the elaborate equipment Alias had set up, and he knew that the operation was in full swing.

The dust they were making was not going to save their lives, but Alias was fast-tracking the production anyway. His plan was to build up a large supply and add the *Yano* as soon as they located it.

"Perfect timing," said Theos when he saw Stefán walk in. "We were just finishing up."

After the others filed out, Stefán bent down over the

map. "You know, Theos, I'd be honored to pitch in and help. Give me a territory, and believe me, I'll scour it."

"I know you would," he said. "You've been a godsend these past months. I don't know how we could have managed without you. But you must be exhausted by now."

"I admit I was feeling pretty pooped there for a while," said Stefán. "But I loved what I was doing and felt I was making a real contribution. Sounds like Greta and Lily will be running things for the time being, though, so I guess I'm expected to go back to managing the teahouse full time." He stared at his shoes. "I wish there was something else I could do. I feel like I've become more valuable. You know I'll do what you want, but honestly, just running the teahouse would feel like a demotion."

"You are valuable, Stefán, and know that I'll keep my eyes open for something else. Listen, if we don't find the *Yano* in the next day or two, I'll definitely fold you into the team."

"Thanks. Um, I also wanted to run something past you." Stefán bit his lip, hoping the suggestion he was about to propose would be received well. "My idea might seem trivial compared to finding *Yano*, but I think it has merit, just the same."

Theos put an arm on his shoulder and led him to the small sitting area. "Let's sit. I'm all ears."

"I'm sure that you're aware of the tension that's been brewing among the fairies. I can't blame them for being out of sorts. As you know, they aren't accustomed to being thrown together with fairies from other kingdoms and living on top of each other and being cooped up."

"I know," said Theos. "Especially the Outliers, although

until we find new space, I'm not sure there's much we can do."

Stefán cleared his throat. "It's not my place to suggest a long-term solution, but my idea might defuse the tension, at least temporarily."

Theos cocked his head. "Hmm. What do you have in mind?"

"A beach party. Well, more like a beach festival. We'd invite the fairies from all three kingdoms, including the Outliers. My idea would be to structure a full day of activities that would get them outside for a while. It would be an opportunity to mix naturally, instead of the forced situation they're in now. We'd have tons of food, sunshine, and plenty of space for a change. It'd be nice to throw in some alcohol, too."

"So, obviously this event would have to be open to the public, right? I mean, if you want to take over the beach."

"It would have to be. And I see that as a positive. The fairies are going to have to learn how to assimilate eventually. Why not in an atmosphere that's fun and non-threatening?"

Theos' face relaxed. "You know, a party is exactly what we need." He leaned in. "Between us, I was planning to lift the quarantine soon anyway, so the timing couldn't be better." He started to bounce his leg and tap his fingers on the tabletop. "You've got my mind racing already. Remember that assimilation course that Dame Gabor was going to present with Greta and Lily that was supposed to help them blend in with the humans?"

Stefán nodded. "Yeah, and as I recall it didn't go over so well." His eyes sparkled. "Tell me if you're thinking what

I'm thinking." He took a breath. "That we should make taking it mandatory to participate in the beach festival."

"Bingo!" said Theos. "Now, I'm thinking it needs to be longer than one day. I was thinking we could include a few contests and maybe a couple exhibitions. I know I could wrangle a few of my kitesurfing buddies to come back here and put on a show. Lily and I might even do a tandem exhibition."

"I was going to ask a few shopkeepers I'm friendly with to see if they'd like to participate. Maybe they'd agree to sponsor some of those contests. What would you say to that?"

Theos got up and paced the floor. "You know, in this country, people love participating in a big event when there's a sponsor or a charity involved. How about we have The Endowment for Oceanic Solutions sponsor the whole thing? We could throw up a big tent and show people all the good things we've been doing around the world."

"And we make the festival so much fun that everyone will want to come. So, what do you think? A whole weekend?" asked Stefán.

"Nah," said Theos. "I think even bigger. A whole *week*long festival, maybe, with fireworks and bonfires. Let's pull out all the stops and close the week with something really big. I expect we'll have new fairy dust by then, so we can call it 'the Day of the Dust,' or something."

Stefán closed his eyes. "I've got it. We call the whole thing the Myers Beach Dust Up."

"Perfect. Now, since I know I can trust you to keep this a secret, I want you to listen carefully."

Theos informed him that they now had only a few

weeks to go before most of the fairies would need dusting with high-powered fairy dust they still didn't have. Some were already seriously behind in their treatments. Greta and Lily had lists of everyone's due dates and were monitoring them closely.

"We're hoping to have new fairy dust by the end of that week. If we do, we'll make the Day of the Dust the biggest celebration we've ever seen. If not, then…well."

"Are you saying that all of us will die in a matter of weeks?"

Theos nodded. "We feel lucky that nobody's died already. And that's why the party needs to last at least a full week. If we're all going to die, I want us to go out with a bang."

Stefán gulped. "Um, when do you see putting all this together? It's a big deal."

Theos smiled. "Next week. Look. We're fairies. All it takes is magic. I'll take care of getting permission from the mayor if you'll handle everything else."

"I'm on it," he replied. "But you still have hope of finding *Yano*, don't you?"

"To be honest? Less and less."

"And if you found it, we could all be saved?"

"I certainly hope so."

CHAPTER THIRTEEN

Theos

I'm upbeat about throwing the beach festival as a way to calm things down around here, and I'm grateful to Stefán for suggesting it. I'd heard that many of the fairies had become restless. I'd even heard rumblings about some of them wanting to abandon ship and go home, back to all of the deserted palaces. Some have even suggested things that would be treasonous, given any other situation. But with things as they are, I can't blame them for having short fuses.

I am not completely surprised that many in each kingdom are at odds with each other. In my opinion, there are several causes for the uptick in nationalism.

Lily and Greta put their finger on one important issue.

There are too many cooks in the kitchens, as it were. Too many kings with laws of their own for everyone to keep track of what they can and can't do. The fairies want separate spaces and rules for their own kingdoms. Alias, Christophe, Zsombor, and I got together to see what measures we could implement to mitigate the tension while we were all sequestered so close together in one small town.

We determined that it might be helpful for the fairies to have something or someone to rally behind, and we discussed appointing a High King—someone who could be in charge of all the fairies, at least temporarily.

Since mine is the largest kingdom, they unanimously gave me that position. My word would be law, with Zsombor and Christophe enforcing it with their people. I have to admit that it sounds like a daunting task. I never expected to rule my own kingdom so early on, let alone all the fairies everywhere. But we had to do something. I fear if we leave them to their own devices, our short-tempered subjects might start causing real trouble.

But unless we find that last element soon, all of this will be in vain. Alias was able to trace tiny, microscopic fragments of it in the ocean, which means it must be in the ground somewhere.

I feel so guilty for not telling the people that we only have a month left to live. But I think revealing that drastic news would cause more harm than good. It would only cause mass panic, which could lead to a whole host of other consequences. But to ease their minds, I'm putting an end to the quarantine and lifting the ban on flying.

Alias had a point—not only would it win the people over to being more accepting of me as High King, but it would also help them relieve some of that pent-up frustration. Plus, if we only have a month left, I'd rather give them time to make the most of it.

I've noticed Julie and Stefán hitting it off. Given what Christophe and Alias have told me about her dating history, I'm glad to see her interested in someone as good as Stefán. I've also seen him and Zoë together, so I just hope he doesn't break any hearts in the process.

Lily and Greta both assure me they'll keep me in the loop. Now that they're back together with Julie, they have reestablished their regular hangouts at the Tiki Hut. That and the fresh air will help reduce the stress, which can't be good for the babies.

I'm just so excited to be a father. With Jamie off at boarding school, I haven't been able to hang around him too much. But I know he'll be the best big brother to his fairy sibling.

CHAPTER FOURTEEN

Stefán was reviewing teahouse receipts when he heard something shatter on the marble floor. He ran out of his office toward the sound and found three fairies in a stand-off. Two women stood close together with their arms crossed glaring at an older male fairy with rage on his face.

"You'd better watch it!" the man shouted.

"Mind your own business," said the woman with golden eyes and shoulder-length blonde curls. Stefán recognized her as one of the Outliers who'd arrived with the recent giant migration. He was not familiar with the other woman with brown eyes and long black hair. Her bronze skin marked her as a fairy from the Third Kingdom, and her defiant gaze told him that she was not to be trifled with.

This wasn't the first squabble to arise between kingdoms, but it was the first that involved the Outliers, and he hoped that heated arguments wouldn't become a trend. He brought up the concern in a staff meeting, but his observation had been met with a yawn. Considering what all the fairies had been through, the staff was willing to give them all a pass.

At that moment, the queens were in a meeting with Alias to discuss options to alleviate the overcrowding, and Stefán was the last line of defense. He didn't mind stepping in, however, because, with Greta and Lily now in charge, he knew it would be one of the last times he'd have to. Running interference in those kinds of matters would no longer be his job, and he was happy about that.

"We were just talking," explained the one with the bronze skin. She pointed at the man. "But then this guy just walked right over and dumped his tea in her lap. Then he smashed her cup on the floor."

The man stepped closer to Stefán and jerked his thumb in the direction of the blonde with the wet shirt. "It's those damned nomads. They get all the best tea before it runs out, and we get stuck with the crap. So, I figured that if I can't have it, neither should they."

"We'd prefer if you used the term 'Outliers,'" said Stefán. "Nomad is a bit…racist."

"Whatever!" The man threw his hands in the air. "They're everywhere. And somehow, they always manage to get all the best stuff before we do." He pointed a finger at the dark-haired fairy. "And that one is a damned Outlier sympathizer."

The blonde lunged at the male fairy. "Screw you!"

"All right, why don't we settle down?" Stefán stretched out his arms to keep them separated. "Belos, maybe you should—"

"Of course you would take their sides," the man, Belos,

said. "We know you've been giving them the best rooms, too."

Stefán was shocked at the accusation. "I have not. What makes you think that? I've never played favorites."

The man scoffed. "They hog all the exercise machines in the spa, too, so we can never use them." He poked a finger into Stefán's chest. "It's obvious that they're getting special treatment. From you."

Stefán backed away. "You're wrong."

"What's the meaning of this?" He breathed a sigh of relief at the sound of Greta's commanding voice behind him. He turned and saw Lily and Alias standing by her side looking like disappointed parents.

"Thank you, Stefán," Greta said, as she stepped forward to squeeze his shoulder in thanks. "Lily and I will take it from here."

Alias shot Stefán a bright, friendly smile and escorted him back to his office. Lately, defusing the tensions had become one headache after another, and he was relieved to have the help of the royals.

"We've gotta figure out a better solution." Stefán sighed as he eased himself down in his desk chair. "The squabbles have started to turn into actual fights." He stretched his head from side to side to pop the tense muscles in his neck.

"I heard that Zsombor and Greta's people are angry because they're nowhere near a forest. Can that be?"

"Yes, and your old kingdom's fairies are upset that they can't use the beach. Since nobody is allowed out of the building, being cooped up is causing them to lash out not only at us but also at one another." He pinched the bridge of his nose. "And sorry to say, but the Outliers have only added to the tension."

Alias leaned against the doorframe and nodded. "Well, then everyone should love hearing Theos announce that he's lifting the quarantine in a couple days. He's going to tell them about the festival you're working on, too, Stefán, so that's going to lift their spirits."

"That was the idea," said Stefán. "But it'll only be temporary. It's not going to address the root cause...the overcrowding crisis."

Alias looked out into the hallway, and when he saw that the coast was clear of prying eyes and ears, he looked back.

"You didn't hear this from me, but I've been helping Theos renovate his compound to make room for their fairies. He wants to move them as soon as possible. That should give Zsombor and Greta's kingdom a fair amount of breathing room."

"Fantastic," Stefán agreed, sitting forward. "I have a lead on someone who controls a couple other buildings on the boardwalk, and I'm hoping we can work out an arrangement to house the Outliers. It's early stages, and I don't know of their availability yet, but I'm pursuing it."

Alias hadn't been gone more than a couple of minutes when Dame Gabor flounced in unannounced and folded herself into one of the plush blue chairs that faced Stefán's desk.

"Well, that was quite a show down there." She nodded her head toward the door to indicate the commotion Lily and Greta were handling in the common room. She crossed her legs and looked exasperated. "I need a drink. Anyone want to join me?"

"Count me in," said Stefán, "but don't make me one of your martinis. They're way too strong."

"No problem. I gave them up. It's strictly bubbles for me from now on. Man, you wouldn't believe what I just passed through to get here."

"I'll bite," said Stefán.

"I overheard a group of fairies talking about staging a hunger strike. Can you believe it? I thought I was hearing things myself until I saw some of them painting signs."

"Why would they do that?" he asked. "We just gave them really great news."

"This is the sad part. Apparently, they're not going to eat again until the Outliers are truly out of the building."

"Yeah, I've taken down more than a few posters already," said Stefán. "And I can't believe the insensitivity. They're using capital o, u, and t to spell Outlier." He took a drink. "But the lowest point of the meeting for me was when that fairy of the Third Kingdom accused me of playing favorites. I never do, and believe me, it's tempting sometimes."

Dame Gabor poured herself a second glass. "I recognized him. He's new, and a mischievous little pistol. You both know who I mean. I see him in the tea house most nights when I'm on stage. He always has an entourage, and they all seem to have one thing in common. They don't like the Outliers."

"Yeah, I know him," added Stefán. "It doesn't stop there. Whenever you hear an argument breaking out he seems to be around, if you get where I'm going with this."

"I'd rather not talk about the dissension in the ranks. I try not to let their negativity pollute my mind. Besides, I came up here for a different reason. I came to pitch you an idea."

"Why me? I'm just a simple teahouse manager."

She pretended to knock on a door. "Hello? Aren't you in charge of the beach festival?"

He laughed and sat back. "Whatcha got? I'm all ears."

She stood and moved her chair and two others against the wall.

"Wait! What are you doing to my office?" he yelped.

"Oh, brother!" She snapped her fingers and produced a chilled bottle of prosecco and two flutes on a rosewood tray. "I can see you're going to need this."

She spread out her arms. "Picture this. A loving household. Mom, Dad, and three children. A girl and two boys. We're in the children's bedroom. It's huge, big enough for all three kids. Through the tall windows, we look out over the tiled rooftops of London. White smoke filtering out of people's chimneys. That kind of thing. Dog has his own bed on the floor. Maybe there's a—"

"I get it. I get it," said Stefán. He rolled his hand to get her to move it along.

"So the mom reads them a bedtime story, and later, in the middle of the night, a boy shows up at their window and the girl lets him in." Dame Gabor pantomimed opening the window and then she scampered around Stefán's office flapping her arms as she described the kids zooming around their bedroom in their pajamas after the boy teaches them how to fly.

"The next part is crucial. The boy has the cutest sidekick, a beautiful petite fairy, with a wand, and fairy dust which she throws around all the time and everything. So the boy talks them into flying with them to this magical island, where they have one adventure after another."

She twirled a pretend mustache in Stefán's face and then mimicked a sword fight when she asked him to imagine the villain, pirates, and a man-eating crocodile.

"The boy is the hero, and the girl is kind of his love interest, but the star of the show is really the fairy, of course."

Stefán stared at her with a blank face. "Did you really think you needed to tell me the story of Peter Pan? It was the only book I remember my mother reading to me."

"Did you know it started as a play?"

"No. I can't say that I did. Why?"

She returned the chairs to their original places in front of his desk. "Because I want to stage it. I want to put on the play as part of the beach festival. The themes and conflicts are classic. The challenges we face growing up and the tragedy of having to leave our childhood innocence behind. The kids will love it. It'll be a huge draw. I'll rewrite it as a comedy, of course."

He scratched his chin. "You know, I think you're on to something. We'd have to tweak it, of course. It's a big production."

"Yeah, and that's no problem. The author, J. M. Barrie, supposedly tweaked it for ages before she finished the novel. For starters, instead of the magical island, obviously, we'd substitute magical Myers Beach."

"Yes, I follow, but we don't have a stage big enough. You're talking lots of sets."

"I'm talking about making the play take place over the whole darn beach. We've got everything we need, the jetty and the lighthouse to use for the dangerous scenes. We can create a pirate ship with the snap of our fingers. The critics will go nuts at our innovation!"

"You know, Dame Gabor, your play might just be the splash I was looking for as the grand finale. Theos designated that Sunday as the official 'Day of the Dust.' You're a genius! Who are you going to get to act in it?"

She poured herself a flute of prosecco.

"I thought you'd never ask. Casting is crucial. I think if we do it right, we can get this play to do more than just entertain. Look. I think we can agree that the fairies are fed up. What if we got some of the royals to act in it? Think about it for a minute. Seeing their kings and queens being silly on stage could humanize them. We'd all have fun."

Stefán got up from his chair and walked around the desk.

"Ok, this is fun. I can tell that you've given it a lot of thought."

She took a sip. "I'd play Tinkerbell, of course. Julie's not a royal, but she'd be perfect as Wendy. Theos and Alias could play the two younger brothers. Maybe cast Lily against type as Captain Hook. For fun, we could cast his first mate, Smee, as a woman. Greta could pull it off. She has theatrical experience. And we'd ask Zsombor to narrate. He's got the best voice."

"Hmm. I like it. But if you're playing Tinkerbell, who would play Peter?"

"I've played Peter plenty of times. You know his character is generally played by a female. But the author always wanted to have a male play him. We could grant her wish by casting you."

"Me? Wow. I've never acted before. Are you sure I've got what it takes to play the lead?"

"With me as your coach? Come on. And with your good looks and personality, in a few sessions I'll have you delivering such an award-winning performance Theos will want to give you a knighthood. Let's pencil in a few times right now, while we're thinking of it."

"Good plan. Speaking of Theos, we'd better get downstairs. His announcement will start any moment."

CHAPTER FIFTEEN

It was standing room only. Staff had removed all the tables and chairs from the dining hall, and fairies from all three kingdoms and the Outliers lined up in their six-inch forms across the floor. After a long drum roll and even longer brass fanfare, Theos took the stage in a display of majesty befitting a High King. Kings Zsombor and Christophe flanked him on either side.

"First of all, we want to thank you for being so patient with us. We know you understand that the situation has not been ideal, but we also know that given the threat level and the disastrous fairy dust circumstances, our abrupt move was necessary."

"Liar!" a male voice boomed through the dining hall. Everyone turned toward the back of the room to see who was responsible, but the disruptor did not identify himself.

Theos continued without missing a beat. "We want to assure you that your kings and queens want to do what we can to make things as comfortable as possible for everyone. We recently put our heads together and arrived at two decisions." He cued the drums. "The first is that for the purposes of fairness—"

"You wouldn't know fairness if it slapped you in the ass!" yelled the same voice. This time Belos held up his arms and gave a slight bow. Murmurs filled the room, but it was impossible to gauge whether the reactions were positive or negative.

Theos repeated. "For the purposes of fairness and streamlined messaging, we decided to pick one of us to be High King, and he will make the final decisions on policy. And while any of us could do the job equally well, I was selected." Theos quickly gathered everyone's attention by cueing a second drum roll which again brought the audience to silence. "King Zsombor will tell you our second decision." There were groans from the audience. "Which I think you'll like much more than the first.

Zsombor took the microphone. "In two days, we will be lifting the quarantine." The audience stomped their feet, and the room filled with scattered cheers. Some took a little longer to join in because at first they couldn't believe that the good news was true. "Yes. In two days you'll be free to come and go as you please."

This time cheers filled the room, and to keep the momentum going, Zsombor signaled the band to play a fairy marching song. He and Theos and the royals clapped along with the audience until it was time to add his small caveat.

"But it comes at a cost," said Zsombor. "We must all remember that it is absolutely imperative that we continue to fly under the radar of the humans. So, before we let you loose on Myers Beach, we want you to be prepared to blend into society. With that in mind, everyone's favorite lounge singer and actress, Dame Gabor, under the sponsorship of the queens, has agreed to run classes that will cover tips and strategies. Completion of the course is mandatory to receive your passport to Myers Beach!"

A collective moan ran through the room, but Theos brought Stefán forward, and their bright smiles quieted the room.

"And to celebrate, Stefán is arranging a weeklong beach festival." Theos encouraged the crowd to cheer. "The whole of Myers Beach will be invited, so it'll be a fun and easy way to begin your assimilation with the humans."

He and Stefán raised their hands and clapped, which prompted the rest of the audience to follow suit. Soon they began to chant. "Stefán, Stefán!"

Theos continued. "And speaking of flying under the radar…." He waited for the drum roll again. "We're also lifting the ban on flying!"

Whistles and cheers of "Long Live the Kings and Queens" filled the room. After they all took their bows, they left Stefán alone on stage to take care of some housekeeping items. He instructed them on how to sign up for the assimilation certification classes and then gave an overview of the exciting weeklong beach festival.

When he was finished on stage, he escaped into the kitchen and leaned against one of the butcher block counters. While he'd trained in hospitality and loved to exercise by playing sports, he was not a fan of public speaking. Every time he was forced to do it, he needed time to decompress afterward. He took a deep, calming breath and was about to go back to the common room when Zoë appeared.

"Everything okay?" she asked. Her pinched brows conveyed her concern.

He grimaced. "Yeah, it's just…public speaking."

She stepped close and was rubbing his shoulder when the doors swung open and Julie stepped in. She stopped short when she saw them huddled close together.

Her face turned bright red. "Oh, I'm sorry. I just wanted to…oh, I guess I'll just go, then."

CHAPTER SIXTEEN

The next day, Stefán was on his way to the front of the bookstore to pay for the book on mindfulness he'd just found, when he noticed Julie on her tiptoes, straining to reach a book on the highest shelf in the young adult fiction section. Her face was red from effort.

"Here, let me." He stepped in close and easily grabbed the book she was after. "It helps to be over six feet." He smiled and nodded at the cover as he handed it to her. "What's it about? Must be good if you were working so hard to get it."

She grinned. "It definitely is. It's about a closed-off girl who moves to New York City to get away from her mom and meets the greatest cast of funny, quirky characters that show her how to open up again." She leaned closer to whisper, "Spoiler alert, the love interest is a time-traveling ghost that only has a short time to live on the subway before being destroyed forever."

She clutched the pink and purple book to her chest. "It's one of my favorites, but I was actually getting a copy for

Zoë." She stood on her toes to look at the shelf again. "This writer has a few more books, but it looks like I'll have to wait until they get them in. I wish I could bring the others to her today."

He looked behind them, and when he saw that they were alone, he bopped her on the nose. "Your wish is my command. *Poof*."

Julie pushed his hand away and rolled her eyes. "Come on. That can't be how it really works." Stefán grinned and pointed up at the bright green book and another pink one, both shelved under the name of the author she was looking for.

Her hand went to his wrist. "You know, I'm still not used to this. During all that time I spent with Christophe, he never let on that he was a fairy," she whispered. "And so he never used magic around me. At least, not that I knew of."

"Still want them?" he asked. She nodded, and so that he wouldn't have to break the connection of her hand on his wrist, he didn't bother to reach up for them. Instead, he pressed close to her and flicked a finger, causing the two new books to fall from the shelf into his other hand.

He playfully waved them in circles above her and laughed as she jumped to try to get them. Then he stopped clowning and held them defiantly in crossed arms against his body. She reached again, and when he felt her knuckles brush against his hard chest, he wondered if she was aware that her touch sent shivers down his spine.

She was still holding onto his wrist, and their faces flushed when his light blue eyes met her hazel ones. A clatter and shout from the front of the store broke them out of their impromptu staring contest, and Stefán backed up to put some distance between them.

Julie turned away and rubbed the cover of one of the books. "Zoë will love these," she stammered. "I think we've started a bit of a book club, to be honest." She placed her books on the cashier's counter. "After buying these, she and I are actually supposed to meet at the High Tide Tavern, the board game bar up the boardwalk. Do you know it?" He nodded. "Alias and Christophe are meeting us there so we can play a couple of games. Want to come?" She stepped to the side so they could ring up his purchase.

"Ordinarily I would love to, but I have some things to take care of for the big beach festival. After that, though, I'll have a bit more time now that Lily and Greta have taken over most of The Fairy Kingdom operations. After the Dust Up, I'll only have the teahouse to run."

"Time to find new hobbies, then, huh?" She stuffed her wallet into the back pocket of her jeans and grabbed the books. The sun was shining high in the sky when they made their way out of the store.

Stefán looked longingly at her, as she turned to head toward the High Tide Tavern. He wasn't ready to leave her yet, and even though The Fairy Kingdom was in the opposite direction, he walked with her.

"I'm hoping Zoë will make some new friends from the game bar," she said. "I feel so bad for her, sometimes. Her magic is just…gone, and I can't imagine how depressed she must be because of it."

Stefán took her hand. "I can't either. A fairy without magic…it would be torture for me."

"And then her wings...well." She shook herself. "Not that I know what that is like, or anything, either."

Stefán nodded. The loss of a fairy's wings was a huge deal in their culture. A wingless fairy was seen as maimed and deformed. Centuries ago, the horrible practice of shearing a fairy's wings off had been a punishment for the worst crimes until the kings finally came to their senses and realized the practice was too cruel and unusual to continue. Zsa Zsa's taking of Zoë's wings had been the ultimate act of malice.

"I can tell you that everyone is so grateful that you've become her friend, especially Christophe."

They stopped at the door to the bar. "Are you sure you can't stay?" she asked.

He saw what he thought was hope in her expression, and he reminded himself that he was a fairy and could make almost anything happen. Whatever responsibilities were waiting for him at The Fairy Kingdom to fix, could wait.

Stefán had never had a reason to patronize the bar before, not being the bar type or familiar with board games, and he was shocked to find the indoor venue buzzing with so much activity on such a beautiful, sunny afternoon. She led him past dozens of gamers of all ages who were sitting across from each other on padded benches at long wooden tables that filled the main room.

Then she pointed to the floor-to-ceiling shelves.

"I had no idea there were that many different games," he

said. "Or, that they were so popular." He wondered if perhaps Greta and Lily might consider converting a small section of their lounge into a game room, and walked along the tables to see which games people were playing the most.

Facing the glass storefront was the tiniest bar counter he'd seen in Myers Beach, and he wondered how the cheerful bartender could possibly make and serve the lengthy list of drink options written on the black chalkboard behind her.

He wandered over to the medieval-style door to the left of the bar, labeled "The Alexandria Librarians." Julie must have sensed his confusion at both the name of the room and the sign in a cursive font next to the door, which read, "Speak friend, and enter."

She leaned over. "That's where the local, serious Dungeons and Dragons players meet." When his face still registered confusion, she beckoned him to another set of tables. "We usually meet by the windows, over here. Look, there they are."

He followed her pointed finger to see the fairy princess, garbed in a cropped, gray band T-shirt and heavily ripped and paint-splattered jeans, which she'd paired with a black leather jacket that seemed like it had been tailor-made for her. Her heavy black biker boots solidified the idea that she was definitely dressed for a bar, though one that served a more rough-and-tumble clientele and less like the nerdy vibe of the one they were in. Either way, he had to admit that the look suited her personality.

Sitting next to her was someone about her same age, with short blond hair tucked up into a gray beanie that left bangs falling into a pair of golden eyes. They wore a black henley and simple jeans rolled at the ankles to show off a pair of boots similar to Zoë's.

Stefán was dying to know how the person fit into her small circle of friends, but he didn't have to ask. Zoë said something to the stranger, and they gazed back at her like they were star-struck. Then the newcomer stood and as they walked toward the table, even at a distance, Stefán's fae-dar went off. The stranger was one of them. An Outlier.

"I got those books we were talking about!" Julie dropped the three new paperbacks on the table.

"Awesome! Thanks." Zoë waved at Stefán as he sank into a chair next to her. "Here to join our book club?" she asked him.

"Probably not. Julie mentioned meeting you here, and since I hadn't been in this place before. I got curious."

"Speaking of curiosity," Julie wiggled her eyebrows in the direction of the blond stranger. "Who was that?"

Stefán hadn't seen Zoë blush before then. "Uhm, their name is Briar." She looked down at her lap. "They said they'd like to play a game of *Sorry* with us before we start talking about the books, if that's cool?" She ran a hand over her hair, careful not to disturb the perfect curls she'd wrangled her hair into. "They've read the book, and it'll be their first time meeting my brother. I could use the backup."

"Of course!" Julie said. "Stefán, do you want to join us?"

"Sorry." He smiled at his own pun and the girls laughed too. "Like I said, I've got a ton of things left to do for the big beach festival." He stood. "Rain check?"

CHAPTER SEVENTEEN

Later the next afternoon, Greta and Lily asked Julie out for ice cream in the name of pregnancy cravings, friendship, and bonding time. With cones in hand for the queens and a strawberry sundae for Julie, they stepped off the board-walk onto the beach and strolled along the water's edge from the Hersey Lighthouse all the way to the jetty at the north end.

"Hey," said Greta. "Since we're so close, let's show Lily the skatepark you had a hand in setting up."

Julie was thrilled at their interest, and the side trip worked out well, too, because she was going to meet Zoë there later anyway. They took a left at the jetty and walked the short distance to the park, and Greta showed Lily the plaque that acknowledged Julie for coming up with the idea and shepherding the project through to the end.

Seeing groups of happy people occupying nearly every picnic table on the grassy area surrounding the ramp made Julie beam. The tables had been her idea, too, because she knew from experience that skateboarders had friends and family who didn't ride and needed a place to hang out and watch those who did.

They found an empty table in the shade of a large tree with an excellent view of the ramp, and as boarders raced up and down, they asked Julie to break down what they were doing and what to watch for.

She was licking ice cream off her finger and explaining how one of the boarders was grinding on the concrete coping on the lip so they could pop away and do airs when Greta interrupted her and pointed to the other side.

"Hey, isn't that Stefán?"

"And Zoë?" added Lily.

Julie spun around in time to see Stefán wobble off a skateboard into Zoë's waiting arms. She rolled her eyes and looked away, unwilling to witness what was sure to be a loving look or some other act of intimacy between the two.

"They look pretty cozy," Greta said, looking over at Julie.

"Now I'm really confused." Julie let out a huff of frustration. "I thought she was more into Briar."

Lily bit into her cone. "Have you asked him out? I mean, on an official date? Not just a...what are you kids calling it?"

"A hangout," Greta supplied, snapping her fingers and shooting Julie a silly look.

Julie laughed at their antics to cheer her up, but she took Lily's comment seriously. None of their hangouts had been official, and maybe it was time to make things more clear that she was interested in being more than just friends. She handed Lily her sundae.

"All right. I'm going over."

When she got close enough to overhear their conversation, Zoë noticed her and waved.

"Oh, hey. Yeah, I got here early, too," she said. She flipped her board up to her hands. "Stefán said he wanted to improve his technique, and since he and I were hanging out today anyway and I was coming here to meet you, I offered to show him a few of the basics."

"I thought snowboarding was your passion," said Julie. As a champion skateboarder, she was offended that he had looked to Zoë for instruction.

"Yeah, well both, really. Of course, I'm nowhere as good as you on a skateboard."

Julie turned to Stefán. "And I thought you had work to do on your beach festival?"

Stefán walked off the ramp and laughed. "Listen, I have to go. But as uncoordinated as I was out there, there's plenty of opportunity for both of you to teach me."

Before he got too far away, Zoë called to him. "Speaking of teaching, are we still on for tonight's cooking class?"

Julie's heart sank. Was anything they'd done together special? She looked at her smartwatch and affected an urgent air.

"Oh no, Zoë!" She waved goodbye to Lily and Greta, who were still at the table across the way. "Something's come up and I can't stay, after all."

CHAPTER EIGHTEEN

Julie woke early Friday morning to the tolling of church bells. She'd not heard them from her loft before, and she struggled to place the source that was becoming louder and more elaborate. She knew there were a few churches within the city limits, but she wasn't aware that any of them rang bells anymore.

Half-asleep and still in a brain fog, she stumbled out of bed and slid open the metal barn door that served as the entrance to her bedroom. That's when she felt the full effect and majesty of all twenty of Notre Dame's bells reverberating throughout her penthouse loft.

She recognized them from a recording Christophe had played for her. He'd made it years ago one Christmas evening, before the tragic fire. He'd described how on those special occasions, all eight bells in the north tower, the two in the south tower, seven in the spire, and another three in the roof of the north transept would ring at once. She'd heard the three-ton Emmanuel bell ring once before. He'd taken her past the cathedral after the anniversary of the tragedy, and she'd never forgotten how even from across the square the vibration of its deep F sharp pounded against her chest.

Upgrading the security system in her penthouse had been Alias and Christophe's idea, and while they were at it, they took the liberty of upgrading her doorbell sound. They'd chosen the Notre Dame bells, not only because Christophe had taken Julie there, but because it was during the ringing of those bells that he and Alias had first kissed.

She'd never heard the glorious sound in her apartment, since that morning was the first occasion that someone used her doorbell, and she certainly wasn't expecting Stefán to be on the other side of the door.

He squinted when he saw how she was dressed. She'd stolen the pair of black plaid boxer shorts from her brother before he'd ever had a chance to wear them, and the well-worn T-shirt with the phrase "Death Before Decaf" had been a gift from Greta.

She suddenly felt self-conscious about the holes in the old shirt, and she hugged her stomach to hide them until it dawned on her that those were the least of her problems. The shorts sat high on her thighs because she'd rolled them at the waist so they'd fit and wouldn't fall off while she slept.

"Um, was I supposed to know you were stopping by?" She ran a hand through her short hair in an effort to tame the strands from their current "electrified by a socket" look.

From behind his back, he produced two large bags, and she could see that sticking out of one of them were handles of what appeared to be pots and pans. The other seemed to be full of food and ingredients. He nodded toward the kitchen island behind her, and she stepped aside to let him pass.

"I thought we agreed that we would do a little cooking together, today. Didn't we say eight o'clock?"

Her eyes narrowed as she watched Stefán unload the canvas bags. "Yeah," she croaked. She smiled, but her voice was hoarse from disuse. "I assumed that meant this evening."

Stefán stopped organizing the jars and tins. "Gosh, I'm sorry. I can come back tonight if you'd rather."

"No. No. I'm up, and it's fine. Perfect, really. It's just that at this hour, what I could use is some caffeine."

"Well, you're in luck." He reached into the bag and handed her a travel mug which was still ice cold to her touch.

"Oh, man. You made me one of your frappuccinos already this morning?" She took off the lid and saw the perfectly symmetrical whipped top. "I almost hate to ruin this," she joked before taking a large sip. By the time she'd had enough to start to feel human again, Stefán had lined up everything he'd brought in neat little rows.

"I wasn't quite sure what you had." His eyes lit on the empty hooks above the island and on the wall above the stove. "So I brought everything we'd need."

Julie laughed and flung open the door to the pantry that revealed empty shelves. "Yeah, when Greta took me shopping for furniture for this place, I only bought a few things for the kitchen, because at the time I usually just ordered takeout. And then I left for Europe right away, so I didn't ever pick up, you know, basic ingredients."

Stefán's eyes crinkled with a smile that looked like he was trying his best to hold back a snicker at the lack of anything to work with. He could have conjured up whatever he needed, but he wanted to show her how to do it on her own.

"Today, I thought I'd show you how to make something that you can serve to others if you ever invite people over. It's quick to make and doesn't take a lot of prep. The first dish is spaghetti puttanesca. The second is both a dessert and light breakfast—a caramel-nut cake."

"So…are we starting now?" She pulled out a stool for him and waved at her T-shirt. "Because I think I should change first."

She opened a door next to the industrial glass-fronted fridge and grabbed the gag-gift aprons Greta and Alias had gotten her as housewarming gifts that she'd never had an excuse to use. One was all black, with huge white lettering that said, "I like to get HIGH." In smaller letters directly under it was the clarification: "quality ingredients." The other apron was all blue with "Oh Crepe!" in pink lettering across the chest. She handed both to Stefán.

"Take your pick of these, and I'll wear whichever, when I finish changing."

She beat a hasty retreat back to her room and slid into a pair of jeans and a loose button-up blouse. As she ran a brush through her hair, she considered how thoughtful it had been for him to bring everything and take the time to teach her. Conversing with him had already become so easy, especially with their time in the mornings when he brought her his infamous frappuccinos, and she loved that they could tease each other and get away with it.

Even after learning that most of her friends either were fairies or had married them, she hadn't thought of dating one. It was different for her. Lily and Greta had fallen for their guys before they knew.

She hadn't personally spent much time alone with Stefán, but because he'd worked next door to Greta for so long, she felt in a way that they were old friends. While she wasn't in the market for a man, he was kind and generous, steadfast and smart, loyal and funny—all the qualities to make someone a good husband one day. She just had to make it clear she was interested in him for more than just being friends, otherwise she might accidentally push him into Zoë's arms.

By the time she made it back out into the kitchen, Stefán had laid out all the ingredients and set out the skillets and saucepans. She laughed when she saw that he'd picked the blue apron with the French pun, leaving the other one for her. She made quick work of tying it around her waist and stepped up to the counter next to him.

"Did you know that pasta puttanesca was one of my favorites? Christophe and I ate our way through Italy on it. I'm surprised you picked that to start. It tastes complicated."

"That's the beauty of it," said Stefán. "It's full of flavors and yet it only takes about twenty minutes to make."

"So, where do we start, chef?"

He measured out a cup of black olives. "We need to chop these in half. They're already pitted, which I suggest you remember to get if you make this on your own."

He glanced around the kitchen and Julie pointed to the knife block by the double cast iron sink. "Knives are there," she said. "And since the counters are butcher block, we can just chop right on them."

"That would be you doing the chopping, Julie. Do you know how to work a knife?"

"Actually, yes." She selected the right size. "My brother showed me how. But, during all those years that I worked for Lily, I was in college and I hardly ever cooked more than noodles, so I don't exactly chop like one of those chefs on television."

"I can show you the technique they all use. It'll keep you from cutting off your fingers. Don't worry about going fast. The speed comes with practice, and for this recipe, you don't need to cut them precisely, anyway." They made quick work of it and after they scooped them into a small bowl, he broke off four garlic cloves and demonstrated how to smash one and remove the peel. "You talk about your brother a lot. Are you guys close?"

"He was basically my only friend when we were growing up. He's the one who got me into skateboarding." She smiled as she remembered how he picked her up after wiping out on her board one summer and how he encouraged her to keep going.

"Where is he now?" asked Stefán.

Once Julie got the hang of the movement, she found that some of her attention could be freed up and she could carry on a conversation while she worked.

"Gosh. All over the place. He's an adventurer and a conservationist. He's also a filmmaker who sort of doubles as an environmental activist. He's—well, if you ever meet him, don't tell him this…but he's kind of my hero. He's the reason I want to help change the world and make it a better place."

Stefán smiled and moved on to heating the oil in a skillet.

"What about you," she prompted. "What motivates you?"

He thought for a moment. "Honestly, I loved my life as manager of The Fairy Kingdom." He stirred in the garlic for a minute before adding the anchovies. "It's weird because I like the order that comes with making decisions, and I loved helping out the fairies when they migrated over."

Julie saw him nod to the skillet and she added the olives and the tomatoes and capers. "You said 'loved.' What's changed?"

"Well, because now…now, I don't really know where I stand. Lily and Greta have taken over and I'm back to just running the teahouse. I understand why it has to be, but I can't help feeling like after being in charge of the whole place, it's a bit of a demotion."

Their eyes met and Julie was overcome with an intense fondness for the man next to her. She gently squeezed his arm. "Thank you for opening up to me like that." Before she took the potentially embarrassing next step of kissing him, she cleared her throat and turned away. "By the way, did you say this stuff needed to simmer for about fifteen minutes?"

He nodded and as the spicy fragrance of the puttanesca sauce filled the loft, Julie decided to lighten the mood. She asked Alexa to play "Sway" by Michael Bublé and then pulled Stefán into an impromptu dance that ended up a combination of Rumba and Cha Cha.

He lowered her into a dramatic dip, and when he brought her back up, he whispered in her ear. "I'm still your cooking coach, so I want to remind you not to forget the spaghetti. The water is already boiling, so all you have to do is drop it in."

Julie pulled out a serving bowl she'd bought with Greta, and he took out a baguette that he'd secretly warmed in her oven. Then, he placed his hands over the table, which produced an authentic Tuscan tablecloth. With a snap of his fingers, plates and silverware appeared.

He gestured for her to sit across from him, and as she lifted her first forkful, she burst out laughing.

"This has been great fun," she said. "And I can't thank you enough for showing me how to make one of my favorite dishes." She lowered her head and looked up into his eyes. "But you do realize that it isn't quite nine o'clock in the morning, and we're already eating dinner."

He winked. "Yes, well some people say that breakfast is the most important meal of the day, so wouldn't you want it also to be your favorite?"

"Good point. So, when are we going to make the second recipe, the caramel-nut breakfast cake?"

"How about tomorrow night?"

Even from across the room, Stefán knew that the group of three seated at the table near the window were Magda and her two friends, not because he recognized them, but because he'd expected them in The Fairy Kingdom Teahouse at that precise time. He giggled to himself. Once again, their disguises were perfect. By then, he'd met with them enough times that even without his fairy intuition he could easily tell which was which. Since they'd never offered their real names, he privately referred to them by the ones he'd given them at their first meeting.

"Tea for three, please," said the woman wearing the tasteful scarf and who spoke with a French accent. Stefán recognized her immediately as Cropped Hair Guy because she pursed her lips at the end of her sentences in the same way he always did. The teenage boy with the blond bangs and painted fingernails was biting his lip just as remembered Eye Patch Man doing, which meant that the grandfatherly gentleman who did most of the talking, also with a French accent, was probably Magda. He carried a silver-tipped cane.

Stefán had suggested the mid-morning meeting time, because generally there were fewer customers at that hour, and he'd likely have the opportunity to join them at their table at least part of the time.

He brought a samovar of tea and a tray of cookies, and as there were still a couple of humans in the room, he turned up the volume on the ambient music. Then, in a low voice, he passed on the information they sought.

"The meeting you requested with the royals is confirmed."

CHAPTER NINETEEN

Györfi's time serving as a waiter in Gabriella's bar had not been a total waste. He'd kept his eyes open and taken notes. When he'd first arrived in New York City, albeit not of his own choosing, he'd been naive about American customs and language, and determined not to make the same mistakes again.

Customers of all stripes came to the bar, and he'd learned to recognize which of their mannerisms and slang were worth imitating. From them, he also developed a hip sense of style, and he found out how to duplicate their looks by chatting them up and discovering the brands they wore and where they bought them. He also figured out a way to order clothes and accessories and have them delivered.

First, he'd had to lose weight and get in shape. He suddenly had access to cash, and at the recommendation of a customer he'd hired the personal trainer they all seemed to use. Since he was confined to the bar, he'd paid the trainer to come to him, and his efforts paid off. He didn't exactly become buff, but he went from a size extra-large to a medium.

He made the bar manager so miserable that the man quit, and with Györfi now in charge, he could make the decisions. Without Zsa Zsa as a headliner, he set about to change the theme of the bar, and by paying attention to his customers and a fair amount of trial and error, he eventually transformed Gabriella's into a trendy New York club.

Dressed in the latest cool clothes and fluent in a more modern vernacular, in time he passed as the smart and sophisticated owner. He'd also created an entirely new back story whereby he claimed to be a former rock and roll record producer with several gold albums under his belt as well as a long list of celebrity friends. Using the bar computer, he'd printed photos of himself at parties and on red carpets and hung them in frames throughout the bar.

By the time he'd arrived in Myers Beach, Györfi had developed so much self-confidence that he ended up believing his own made-up nonsense. Gone was the stuffy Lord Birnam-Wood that he'd wrongly thought would appeal to Zsa Zsa. He was still partial to the name, but in his hip new-and-improved version he palmed himself off as an obscure billionaire jet-setting aristocrat who, thanks to Chet, looked good with his shirt off.

And that's how he spent his afternoons. Sitting on his favorite bench wearing nothing but a Speedo watching the men's volleyball games. Every day he held out hope that he'd spy Alias on one of the teams. He was sure he'd recognize him, even after all these years. And he was in no rush. He had all the time in the world.

He looked down at his empty bag of french fries. Then

he flicked his finger and chuckled when it was instantly filled with a new batch. Goal number one? Check.

Before he left Zsa Zsa's club and while she was peeling hot candle wax from her face, on the spur of the moment, he'd rubbed the pendant stone, snuck up behind her, and became one with her body. Simply locking her up wouldn't have been enough. She had fairy princess magic. Furthermore, she lived for revenge, and he knew that she'd never stop chasing him.

For the first time, he could do fairy things. Lots of silly things, like making things appear and disappear. He'd been practicing his magic for a couple of days and found he was getting pretty good.

So, all in all, Györfi was pleased with the way things had turned out. All that stood in the way of his complete happiness was his second goal: to make Alias his lover. While he waited, he would enjoy the sweaty, shirtless men thirty feet away who never failed to turn him on.

He was taking a bite from his sandwich when he heard a voice behind him mentioning that the surf wasn't as high as he'd thought. Two men carrying surfboards walked past him and skipped down the boardwalk steps to the beach. From the back, the brunette looked like he could have been Alias—same height, same shaggy hair, long legs, perfect body. Of course, he couldn't be sure.

Györfi tossed the last of his sandwich into the air and snapped his fingers. Suddenly, two seagulls dove for it at the same time, and when they collided, their squawking was loud enough to attract the guys' attention. They turned around briefly at the commotion and then continued to the water, but in that one split second, Györfi's heart pounded and his mouth went dry when he recognized Alias and the young Third King. He couldn't believe his luck.

He watched them toss their boards into the water and paddle out. The moment he'd been waiting for had arrived. He pointed at the surf and flicked his finger sending enough princess power to create some impressive swells. Then, when nobody was looking, he manifested a board and headed out after them.

For the next hour, he rode in one huge wave after another. They could see how good he was, too, he made sure of that. In time, they'd wave to each other, and sometimes they'd race to see who could get back out to catch the next wave the fastest. For never having surfed in his previous nerdy life, Györfi was ecstatic. Being a jock around Alias was a dream.

All three dragged themselves back to shore at the same time, and when he saw Alias and Christophe tilting their heads back and squeezing the water from their hair, he waited until they looked in his direction and then did the same. He also made a point of flicking water and sand off his chest to draw attention to his well-developed six-pack. He took a moment to thank Chet again.

"Hey, friend. That was fun!" Alias walked up and gave him a quick pat on the shoulders. "We were going to Joe's Java Joint for a coffee. Want to join us?"

Györfi looked at the dive watch he quickly manifested on his wrist, and turned toward them to make sure they could see that he was wearing the Panerai Submersible S Brabus Experience Edition.

"Um, let me check the time," he said. "I have a couple

of…oh, never mind. It's not that late. Yes! I'd love to join you."

They ditched their boards and took a table outside. Alias and Christophe were introducing themselves when Derek came to take their order.

"Well, if it isn't Lord Binghamton again. I wasn't sure you'd be back."

"It's Birnam-Wood," Györfi corrected again.

"Lord?" Christophe and Alias asked in unison. When he saw their shocked expressions, he coughed and laughed it away.

"Oh, that. Yes, I'm afraid it's true. This young man insisted on calling me by my full name, but of course, nobody else does, especially my friends. He thought quickly. "Call me Monty."

"Monty?" asked Derek. "Now you want me to start calling you Monty? Okay, whatever. Regular coffees all around, guys?" They nodded and when he left, Györfi leaned back in his chair.

"Short for Montgomery," he said.

With names under their belts, they started to recap the last hour, and the epic waves and their close calls. When they asked, Györfi explained he was eager to make a change, and he'd come to town to see if he might make Myers Beach his new home base.

Christophe made his apologies for having to leave early, and Györfi ordered another round of coffees for him and Alias.

"Those were some waves," said Alias. "We generally don't get such big ones this time of day."

Györfi winked. "Then I guess we got lucky, huh?"

"Yup. So, you must have been surfing for a long time. It takes a lot of experience and stamina to take on monsters like those."

"Yeah. Well, I try to keep in shape." He wiped a hand across his chest. "Speaking of which. I'm looking for a gym. By the looks of your six-pack, you obviously work out. Can you point me in the right direction?"

Alias smiled. "Um, actually, I don't go to a gym. What you see is what you get, I'm afraid."

"Gosh, why do you say 'afraid?' You've got an amazing body...Alias." Györfi's voice wavered when pronounced the name. For too many years as Alias' tutor, he'd been forced to refer to him as 'highness.'

"And you, Lord Monty, have an awesome watch! May I?" Györfi turned his arm so Alias could get a closer look. "Very nice," he said as he traced a finger over the face. "I might have to get one like it."

"I'd be happy to show you my other one," said Györfi. He brought his finger to the watch face and made a point of accidentally grazing against Alias.' "It's just down the boardwalk...in my room at the Sandpiper."

Alias pulled his hand away and finished his coffee in one gulp and pushed his chair away from the table.

"You're a very cool guy, Monty," he said, standing up. "But I think you may have misinterpreted my easygoing personality. I'm very much a married man. In fact, Christophe, the other cool guy who was surfing with us, is my husband."

Györfi sat alone at Joe's, letting sink in the uncomfortable feeling of having been rejected a second time by Alias the beautiful. Looking back, he realized the first time had been his own fault. He'd been an overweight and sloppy drunk trying to seduce a Greek god. This time, at least, he felt he'd gotten to first base.

It was time to regroup and rethink his strategy. Sadly, to make another stab at Alias, it would mean abandoning Chet's body and ditching his other favorite alias, Lord Birnam-Wood. He'd need to eliminate Christophe too, and when he remembered Zsa Zsa wanting to take down the fairies by getting the royals to turn on each other, he smiled and thought that perhaps she had the right idea, after all.

CHAPTER TWENTY

"Thank you, thank you. You've been a great audience." Dame Gabor had just finished her set with a cover of *My Heart Will Go On* to the usual warm applause. As a regular performer, she knew how to milk an audience, and she'd developed a new signature bow which included clutching her hand to her heart, a second homage to Celine Dion. "I'm going to take a little break and I'll be back up here soon, so don't go anywhere."

She blew a kiss and walked to the crowded bar. This was Györfi's third night at The Fairy Kingdom piano bar. To be sure he was noticed, he wore the same skinny jeans and Gucci loafers with no socks, along with an Armani unconstructed jacket over a different graphic T-shirt every night. Because Alias had admired his expensive dive watch earlier in the day, Györfi decided that wearing a luxury watch was a must, and he pushed back the sleeves of his jacket to show off the Jaeger-LeCoultre Master Control Geographic Automatic Stainless Steel and Leather watch he'd seen online and conjured for the occasion.

Until he worked up another persona, he was walking around in Chet's body, thinking that on the off chance that Alias might pop in and see him, he might give Györfi one more chance. At the least, if Alias was as well-known as he expected, he hoped to learn more about the man so he could plan his seduction better.

He also wanted to find out all he could about Christophe and learn where he hung out and when, because Györfi had added another box to his checklist: eliminating him so Alias would be available.

From his experience at Gabriella's, he was aware of the tug-of-war patrons played with the entertainers. Customers got bragging rights for being seen in conversation with celebrities, especially for the inside gossip they'd bring home, and he knew that entertainers responded well to flattery and tips, not necessarily in that order.

"Your voice gives me goosebumps," he said to Dame Gabor when she sidled up.

"So does yours," she replied. "It's one of the sexiest I've heard. Are you an actor?"

He realized how little he knew about the man's body he inhabited. But he had to agree with her. He'd miss speaking through the man's incredible vocal cords.

"What can I tell the bartender you're drinking?" he asked.

She eyed his tanned face and slim figure. "Oh, he knows." She raised a bejeweled finger at the bartender, and he slid over the lemon drop martini he'd already made her.

"It's on me," he said with a grin.

She raised her glass. "Thanks. I've seen you here a couple of times. Got a name?"

He took a breath and this time had fun mimicking Sean Connery. "Wood. Birnam-Wood." Then for fun he added, "At your service."

"Pleased to meet you, Birnam." She eyed his clothes. "Anything you'd like me to sing? You look like a hip kind of guy. I may not look like it, but I do hip-hop."

Györfi was tired of explaining his name, so he didn't correct her. But he quietly vowed to make sure the next one he chose would be easy for people to regurgitate. He clinked his glass against hers and gestured at his shirt and jeans.

"Yes. But looks can be deceiving. I happen to be into very specific retro music...by artists you're much too young to have even heard of."

She batted her eyes at the compliment. "Try me."

"Okay. Here's one. *Are You—*"

"*—Lonesome Tonight?* It's one of my absolute favorites. I sang it just the other night. I guess it was one of the nights you weren't here."

"I must not have been, because I certainly would have remembered." He slid her a fifty-dollar bill. "Would you sing it for me tonight?"

She batted her eyelashes again. "Next set, if you're nice. But I should warn you that I don't sing the Elvis version. I like how they sang it in the late nineteen-twenties and early thirties. In the style of Vaughn De Leath."

"Yes," Györfi nodded. "Or Zsa Zsa Hajdu?"

Dame Gabor arched a brow. "Yeah, her. Not a fan."

He gazed around the lounge and hooked his thumb at a table in a corner. "How about joining me over there? It's more private."

He got two fresh drinks and carried them over.

"So, what brings you to Myers Beach?" she asked.

"Hoping to spend some time with an old friend." Then he looked her straight in the eye. "Maybe looking to make a new one."

She touched his hand. "Anybody I might know?"

"It's unlikely. He's quite a bit younger than we are."

She winked. "You never know."

"His name is a bit unusual. Goes by Alias."

Dame Gabor gulped. "Tall? Extremely good-looking? Patrician?" She watched him nod in acknowledgment. "My goodness, Birnam, another coincidence. You are certainly a curious man."

He gave his name one last chance. "Birnam's not my first name," he said. "I'm actually Lord Birnam-Wood. But please, call me Monty."

She sighed. "Somehow I'm not a bit surprised that Alias would have a titled friend. But since we're friends, now, how about I drop the *lord*, and you drop the *dame*? Call me Rita."

"Deal," he answered.

The stage lights went back on. "Listen, I'm up now. Will you be here after my set?"

"Of course."

She opened with his favorite song, which she dedicated to her friend, Monty. He smiled when the spotlight hit him for that one instant, but he only listened with one ear. Instead, he focused on his new next move. Getting closer to Rita and gaining her trust had become crucial.

The votive in the center of the table reminded him of Zsa Zsa and made him chuckle. But when he looked around the lounge, he noticed that the candle was the only one in the house that was unlit. When he was certain that no one was looking, he snapped his fingers and produced the flame. He giggled again. Even Zsa Zsa would have been impressed.

"So, how do you know him, our mutual friend, Alias?" Dame Gabor asked when she rejoined him.

Her reminder of his new conduit to Alias rekindled his excitement and sputtered out his response. "I…well, I knew him when he was younger."

She reached across and traced her finger down his shirt. "So that's how he got his awesome body, huh? You taught him to lift weights?"

Györfi blushed. "Something like that. We did play sports together."

She lowered her voice. "Did you make magic together, too?" He blushed. "I saw you light the candle from the stage. I suspected you were a fairy, but one never knows. You must have come with that last migration."

Györfi coughed. "Guilty as charged.'

"So you're one of those!" She touched his hand again and her eyes got wide. "I confess that I find Outliers absolutely captivating."

"And you're a fairy, too, then?"

"Yes, of course. And now that we got that out of the way, let's talk about Alias. I suppose you know that he's a king now, by marriage to the Third King?" she asked. He felt a chill when he heard the words fall from her lips, and he nodded to pretend to be current.

"So, it sounds like you know him well."

"Yes, and *entre nous*, we're especially tight. I'm what one might call his confidante."

Györfi could hardly contain himself at his good fortune to meet someone who would be so helpful, and he had to force the next words out.

"I'd love to meet King Christophe. Do you know him, by chance?"

"Not to brag, but I'm terribly close to all of the kings… and queens. I'm sort of a celebrity around here, and we hang out together quite a lot. If you like, I'd be happy to arrange a little get-together to introduce you. It's no problem." She tilted her head. "As a matter of fact, I'm meeting Alias in two days," she said. "Right here. Shall I tell him you're looking for him and try to set something up?"

"That would be most generous," he said.

CHAPTER TWENTY-ONE

"I hope you won't be upset if we don't bow, Your Highnesses," Magda said as her guests entered the spacious vestibule. Stefán easily identified the two men standing rigid at her side as Cropped Hair Guy and Eye Patch Man. "My friends and I gave that up long ago."

"No worries," said Theos warmly. "And I believe I can speak for Christophe and Zsombor. We understand your politics."

For eschewing the trappings of royalty, Magda nevertheless presented as a patrician in a dark navy Chanel suit and a simple gold necklace over a slender body with ramrod-straight posture. She held out a hand and nodded to Stefán as a sign to begin the formal introductions.

The kings and queens formed a line and waited patiently as she greeted each one and passed them on to an awaiting assistant who showed them the wide curved stairway that led to the mezzanine where they would all gather.

Lily was first in line.

"Oh, Lily. How I miss your old store. I think I've got one of everything you sold." She gestured to a room closed with double doors. "They're on display in the next room, and I'd love to show them to you later." When Lily's face didn't show that she recognized the woman, Magda smiled. "Please don't bother to try to place me. It will be futile…I'll tell you why, later."

Magda's hand moved her on so she could greet Theos, who was next in line.

"Theos, the king! My goodness. Even more handsome than I remember. I watched you kitesurf every day during the exhibition. Front row on the beach. Didn't miss a single event. You cut your hair—it used to reach your shoulders. But you've still got those same eyes." She turned to one of the men standing at her side. "Please remind me to get his autograph for someone on my staff, will you?"

"And Greta, my goodness. You kept me in stitches every weekend with your skits. I keep one of your wands on my desk. With everything you're doing now as a queen, I'm so pleased to hear that you've kept up with your many local charities."

Greta looked surprised. "You know about them?"

Magda nodded. "Why yes. I helped deliver your school supplies to needy kids. I was a volunteer for years."

Greta tilted her head and squinted to place her. "Hmm. Maybe it's the hair color," she finally said.

"Most definitely," Magda laughed.

"Zsombor, I haven't seen you since the opening gala of The Fairy Kingdom. It was a lovely party and the Piano Bar Lounge is a wonderful addition to our boardwalk." She gave him a wink. "Marrying Greta was a fine choice."

Christophe and Alias came forward together. She had not met either, but she knew a great deal about them.

"Alias, a prince and now a king! Congratulations on your marriage to this handsome man, the Third King." She dropped his hand and took Christophe's. "I remember you when you were born. Welcome to my humble abode." She led them up the marble staircase where she directed everyone to a large and comfortable-looking semi-circular sofa that faced the ocean.

"My goodness. What a view!" exclaimed Greta. "Look, Zsombor. It rivals the one from Julie's penthouse, don't you think?"

As they filtered in and took their seats, Christophe stopped to admire a bronze bust that sat on a marble pedestal.

"Stephen the First, am I right?" he asked.

"Yes. You're spot on," said Magda. "The last Grand Prince of the Hungarians. You probably know that this bronze was cast to commemorate his ascension to the throne as the first King of Hungary. It's been in the family for over a thousand years."

"I thought so. We have a similar bust in our palace library," he said.

"Identical, I should think. Your grandfather and I were given them at the same time on that festive occasion. Zsombor and Theos should have one as well." They nodded.

"I'm amazed that you knew our families," said Christophe.

"Goodness. Everyone knew everyone back then."

Stefán spoke up. "Well, I'm very familiar with the bust

in Christophe's library. Not long ago, I had the misfortune of someone dropping it on my head!"

Magda raised her eyebrows. "Do tell!"

He looked to Christophe for permission to relate the incident. When he nodded, Stefán went on to give a thumbnail of how Zsa Zsa had taken over Zoë's body and caused such mayhem, which culminated in their battle in the palace. Magda listened with great interest. Two large pink teapots and the exact number of cups and saucers had been artfully arranged on the long glass coffee table, and when Magda gave a nod, one of the men removed the tea cozies and poured.

"Hajdu? That Zsa Zsa?" she asked.

"How would you know about her?" asked Theos. "She's not a fairy."

Magda waved a dismissive hand in the air. "I didn't mean that we were friends or anything. I made an educated guess on pieces of recent gossip I put together. She's become quite infamous, and well, there aren't many Zsa Zsas around."

"Yes, we can agree on that," said Stefán. "But as I mentioned, this get-together is a social call and has no agenda other than a chance to get to know each other. Thank you, Magda, for hosting, and to the rest of you for coming."

"We were certainly intrigued when Stefán mentioned that you and a few other fairies had been living in Myers Beach before us," said Zsombor. "And I was surprised that you said you'd been at the gala we hosted at The Fairy Kingdom Teahouse. I don't mean to be rude, but you seem to know a lot about us, and yet none of us recognizes you."

"But we were there." Magda looked at Greta. "We were on the pink carpet right behind you."

Magda walked to the huge round window that looked out on the ocean. "I've already shared our story with Stefán, but I've decided to share it with you as well. It's a major part of who we are today and I think it'll give you a better insight into our people." She took a sip of tea. "We left our homelands, such as they were, over a century ago, to escape tyranny, and we were lucky enough to find this marvelous refuge here on the Pacific. So as not to draw attention to the differences between us and our human neighbors, I hope you understand that we've gone out of our way to change our appearance on a daily basis."

Theos cleared his throat. "We feel the same way. Staying under the radar is obviously paramount to our survival as well."

"Pardon our skepticism," Magda continued. "But missteps by members of your various kingdoms have already brought media coverage and scrutiny to Myers Beach that we'd never experienced, and frankly we're worried. With so many of you in town now, more slip-ups will inevitably occur, and we fear our calm oasis will cease to exist."

Alias added, "We'd like to reassure you. Every fairy allowed to leave the confines of our building now has to complete a course that instructs them how to assimilate. Award-winning actress Dame Gabor gives the classes personally, assisted by our queens," he gestured at Lily and Greta. "We're confident our fairies will leave with a full set of strategies to fit in."

"Ah yes, Dame Gabor," said Eye Patch Man. "A good choice. She likes going out in disguises as much as we do."

"Yes, we frequently listen to her sing at The Fairy Kingdom Lounge," said Cropped Hair Guy. "By the way, can any of you shed light on the very hip and handsome younger man she's hanging around."

Alias jerked his head at Stefán and smiled. "She hasn't told me a thing about a guy. You?" Stefán shook his head. "Well, good on her. Anyway, I'm seeing her tomorrow morning. I'll try to work it into the conversation."

Magda spoke again. "On a more sober note, Stefán tells me that overcrowding in The Fairy Kingdom has become a pressing issue. From our point of view, that can lead to unhappiness and increased tempers, and we see that as a recipe for disaster."

"Yes," said Lily. "We're currently looking for new space, though I know all too well that the Myers Beach real estate market is tight."

"And we'd ultimately like each kingdom to have its own building. For obvious reasons," Zsombor added. "To avoid scrutiny, we need to keep the main floor of The Fairy Kingdom open to the public, as it currently is, but we'd have plenty of room for our fairies if we relocate the others."

"Lily and I are working on finding enough space up in our compound," added Theos. "It's going to be tight at first, but there are other areas within the cliff itself that we haven't completely explored."

"Which leaves us looking for new quarters for the Outliers," added Stefán.

Magda gestured to her two friends. "Among the three

of us, we own considerable property in and around the beach. Candidly, we see it in our best interests to offer them up as options, if you'd be interested."

"They've already shown me a couple buildings," said Stefán. "And honestly either one would be suitable to house the Outliers."

Theos shifted in his chair. "I'd like to go off-topic for a moment and ask a question that's been bugging me since I met my first Outlier." Magda nodded for him to go ahead. "Forgive me if it's too personal, but I wonder how you've managed to stay alive without fairy dust? Do you have your own supply? I mean, I assume you heard about the pandemic."

"Of course. It broke our hearts when we heard. But like I said. It's the air and the water around here that sustains us," said Magda. "We can't do as much magic as you and the other fairies, but we can do enough. Considering that humans can't do any, what we can muster up makes us kings of the mountain around here, though being kings of anything is not an expression we particularly like to use."

"For centuries our people had limited access to fairy dust anyway," added Cropped Hair Guy. "So we've gotten used to doing without it. Not sure how your fairies will manage, though. It sucks."

"Still," said Eye Patch Man, "I'd be lying if I didn't admit to a secret desire to experiment with some, you know, even just to feel the power. I mean, I remember hearing from my grandparents how back in the day, people had candy dishes full of fairy dust sitting on top of tables all over the house."

Stefán smiled as a bittersweet feeling swept through him. He hoped they'd all have enough to go around, one day. And in an effort to help add to the spirit of the meeting, he suggested, "Well, once we make a breakthrough with the dust, maybe we'll be able to give you all some so you can do a little more?" He looked at the surrounding kings and queens to gauge their reaction to the offer, and they all seemed amenable.

Magda's lips curled into a genuine grin. "That would be lovely, Stefán, dear."

CHAPTER TWENTY-TWO

Julie was soaking up the sun when drops of cold water splashed against her warm thigh. She jumped up and spotted Alias racing back into the surf laughing like a hyena.

"You're the worst!" she shrieked. As she settled back against her lounge chair she watched him dunk his head into the surf and then squeeze his hair back into a messy bun.

A little while earlier, she'd caught him racing out of The Fairy Kingdom down the boardwalk. He'd been on his way to see Christophe when she'd stepped in front of him and held out her arms to block his path. She'd directed him to a bench that faced the water and had made him sit down and stop rushing around.

They could both use a break, she'd insisted. She was still running the fairy figurine and foundry business Lily had left her, and Alias was always in the lab or out scouting the *Yano*, and they hardly ever saw each other. Before long, she convinced him to take an hour out of his day and relax with her on the beach. Since she was already wearing her bathing suit under her sweats, all he'd had to do was conjure up a couple of chairs and towels.

At mid-morning, there were not a lot of sunbathers, and they mostly congregated in the central area around the lifeguard tower. Off to either side, away from the guard's whistle and people playing Frisbee, there was plenty of space where the two of them could unwind in relative privacy.

He waded back to shore and flopped onto the lounge chair next to hers. "I could hear you thinking all the way back in the surf," he said. "I thought we were taking a break. What's got you so glum? Nice shades, by the way."

She sighed and lowered the hot pink sunglasses that he'd left on his towel when he went into the water.

"Geez, I didn't know it showed. I'm so confused. I don't know where anyone stands anymore."

"Hmm. I'm not sure who you're referring to?"

"I don't know. Maybe it's silly but I'm worried that Stefán and Zoë are together."

He turned onto his side so he could look into her sad eyes. "You mean like together, together?"

"Yeah. That kind."

"Hmm. That's the first I've heard of it, but Stefán and I don't talk much about our personal lives. What makes you think they're a thing?"

"For starters, they've been spending a lot of time together, you know, just the two of them. He's been showing her how to cook, and I've seen them out shopping. Once I saw her teaching him to skateboard, which I swear he asked me to do."

"I wouldn't read too much into that. Everyone is trying their best to keep Zoë's spirits up. After she learned she didn't have magic, on top of not having wings, it's been harder and harder for her to stay positive."

All the tension left Julie in an instant and she sighed. "Yeah, I guess that's true."

A glint of light that ricocheted from something shiny peeking out from her top hit his eye, and when she saw him looking closely at her chest, she pulled out the pendant. "Oh. I see that Christophe gave it to you," he said.

.She nodded and put the pendant back under her top so the sun wouldn't turn the metal too hot. "He was so cute. He said the thing had brought you together, and that was all the luck he needed. So he passed it on to me. I guess you approved?"

"Of course. I'm glad to see he followed through and gave it to you."

"Yeah, yesterday. He caught up with me right after I had seen Stefán and Zoë goofing around for the millionth time, and I guess I looked pathetic and needy." She gave it a rub with her thumb, over her top. "I hope it works."

Alias reached for one of the water bottles they'd stashed between their chairs and rolled over on his back again. "Aah. I really need this. Things aren't so great at the compound, either." He let out a sigh of his own. "Theos and I have been trying to accommodate all the fairies, but there's still not enough space. So that's an ongoing challenge."

Julie fiddled with her sun hat. "Hmm. Listen to us. A couple of Debbie Downers today."

He snickered. "Yeah. It's not exactly how I thought this relaxing break you talked me into would turn out."

Julie was about to reply when they heard Dame Gabor's voice.

"Well, I'm surprised to see you two down here. I didn't think you left the lab, Alias. Am I interrupting anything?"

"Nah. Julie said we both needed a break, and she was right. What are you doing here? I thought they had you tied up all day teaching the assimilation classes."

"True that." She looked at her dive watch. "In a few minutes, I'm giving a module about interacting on the beach, and I'm a little early. I saw you and thought I might catch some rays while I'm waiting."

"Is that a new watch?" asked Alias. "I don't think I've ever seen you wear one."

"I never used to, but last night I saw a customer at the lounge wearing it, and when I mentioned liking it, he just gave it to me. "

Alias raised his eyebrows. "Would this *customer* be the same guy people tell me you've been seeing?"

"Who's saying that?" She spread out her towel. "Whatever happened to the concept that 'What happens at The Fairy Kingdom Lounge, stays in The Fairy Kingdom Lounge?'"

"Well, apparently it doesn't," he said. "If I heard it. Anyway, I ask because it looks like the exact same one I saw a guy wearing yesterday." He brought his face close to her watch dial. "Yup. I thought so."

Dame Gabor laughed. "I'm not surprised. The town's gotten full of high rollers." She reached for Julie's sunblock and when Julie nodded her approval, she squeezed some out and lathered her face. "What did he look like?"

"Good-looking dude. You know, buff, tan, all that. He was out surfing with Christophe and me. He was pretty hip, actually."

"And probably loaded. I looked the thing up online. They're super expensive. I'm glad I didn't have to pay for it."

"I don't think he had to, either."

"What makes you think so?"

"When he was riding in on a big one, Christophe told me he saw what looked like a wing scar, so later I gave him a bro pat on the shoulders and felt it. Since we hadn't seen him before, we assumed he was one of the Outliers."

"Sounds like he might be the same guy," said Julie. "Was he a fairy, Dame Gabor? You didn't say."

"Actually, he is," said Dame Gabor. "And he's quite handsome if I do say so myself. And sophisticated. He's got some title, too. Lord something or other."

"Ah, that's him," Said Alias. "Lord Birnam-Wood. Definitely cool, but full of crap, right? Since when are there such things as fairy lords?"

Dame Gabor coughed. "Ahem. I beg to differ, your H. I recall a rather madcap dalliance I had with a handsome one. Of course that was a millennium ago. Back when there was a Fourth Kingdom."

Julie perked up. "So, you were around then? Zoë showed me a book that talks about it," she said. "Do you remember the lord's name?"

Dame Gabor fanned herself. "Young lady, you can't get anywhere in life if you can't remember names and faces. Of course I do. Lord Steffon, and a real dreamboat, as we used to call guys like him."

Julie probed further. "Did he look like our Stefán, by any chance?"

Dame Gabor closed her eyes. "Hmm. As a matter of fact, yes. I can see a strong resemblance. Different spellings of the name, of course." She hummed a bit. "A shame that the little coup to overthrow that beastly grandfather of his ended in his throat getting slit."

"Yeah, I know about that since we studied it in history. I'd really like to get back our mutual friend, the lord," said Alias. "Do you mind my asking if he made, how shall I put it, advances?" Dame Gabor squirmed but didn't answer. "Because he hit on me."

She sat up on her towel, and the color drained from her face. "Wait? Really? No. He said you two were old friends. That he knew you when you were little." Chatter from the class assembling down the beach interrupted the conversation. "Fun's over for now," she said. "Why don't we pick this convo up in the morning, your H. We're still having coffee, aren't we?"

He nodded and lay back down. "Yup."

Alias and Julie dozed off, and when Julie sat up later to reapply sunblock, she glanced down the beach to the group that surrounded Dame Gabor and then craned her neck. "I thought she said she was giving a class to fairies. Those people look like humans."

"Good," said Alias. "Then she's doing her job. They're fairies disguised as humans. Can you see? Some of them are taking notes." He closed his eyelids.

"Wow. She is good. They fooled me."

Someone in the group started shouting and Alias jerked his head up. The man sounded angry, and when Julie squinted, she reported that the man was Belos.

"I recognize him. He's the one who caused a fight a few days ago." They were too far away to hear what he was yelling about, but they could tell he was arguing with someone, because he raised his voice. "And if I'm right, it can't be good."

Alias frowned at the disruption of his nap, and he heaved himself out of his chair. "I better check that out, before things get worse."

"No, I'm telling you, it's true," yelled Belos. "We're all gonna die in a month!" When Alias stepped into the conversation to ask what was going on, most of the fairies gave a slight head bow. Belos didn't and pointed at him, instead. "You! You and your brother. You're part of the problem! You've been lying to us all along."

Julie tugged at Alias' arm. "What's he talking about?"

"It's complicated." Alias turned to Belos. "Nobody's been lying to anyone."

"Don't split words with me. Maybe not lying, but you haven't been telling us the whole truth. We just heard about the fairy dust." He waved his hands in the air to make a point. "And that there's less than a month left to live!"

"Who told you that?" asked Alias.

"What does it matter? Everybody knows, and we're all scared out of our minds. It's all anyone has been talking about today."

Julie's face turned white. "Is this true, Alias?"

He bit his lip and looked at her, but she was too shocked to speak.

Belos started in again. "What are you looking at her for? Why would she care? She's not a fairy."

"Listen," said Alias. He reached to place a friendly hand on Belos' shoulder. "I know it sounds dire, but all the kings are on this. We've been working day and night."

Belos pulled away. "Yeah, so you say. But face it, you've failed. You're no closer to making proper fairy dust than you were months ago!"

Julie blinked as the weight of the news crashed down on her. If what Belos said was true, then all her friends would die too. No more dinners with Alias and Christophe. Or rom-com marathons and game nights where they get to laugh over stupid jokes and poke fun at each other the way they always had. She'd lose Lily, Greta, and her unborn godchildren in one fell swoop. She wouldn't be able to help them set up their nurseries, and she'd never get to be the cool aunt who brought the kids presents from her worldly travels. Zoë would be gone, too, just as they were becoming best friends.

And Stefán. She wondered if he knew. The thought wracked through her body, and without looking back she left Alias and tore across the beach and burst into his office at The Fairy Kingdom.

"You're going to… die," she wanted to yell, but the words got stuck in her throat.

"Huh?" His smile turned into apprehension when he saw the tears leaking from her eyes.

She grabbed his hand. "You're going to die," she repeated. "I heard some fairies talking about it. Something about running out of fairy dust in a month."

"Ah, that." He smoothed his thumb over the back of her knuckles where they touched.

She jerked her hand away and ran it through her short hair. "Huh? I'm freaking out and all you can say is, 'ah'?"

"Listen. Theos and the others didn't want people to panic, or worry, unnecessarily, so—"

"Wait! You knew?" The guilt she saw reflected in his blue eyes told her he had, probably for some time, and her panic turned into anger. "I can't believe you didn't tell me."

He swallowed. "We've been trying hard to keep that whole thing under wraps. Now I have to wonder how it got out. Look—"

"No, you look." Tears streamed down her cheeks. "If it's true, who cares how. I—I just wish I'd known."

"And what would you have done? Found the last element that everyone and their brother have been searching for?"

"No. Not that!" She pounded her fist on the desk. "Oh. I'm so mad at you!"

"Hold on!" He spun around in his desk chair and stood. Then he gently cupped his hand under her chin and tilted up her head so he could look into her eyes. "Why are you mad? Please tell me."

Her face softened and her shoulders sagged in defeat, as the built-up anger drained from her all at once.

"What I was going to say was that, if I had known...I wouldn't have let you make me fall in love with you."

She leaned up on her tiptoes, and when she reached him their lips crashed together in the longest and most passionate kiss of her life. With that news and that kiss, nothing would be the same, and given the ticking clock that she now realized loomed over his head, she was determined to spend as much time with him as possible and make the most of their remaining weeks.

She nestled her head on his shoulder and heard him whisper that he wanted to take her to The Sea Catch for a nice romantic dinner.

"I'll get us the best table with the best view."

"No. I want to be alone with you. Come to my place and I'll cook dinner. Someone recently taught me how to make a wicked pasta. And for dessert…well, it's not going to be breakfast cake." She stood on her tiptoes and they kissed again. "And I promise you won't be disappointed in the view."

CHAPTER TWENTY-THREE

Stefán was flying high. Literally. After a lazy morning spent exploring each other's bodies, he'd finally forced himself to leave the comfort of Julie's bed and the safety of her loft to make her special frappuccino at The Fairy Kingdom.

Once outside, he couldn't contain his happiness and decided that flying would help him burn off some excess energy. He'd popped out his wings and zoomed over Myers Beach from one end to the other. He even did fancy backflips and raced along upside down like a teenager ecstatic over losing his virginity—which he had just done.

Putting off a relationship hadn't been intentional. He just hadn't gotten around to it. Being orphaned at an early age left him with the need to take his education and career more seriously than his peers, and he'd neither sought a relationship nor found himself in a situation where sparks had flown or bells had rung.

Until that morning in the sick bay. He'd been staying up day and night caring for Zoë, when by the simple act of bringing him that frappuccino, Julie had touched his heart. They'd hardly known each other, but she later explained that even from across the room she could see in his exhausted eyes that he was a keeper. He'd been trying to overcome his lack of dating experience ever since and tried his best to be around her whenever possible and show that he was interested in her.

He started by making his special drink every morning and delivering it to her apartment. Sometimes she'd invite him in, and they'd spend a little time in exploratory chitchat, talking about the things that made them each tick. Sometimes they'd sit outside on the front stairway saying nothing but enjoying each other's presence just as much.

By normal standards, as he understood them, their get-togethers hadn't qualified as actual dates, but in the end, he lucked out with his clumsy strategy. Julie and he were together, an item, and they no longer had to waste time tiptoeing around each other's feelings.

Clearly, they both knew that the abrupt pivot in their passion was a result of the earth-shattering news, but he didn't consider it in any way a dilution of their true feelings. In his mind, they'd already been close to the couple stage goalpost, and the fairy dust revelation was merely the catalyst that brought them over the line.

He wondered how she'd gotten the impression that he preferred Zoë's company, and he searched his mind for things he'd said or decisions he'd made that might have led her to arrive at that conclusion. Certainly, Zoë was attractive, but they weren't compatible in any other way that mattered to him. Even if they had been, apart from the additional awkwardness of dating Christophe's kid sister, she was also a princess, and way above his station.

What was true, however, was that she would always be a dear friend. He hoped that things would work out between her and Briar. A union between a princess of the Third Kingdom and an Outlier would go a long way in normalizing relations between them, and might even help defuse suspicions the Outliers continued to hold about governments and authority. Had Zoë not told him that things had been heating up between them in confidence, he might have shared the information with Julie, which would have eliminated her worries.

That morning, he was eager to go to the Third Kingdom palace library and study the ancestry book Julie talked about and see for himself the photograph of Lord Steffon whom everyone mentioned looked so much like him. Before going there, however, he needed to stop by his office to make a brief check-in.

When he arrived, he found The Fairy Kingdom in a state of panic over the fairy dust leak. Greta pulled him aside and led him to a conference room where Theos had called the royals together to discuss the emergency and share the various levels of hysteria that they'd seen playing out in all three kingdoms.

Stefán learned that a small percentage were reacting to the fear of imminent death with depression and had confined themselves to their rooms. Furious at Theos and the other kings for not informing them earlier, a few fairies were even taking out their anger in more militant ways. Lily reported several acts of insubordination and destruction of property.

Infuriated elders promised hunger strikes, and panicked mothers with young or unborn children were devising plans to return to their homelands and had already begun to form groups that would be large enough to reconstitute and sustain their former villages. As expectant mothers themselves, Lily and Greta had spent hours trying to persuade them to stick it out.

Under the guise of trying to make the best of a terrible situation, a surprisingly large number of fairies were copulating in the halls and in other public spaces, and Greta and Lily asked for Stefán's immediate assistance in herding them back into their rooms.

Zsombor and Christophe had already begun to make inquiries about the source of the leak, and though very few individuals would have been privy to that sensitive information, they had yet to come up with a name. With no other recourse, Alias suggested using his time cube technology to corroborate everyone's stories.

"We love the tech," Greta said, shooting Alias a small smile. "But don't you think this invasion of our privacy is going a little too far?"

Theos protested as well, reminding everyone that some time ago they'd all agreed *not* to use the technology on each other, and Lily worried about the lack of trust.

Christophe shot them an apologetic frown. "Listen. It's not that we don't trust you. It's that we can't be sure of who else might've been around to overhear us."

His comment only added to the irritation, and Stefán stepped in with a request for clarification. As someone also privy to the secret, they'd be viewing his actions and whereabouts as well. "So, you're only looking for eaves-droppers, nothing more?"

"It's an invasion of privacy, flat and simple," Greta said. She stood and crossed her arms.

"Honey," Zsombor rested a hand on her shoulder. "We know you have nothing to hide. We just have to be fair to everyone. It'll be okay."

Lily sighed. "I don't like it, either, one bit." Theos pulled her close and she relented. "Fine."

Christophe and Zsombor left to review the footage, and they returned only an hour later to confirm that none of them had let anything slip and that they'd have to widen their search. In the meantime, they fanned out to ask for a pause in the violence and to gather for an address by Theos.

He tried to reassure the unruly crowd that he and the other kings were working around the clock to address the problem and prevent the unthinkable, but from the jeers and boos from the audience, it was obvious that his words had not been enough to assuage their fears.

CHAPTER TWENTY-FOUR

Following Theos' address, Stefán tied up a few loose ends and then left to devote the rest of the day to Julie. Given the serious new development, he was thrilled that he was no longer in charge. Keeping the peace was up to the queens.

He suggested to Julie that they start with some private time on the beach directly below the compound. Since Theos and Lily would be occupied for the rest of the afternoon, he knew they'd have the beach to themselves.

Before Theos bought the property, it had been strictly off-limits, and it was alleged that the entire compound and beach had belonged to a mysterious arm of the government. A sinister cluster of antennae towered above the installation, which, together with ominous signage everywhere, threatened serious consequences to would-be intruders.

Julie remembered how blown away she and Greta had been when Lily described that small strip of secluded beach when she told them about her steamy kitesurfing escapade with Theos. As Julie stood in the skimpy gold bathing suit she'd bought in St. Martin and gazed down from the edge of the infinity pool at the top of the cliff, she couldn't deny that the prospect of using that same beach as the backdrop for her own romantic frolic gave her a thrill.

She'd never noticed a stairway, and she wondered how people ever got down there from the top of the cliff. Stefán suddenly emerged from the pool house and must have seen her look of confusion. His eyes sparkled.

"Oh. In case you were wondering, we'll be flying."

Her heart pounded, though she wasn't sure if it was from imagining what it would be like to sail through the air in his arms, or from how buff he looked in his Speedo with the sunlight glistening on his olive skin.

She kissed his cheek. "Are you sure you can carry me?"

He winked and rolled his shoulders and popped out golden wings that reminded her of the intricate veins of cicadas. She'd seen Alias and Christophe's wings before, but seeing wings that belonged to her lover took her breath away. They looked every bit as large as the others and shimmered as if the very air currents that caused them to flutter were also magical, and she fought the urge to touch them.

He laughed and scooped her up easily. "As a matter of fact, to illustrate my point, I think we'll take the long way." She let out an excited squeal when one massive flap of his wings sent them soaring into the sky.

They flew behind and over the cliff, and though she'd driven to the top in her car many times, looking down from the sky gave her an astonishing new perspective of the imposing estate and the switchbacks that she remembered had been sometimes dangerous to navigate. When they rounded the cliff and headed down, she noticed for the first time that the sand of the private beach sparkled more than the public beach on the other side of the jetty.

They touched down gently near the shoreline and he lowered her to the sand where the surf swished around their ankles. After a brief kiss, Julie took the lead and dragged him out to where the water was waist-high.

She splashed him first, and before long a full-on water fight ensued, during which they took turns diving underwater to sneak up on each other. Once he swam between her legs and lifted her up on his shoulders, and for the next half hour, she stood on them and dove off with increasingly more difficult flips.

"I didn't know you liked the water so much," he said later as they trod water. "Do you think you might like to learn how to play underwater rugby? It's plenty deep."

"Maybe," she said, spitting out water. "As long as you aren't talking about really being underwater."

"No. I am. How long can you hold your breath?"

"Depends. Probably for close to a minute, anyway. Why? How long would I have to?

"Indefinitely," he said.

"Well, then, I guess then that settles that. Underwater rugby is out."

He grinned. "Not necessarily."

She scrunched her face. "I don't get it. How?"

His eyes sparkled. "Magic. Are you up for it?" They were bobbing chest high in the surf, and she was about to nod in the affirmative when a large wave broke on her from behind and pushed her under. She staggered to stand

and regain her balance when he brought his face toward hers.

She turned her head and spit out more water. Then she laughed. "Wow. Are you suggesting that all it will take is a kiss from a fairy?"

"Not exactly. But something like that. Open wide and let me do the work. It'll only take a second."

He took a deep breath, and then holding the back of her head with one strong hand, he pressed his lips over her mouth. Slowly and deliberately he exhaled into her lungs, and her eyes rolled back in their sockets from the tingle she felt as her chest filled with his breath. They stood breathing quietly with locked lips for close to three minutes.

Finally, he stepped back. "Well?"

She pretended to complain. "You lied. You said the magic would only take a second."

He brushed the hair from her forehead. "That's all it did take. I kept on kissing you because I wanted to. You didn't seem to mind."

She poked him. "I didn't. But I, um, don't feel any different."

"You're not supposed to," he said. "What's probably going to feel weird is inhaling underwater for the first time. Trust me, though. After you get the hang of it, you'll love it."

He did a surface dive and disappeared. Julie took a deep breath and dove in after him. The water was crystal clear, and she could easily track him swimming beneath her along the bottom. With a few strong scissor kicks she caught up and swam along. When she felt she couldn't hold her breath any longer, she tapped him on the shoulder and pointed to the surface.

He shook his head, and she heard him utter a garbled 'no.' But she was desperate for air, and she kicked hard to propel herself up. He put his arm around her waist and rose alongside her until she burst through the surface.

"I can't," she said, gasping for air. The water was well over their heads where she'd come up, and he held her steady as the surf continued to break against their faces.

"Did you try to breathe?" he asked. "It didn't look like it."

"No. You're right. I didn't. I just…couldn't." She coughed. "I was too scared."

"Then let's try something else. Start by floating face down. Relax and keep your mouth closed. When you're ready, breathe in just a tiny bit through your nose. See how that goes."

She flipped on her front and though she was more than capable of floating on her own, she let him hold her steady. Bubbles came to the surface first which signaled that she was emptying her lungs. Suddenly her head turned and she blew water out of her nose.

She put her face back in and a few seconds later he felt her chest expanding and contracting as she began to breathe. He let go of her, and a few minutes later she brought her head back out of the water.

"This is so amazing! It really works! I would stay under all day long if the salt water didn't sting my eyes."

Stefán smacked his forehead. "Crap! I forgot. Sorry." He rubbed his palms together and cupped them over her eyes.

"There," he said when he pulled them away. "Now you should be set."

She gave him another kiss. "So how long will this magic treatment of yours last?"

"The rest of the day," he answered. "But if that's not long enough, we can start all over again at the beginning and go all night."

"Hold that thought," she said, and she dove to the bottom.

CHAPTER TWENTY-FIVE

Breathing underwater wasn't the only skill she acquired that afternoon. She learned that they could converse, too, after a fashion. Their words were a bit garbled, but when they got close they could understand each other better.

One of the first things she said to him was that she wanted to postpone learning rugby. She'd been having too much fun exploring the sea floor and they'd just come upon a sheer rock wall that she didn't want to leave.

They determined that they had made a complete circle and they were facing the bottom of the cliff that led straight up to the compound. They split up and she was examining what she thought were letters and numbers carved into the stone when she heard Stefán call her.

She looked over and saw him pointing to a large dark area on the wall. When they swam closer they realized it was a cave, or at least the entrance to one. He pointed to the surface, and Julie followed him up.

"I came up so we could talk clearly. It looks like a cave down there," he said. "Want to take a look?"

"A date *and* an adventure? Hell yeah!"

"Okay. Cool. I know you're breathing like a champ, but we don't know what we're going to find, and it might get a little scary inside. So let me know if you need help."

He led the way, and they dove back down. At the entrance, Stefán told her to hold out her hand. He conjured two balls of light and transferred one to her, and then holding them out in front of them to illuminate the way, they kicked slowly side by side into the dark.

They ran their hands over the super smooth curved walls and down along the bottom, which they were surprised to find was as finished as the sides. The floor made a gradual incline, and soon they were able to stand up. He conjured a third larger fireball which revealed that they had emerged inside a huge cavern. The rough rock walls glistened from the light as though they were covered in quartz or mica.

"This looks like it was inhabited," he said. "And I'll bet we entered through a giant man-made tube."

She pointed to the ceiling. "Yeah, you're right. See? There are lighting fixtures up there and around on the walls."

"What is this place? It's huge." He walked across toward one wall where it appeared that brickwork had been filled in to seal over a former door. He fingered the edge where the new stonework met the original rock and looked from side to side to get his bearings. "I wonder if Theos knows about this space."

He put his face close to the sparkling fragments. "You know, at first I assumed this was quartz, but now that I'm up close, it's clearly not. It's got a gold sheen to it."

Julie walked toward him, and when she got closer, she felt her pendant vibrate. Then it pulsated so hard, it tingled her breasts, and she raised her hands in confusion.

"What the hell? This thing is going bonkers."

"Alias told me the stone in the pendant always reacted that way when it was near one of the elements," he said.

Suddenly her pendant stone spewed out rich golden light so brightly that they no longer needed his fireballs, and after he extinguished them, they stepped back to drink in the spectacle of a billion specks of gold twinkling against the dark, rough walls. He turned toward Julie and when he saw that her body was suddenly awash in gold, he took her hand and watched the color travel up his arm.

He let out a whoop and punched the air with his fist. "This sparkly stuff. It's *Yano!*" They threw their arms around each other. "We found it! We've got to tell Alias!"

CHAPTER TWENTY-SIX

They swam back through the tunnel tube as fast as they could and then scrambled out of the water onto the shore. To their surprise, Alias was sunning on a lounge chair next to their towels.

"Gosh, what the heck's wrong?" Alias asked. "You're breathless. Did you see a shark or something?"

Stefán bent with his hands on his knees to collect himself from the excitement of their discovery and a few seconds later he managed to sputter out his words.

"We found the *Yano!*"

Alias leapt to his feet. "Really? Where? In the water?"

Stefán nodded and pointed to the cliff where it met the ocean. "Down there in a cavern right under your compound. Can you believe it? There's tons of it. Probably enough to last forever."

"Fantastic. Take me there." Alias turned to Julie. "Listen, Dame Gabor is meeting me here, so would you mind keeping her company until I get back?"

Julie gestured that she would stay put and for them to go ahead. She was walking with them to the water when she saw Dame Gabor flying over the jetty toward them.

"Leave it to her to have the most gorgeous wings," said Julie. "It's been ages since anybody showed me theirs, and now this is the second pair I've seen today."

"Can't be," said Alias. He jerked his head to look up and he frowned when he saw that it wasn't Julie's imagination. "She's not supposed to be doing that. There's still a ban."

Stefán gulped and shot Julie a side-eye. He had taken care to ensure that no one saw him fly with Julie a little earlier, and given Alias' reaction, he didn't plan on admitting that he had.

As Dame Gabor fluttered to the sand, the intricate pattern of her vibrant blue wings trimmed in silver shimmered like gossamer in the bright midday sun.

"Forgive me for my ignorance, Alias," Julie said. "Because let's face it, my experience is limited, but I've only seen such elaborate wings on royals. Does she rate those because she's a dame?"

He shielded his eyes from the sun. "To be honest, I've never seen hers before, so yeah, maybe."

Dame Gabor strutted closer and as their eyes adjusted to the brightness, all three gasped at her floor-length gown.

Julie elbowed Stefán, who in turn elbowed Alias. "A little overdressed for the beach, aren't we?" said Alias.

"Oh, this?" She laughed and gestured to the silver-blue fabric that perfectly matched the colors of her wings.

Julie laughed along. "It's stunning. You look like you just got off the stage."

"Guilty!" said Dame Gabor, as she swaggered closer. "After my last set of the night, I ended up drinking late with friends. I'm a bit embarrassed to say that I fell asleep in my clothes." She pointed at Alias. "That's why I missed my morning coffee with him."

"Yes, well, I'm glad you finally woke up, but unfortunately this is not a good time for our chat," he said. "But… what's gotten into you? You know better than to fly around in public. I hope nobody saw you."

"Oh come on, hot stuff." She grazed a finger across his bare chest. "I was late for you once already today. I wasn't going to make you wait around for me again." He stiffened at her uncharacteristic behavior and brushed her hand away.

"I have to leave with Stefán for a bit."

"What's the rush," she asked. "It's a beautiful day to relax."

"Yeah, well, Julie and I found the *Yano*," said Stefán. "We're super excited, and I was about to show him where it is."

"Congratulations!" said Dame Gabor. "So, we can look forward to having some of that high-test dust any day now, eh?"

"Yes!" said Alias. "And not a moment too soon."

"I'll stay with you until they get back," said Julie. "I doubt they'll be long, and it'll give us a chance to catch up. Maybe run some lines."

"Love to." Dame Gabor snapped her fingers and her dress melted into a tasteful aquamarine one-piece, paired with a lacy white beach cover-up, dark straw sun hat, and tasteful beach sandals. She spun in a slow circle for Julie.

"Better?"

Julie couldn't help but snicker at the antics and clapped. "Like a million bucks."

CHAPTER TWENTY-SEVEN

"It'd be good press," said Stefán. "I could get you on the front page of the *Tattler* for stepping up to the plate."

The sponsor for the jump rope event had pulled out at the last minute which was why Stefán and Alias were scrambling to find another. Zsombor had suggested hitting up Joe's Java Joint, considering how they had patronized the coffee house for so long.

"Hmmm, I'd have to talk it over with my new partner," Joe said. Stefán thought that the way he scratched his chin so exaggeratedly was Joe's way of appearing to give the idea his consideration.

"That's baloney, Joe. Since when do you have to check with anyone to make business decisions?"

"Things around here are different now. Emili is very much involved. Have you met her yet?"

He tapped the shoulder of the tall attractive woman who'd been conversing with customers at the table behind them. When she turned, Stefán took in her long dark hair and bright brown eyes. He'd heard that Joe had taken on someone, but the scuttlebutt on the subject hadn't included a description.

"Alias and Stefán, meet my partner Emili." A customer called out to Joe and he excused himself.

"Nice to meet you gentlemen," she said with a voice that came across as cool and confident. She shook Stefán's hand first, and as soon as he withdrew it, he kicked Alias' foot under the table. Alias caught Stefán's eyes, gesturing at the large ruby-red stone on the woman's middle finger, and he held her handshake longer than normal, so he could get a better view of her ring. "Joe tells me that you're putting on a beach festival that you'd like us to help sponsor."

Stefán handed her a flier and sponsorship form. "Yes, ma'am. But not the whole thing. Just the jump rope competition. We feel Joe's Java Joint would be a natural tie-in."

Alias added to the pitch. "Apart from the exposure to thousands of potential coffee drinkers, think of the fun you'd have with the marketing. I mean, picture this." He held out a mockup of two advertisements. "Jump for Joe's" and "Jumping's Better with Java from Joe's."

"We can personalize the contestants' jump rope handles with your name overnight," Stefán added. "You could sell the jump ropes in your store, too. I know how Joe likes that kind of thing."

She flipped over the one-sheet that outlined the terms. "We'll talk it over. Fair enough?"

"More than fair," said Alias. "But tell Joe not to think about it too long. The festival begins in a couple days."

Stefán had just finished adding a final touch of salesmanship to close the deal and he was thanking Emili for listening to their pitch when Dame Gabor walked in, arm-in-arm with Dr. Lydia Anderson, Alias' head research scientist and co-trustee of the Dust Keeper's Manual.

He elbowed Alias. "I didn't know that they knew each other, did you?"

Alias whispered back. "What I do know is that Lydia loves theater. And we both know that Dame Gabor loves her fans. Do the math."

Stefán stood and gave Alias a signal that it was time to leave. The Outliers were about to move to a new location in one of Magda's recently vacated buildings, and Alias had offered him some of the provisional fairy dust to help speed up their renovations, since those fairies had limited magic at their disposal.

Alias' team had just started incorporating that final ingredient into the new and, he hoped, the final version, so he had offered Stefán some of the stopgap dust. It was more than powerful enough for the Outliers' renovation needs and, since they had it in abundance, he was going to allow Stefán to pick some up from the compound.

"Do you mind if we stick around for a few more minutes? I hardly get to spend social time with Dr. Anderson, and Dame Gabor is always good for a laugh." They stood and invited the women to join them. As they were sitting back down, Alias gave him a wink. "Oh, and don't worry, buddy. Like I was telling you, I'll give you as much you-know-what as you need. Because, before you know it, we'll have enough of the high-potency stuff to last a lifetime."

"Did I just hear what I thought I heard?" asked Dame Gabor. "You've started making the final dust?"

Alias lowered his voice. "Yes. Thanks to finding the *Yano*."

She touched Lydia's wrist. "This is so exciting. You know, I was actually there when Alias discovered it, so it makes me feel like a part of history. "

Alias shook his head and put a finger on his lips to shush her. "Actually Stefán and Julie discovered it," he whispered. "But we don't want to make the announcement until we've made the first batch."

"I just left the lab myself and can report that everything was on track," said Lydia. She pushed her glasses up her nose and looked to Alias for approval to continue. He nodded. "We're still doing some informal testing right now out in the field, so, please, please don't mention it to anyone."

"Ah, yes. My lips are sealed." Dame Gabor looked around the room. "I don't think anyone heard me, Your Highness."

"I don't think so either. Oh, and have you forgotten that you promised not to call me that in public?"

Dame Gabor blushed. "I'm so sorry. I don't know what came over me. It won't happen again."

"I was wondering when rehearsals would start?" Stefán asked. "Any idea?"

When no one responded, Dame Gabor looked around and saw that Alias and Stefán were looking at her.

"Are you talking to me?"

"Um, you're still directing our play aren't you?" asked Stefán.

"What play?" asked Lydia.

When Dame Gabor began stuttering again, Alias

stepped in. "Gosh. She's being so modest. She agreed to collaborate with the local theater to stage *Peter Pan* for the Dust Up Beach Festival. It's going to be a big hit, especially with the kids. We're so excited."

Joe stopped by their table and blanched when he saw that she had joined them.

"You? In my café? Now, that's a surprise. Last time you were here, you reamed me out for being a homophobe in front of my customers." He squinted at her. "I hope you came to apologize."

She had only managed to stutter out a few syllables when he stopped her. "Hey, relax. I'm joking. I'm the one who should be apologizing to you. Thanking you, really, because honestly, you did me a favor." Dame Gabor's face relaxed, though Stefán wasn't convinced that she still was following. "The way I talked about gays was pretty awful, and I'm embarrassed for being so ignorant and so appalling to my own grandson. Maybe you heard that he's gay?"

Dame Gabor suddenly pulled her mouth into a smile. "Of course, Joe. I'm glad I could help and that it all worked out so well for everyone."

He gave her a friendly tap. "So, where's your fancy cigarette holder?" She scrunched her eyebrows together and stared at him with glassy eyes.

"I'm sure I don't know what you mean," she insisted.

"Of course you do. The funny one you used to puff on all the time and blow smoke rings. I always wanted to know how it worked without using an actual cigarette."

She laughed. "Oh. That one." She patted her pockets. "I —I must've left it at home."

Dr. Anderson opened the collar of her blouse and fanned herself with a napkin. "So, how about this heat? She and I were just talking about how with all these people in town for the festival clogging the beach already, it's almost impossible to find a square inch of sand for ourselves."

"Yeah. It'd be nice if we knew someone with a private pool." Dame Gabor turned to Alias. "Do you know anybody with one…wink, wink?"

"Listen," said Alias. "If you'd like to go in a few, Stefán is headed up to the compound. You'd let them in the pool, wouldn't you?" Stefán nodded.

"Are you sure?" Dr. Anderson asked. "Theos and Lily like their privacy, and I know the rules. Employees aren't supposed to use it."

"Yes. That's right, but only if you don't have permission. Besides, he and Lily are away for the day."

Emili approached their table again. "Did I hear something about a pool?"

Stefán saw Alias' encouraging nod. "Yes. Alias just invited the ladies to swim up at his place. Y'know, you should come too. He and his brother have this fantastic infinity pool that stretches way out over the ocean. And since you're new to the town, you'll appreciate the amazing view of the whole beach. Obviously, only a select few get to see it."

Emili raised an eyebrow. "Well, I definitely won't say no. Thanks for the invitation. But I hope you're not just trying to butter me up so we'll say yes to your sponsorship deal," said Emili. "Because that's not how I roll."

Alias laughed. "I can't speak for Stefán, but since Dr. Anderson is going, I won't be doing any of the buttering."

Dame Gabor clapped her hands. "This will be fun. I can't wait to see it myself."

Alias rolled his eyes and poked Stefán. "Gosh, she never lets up, does she?" He turned to the older fairy. "You know, Dame Gabor, if I didn't know better, I might think you're starting to exhibit signs of early onset dementia." He gave her a friendly poke. "Of course you know that I'm kidding, don't you?"

"Yes. But you're right. I don't feel too sharp. What I need is a martini."

Alias shot Stefán a look before he turned to Lydia. "Stefán is picking up some of the old you-know-what. Would you mind showing him where to find it?"

CHAPTER TWENTY-EIGHT

Emili's hand went to her heart when they walked through the gate and took in the scope of the cliffside pool and view. "My god. This is breathtaking. You weren't kidding. And that's the house? Wow. I never would have known all this was up here."

"And look. A bar!" Said Dame Gabor. She set her Hermes bag on a chaise and looked around to get her own bearings.

"Oh, come on, Dame Gabor. Enough with playing dumb," said Stefán. "Alias has told me that you've been up here a million times." He pointed out the pool house to Emili and told her where she could find a dozen bathing suits that she could use and to otherwise make herself completely at home.

As he was dragging two other lounge chairs to set up next to Dame Gabor, she slathered on sunscreen and then sauntered to the bar. Stefán laughed when he saw her return with three lemon drop martinis.

"A little birdie told me that you gave up those." Stefán winked. "I think it was you."

"Oh come on, yourself. You know how resolutions go. Anyway, they're not all for me. One's for Dr. Anderson and another for Emili." When both Lydia and Emili held up their hands to decline the offer, Dame Gabor arranged them on the small table next to her chaise.

"Amateurs," she sniffed. "Oh, well. The more for me."

"I didn't mean to seem ungrateful," said Emili. "But I told Joe I'd take care of the evening rush, and in this sun a martini would go to my head right away. I've got my eye on that pool float."

She dove in and swam a couple of lengths before heaving herself up on the inflatable banana.

"While you're there, if you don't mind, I'm going to borrow Dr. Anderson for a moment," said Stefán. Emili gave him a thumbs up and then leaned back and used her hands to navigate the raft around to get the maximum sun.

Stefán waved his hand at a huge door, and the gigantic glass slid open. As they entered, Dame Gabor snuck in behind them. Dr. Anderson and Stefán started down the spiral staircase, and when they sensed Dame Gabor following behind, they gave each other a worried look.

"Look," said Stefán. "It's fine if you want to stay up in the living room, but Dr. Anderson and I are going down to the lab, so I'm afraid this is where we must leave you. I'm sure you understand."

"Oh, gosh. You don't have to worry about me. Alias has taken me down there many times," she said. "He must have told you that I've been his confidante for some time." She hooked her thumb toward the pool. "And that human out there won't need to know."

"To get your dust, we don't really have to go into the lab, per se," said Dr. Anderson. "So, I don't know, it probably wouldn't hurt if she tagged along. What do you think?"

Stefán hunched his shoulders. The compound and the lab were not under his jurisdiction. Dr. Anderson had seniority, though, and so he acceded to her suggestion.

They reached the door on the first landing, and she asked them to stand aside as she waved her hand in front of the sensor screen. The door swung open, and she flipped on the light. Before them, rows of pouches tied with pink laces nestled side by side in rows that ran the length of the storeroom, which Stefán estimated to be about fifty yards deep.

"This is the dust we've been using lately, and it's the best we have at the moment," Dr. Anderson told Stefán. She pointed at Dame Gabor. "Does she know what you're doing with it?"

He pulled three bags out into the landing. "I don't think so, do you, Dame Gabor?" When he saw her shake her head he briefly explained that he'd be using it to help renovate the Outliers' new building.

"I'm glad you're getting yours now," said Lydia Anderson. "We've been gradually moving all this to the lab where we add the *Yano*. Then we'll distribute the good stuff to the kingdoms as we make it so they can dust everyone. Then, of course, there's an entire other secure vault where we'll store the remainder."

"Interesting," said Stefán. "So, then after today, this room will basically be empty?"

Dr. Anderson looked Stefán directly in the eye. "Yes, until…did Alias tell you about the other thing?"

He stared back. "Yes. If you mean the thing that comes after the first thing."

"Yes. Anyway, this is where we'll keep it."

Stefán nodded. "Listen, let me take these and get to work. We hope to get them moved in another day."

"Wait! You guys are speaking in code. What are you talking about?" asked Dame Gabor.

"I'm afraid we definitely can't tell you that," said Dr. Anderson. "That would get the two of us into trouble." She looked at Stefán.

"What, don't trust me, Lydia?" She leveled a hard look at Dr. Anderson. "I thought we were friends." She uncrossed her arms and turned to Stefán. "Really? After all I've done? The risks I've taken to save all of us?"

Overcome with a sudden fondness for the woman who'd risked her life for them only a few short weeks ago, Stefán relented.

"All right, but if anyone finds out, we'll know who leaked it." He whispered, "In the back of the Fairy Dust Manual, there's a short passage about what they call a 'super dust.' When Alias is done with the regular dust, he wants to make some of that."

CHAPTER TWENTY-NINE

"Julie told me what Dame Gabor said. And since you're so interested in the fairy ancestry book that I showed her the other day, I decided to reread it." Zoë and Stefán had met up early the next morning. They were sitting close to each other on one of the sofas in the Third Kingdom library, balancing the heavy, oversized book across both their knees. "This one is the most comprehensive compendium of fairy history."

Stefán's eyes lit up as she flipped through the pages of the ancient tome, which she'd bookmarked at the headings of each of the three kingdoms.

"The book automatically updates itself every so often, all by itself." She went straight to the last few pages. "See? Lily's already been entered as Theos' queen. Look. Greta's in there, too."

"Amazing!" he said. "All of this interests me, probably because I have no idea where I'm from. I wouldn't even know where to start looking."

"Well, I've read this thing a number of times. I know

you told us a bit about your early life, so I'll see if I can point you to the right parts."

He looked up at her with wet eyes. "That'd be great. It's weird not knowing where we came from as refugees, or even why we had to flee our country. Even after Theos' father adopted me, he never told me anything else about my parents or their families."

Zoë did some calculations in her head and turned to the last section she'd bookmarked. "As you have noticed, this old book is full of photos, and here's the one we all keep saying looks just like you." She stopped at a full-page portrait of an older man. "What do you think?"

He bent over to get a better look. "Hmm. I'm not sure I see it."

"Really? The similarities are blinding." She poked him with her elbow. "Your names are even similar."

"Hmm, maybe Magda will be able to help me figure all this out, since she's the oldest fairy I know, outside of Dame Gabor."

"It's worth a try. In the meantime, you can stay as long as you want, unless you're going to Theos' meeting."

"I do have to run, but I'd love to come back and read it."

"Be my guest. The only caveat is that I can't let you take it with you. As I told Julie, it's a one-of-a-kind and has to stay here in the palace library."

Accommodating all the fairies in the dining room was always a tight fit, but Theos insisted that his announcement was of the utmost importance, and he promised he wouldn't talk long. As the first-floor lounge and dining room filled with fairies, Stefán paid attention to where they chose to sit. Loyalists crowded to the front, and those who were vocally disgusted with the kings and queens for leaving them in the dark gathered in the rear. He heard grumbling from every direction.

"I'm pleased to announce the theme for the festival." He strutted across the stage like a tech giant at a convention. He waved at the giant screen behind him, and instantly the Myers Beach Dust Up's bright silver and gold logo appeared on a black background, accompanied by its catchy theme music booming through the hall.

He waved his hand again, and the logo exploded into tiny bits that fluttered across the screen and eventually came together to form the letters of the tagline, *Myers Beach, where your wishes come true.* The reactions were mixed. Amid the scattered applause, he heard several fairies booing. The loudest complaint came from the back row.

"Why make it look like fairy dust?" roared Belos. "Are you trying to remind us that we're all going to die?" He egged on the fairies around him and got others to join in the booing which soon became loud enough to drown out the Dust Up theme music. Then he led them in a chant, which swept through the room.

"Hey, hey. Ho, ho. Theos the king has got to go. Hey, hey. Ho, ho."

Amid the chaos in the room, only a few fairies noticed that Stefán, Alias, Zsombor, and Christophe had walked on stage. Theos had stopped talking, and the five of them simply stood and gaped at the out-of-control fairies.

When Christophe and Zsombor gave their thumbs up, Theos gestured to Alias, who in turn, thrust out his hand and sent a lightning bolt that crisscrossed the ceiling. The ear-splitting crack that followed brought the noisy fairies to attention, and once again Theos took control of his audience.

He held up his hands. "If that's your wish, I will gladly resign." He paused and then smiled. "But not before I announce that our nightmare is over." He stretched out his arms, and the screen lit up with the words, "We have new fairy dust!"

It took several seconds for the message to sink in, but eventually the hall filled with cheers and applause. Theos gave a summary of how everything had come together in the last few days. The fairies stomped their feet in approval when he related the story of Stefán and Julie finding the last element. Then he acknowledged Alias and his team for their tireless efforts to make it all happen.

"I am officially designating next Sunday the Day of the Dust, a date that we will burnish into our calendars forever," said Theos. "And how appropriate that we memorialize this life-saving victory at the culmination of a weeklong beach party festival celebration. And now, I will turn the microphone over to Stefán, who is going to tell you more about the exciting events he has in store for us."

Alias intercepted the mic. "Yes. But before he does, I'd like to announce that starting tomorrow, we will begin to administer a full and comprehensive dusting to all of you." Everyone cheered, except Belos.

"All?" he yelled. "Even the Outliers?"

As Belos' king, Christophe stepped forward and Alias

passed him the mic. "Yes. This dust will give all fairies in Myers Beach a new chance at life, regardless of their kingdom's affiliation."

"Why?" Belos implored. "They haven't suffered like we have. And they don't use fairy dust anyway."

Christophe waved away the comment, and as all three kings held up their hands in solidarity, behind them on the screen flashed the words, *One fairy. Many kingdoms.*

"Your kings and queens will have the full schedule of dustings," continued Alias. "You may consult with them for your time slot."

Belos pushed his way to the stage. "Prove it. Show us the dust!" he yelled. "Why should we believe you? You're one of them!"

"We're mass-producing the new dust right now, as we speak," said Theos.

"Maybe, but Belos is right. How do we know it's going to work this time?" asked one of the younger fairies. "I hope you're not planning to make us guinea pigs again with this so-called comprehensive dusting of yours."

Theos turned to Alias. "Correct me if I'm wrong, but I understand you and Stefán are giving it a dry run out on the boardwalk any minute now."

Alias nodded.

"So, human testing, huh?" grumbled an older fairy. "Good."

CHAPTER THIRTY

At six in the afternoon, the boardwalk was still bustling with workers finishing up the preparations for Opening Day. A nine-man crew was installing the last few rows of the bleachers, where spectators would view the kitesurfing competition and the various other water events that would take place all week. Those races and matches required lanes and markers which the off-duty lifeguards were helping to set out.

A separate crew was laying down the stage in front of the bleachers where singers and standup comedians would entertain in the evenings after the water events were over. The buzz in town was that at least one top-tier singer was coming to perform. A couple more people were testing the giant spotlights that would light up the sky for the windsurfers.

The south end of the beach, near the Hersey Lighthouse, had been reserved for the larger carnival rides and games, and different crews were at work, erecting their own tents and infrastructures.

Sandwiched wherever they could find space, food vendors who had already popped open their tents in front of their vans were scurrying around in search of electrical outlets to connect to their fat mile-long power cords. Stefán watched the mom-and-pop vendors working up a sweat to build their stalls, and he was relieved that he'd taken care of his in advance.

As the organizer and Grand Marshall of the event, he'd arranged for permission to put theirs up the day before. He'd requested the exemption not to get an unfair jump on the other vendors by opening a day early, but rather so he wouldn't have to construct their booth by hand in the hot sun in front of everyone. Instead, he'd made it appear in the middle of the night when there were no witnesses. He'd done it remotely, too, with a snap of his fingers from the comfort of Julie's bed.

"Close your eyes," he said as he led Alias to the fully operational Fairy Dust Wishing Well, which was firmly and appropriately situated on the boardwalk directly in front of The Fairy Kingdom. As they passed by, Stefán puffed out his chest at a job well done.

They'd wanted the well to attract all ages and genders, and he had struggled to make the design look magical, yet not too frilly or too rustic. He ended up with a traditional circular rough stone well with twelve-foot gleaming wooden posts that supported a peaked slate roof.

"Very cool," said Alias, as he fingered the delicate bucket that hung by a silken rope from a single pulley. "Real gold, isn't it?"

"Yep. We'll keep the dust in it so that whoever is manning the booth can easily reach over and take a pinch.

That's not the most amazing thing, though. Check this out. When people look down into the well, they won't be able to see the bottom." He dropped a pebble, and several long seconds passed before they heard it splash.

"Nice! People will be trying to figure out how that works for days." He patted Stefán on the shoulder. "I'm proud of you. You nailed it, buddy."

To put their plan into practice, they wanted to change their appearances to not only draw customers in, but also so they wouldn't be recognized by the public later on. To create believable versions of beautiful young fairy princesses, Stefán enlisted the services of the top experts in the field of disguise: Eye Patch Man and Cropped Hair Guy.

The older Outliers coached them on how to take shorter strides and carry themselves in a more traditional, womanly way and how to pitch their voices higher to convince the public of their new female genders. They'd already picked outfits that complimented Stefán and Alias' new curves and shapes, and when they were finished, the Outliers beamed at how convincing Stefán and Alias played their parts.

Alias chose to play the blonde, and Stefán went as a brunette. Their tiaras glittered from their long flowing locks, and pastel-colored pointy strap-on fairy wings fluttered from their shoulders against their sparkly gowns. Hanging from golden chains around their necks were signs that read, *Modest Wishes FREE—One-to-a-Customer.*

While they had a blast waving their pink plastic wands and mugging for selfies, they also carried pouches of fairy dust. The point of their escapade was to test the new dust's effectiveness by granting random wishes in a trial run before they opened their booth to hordes of people the following day.

They'd put a lot of thought into the wishing well concept. To measure the dust's true power, they needed to fully grant each wish. At the same time, they had to be mindful of their one major constraint: Theos' admonition not to attract too much attention. Some people would no doubt ask for fancy cars or private jets. They always did, and those would have to be off the table. Big stuff like that appearing instantly in plain sight would grab headlines for sure.

They also knew from experience that humans frequently wished for things that took time to come true, like their team winning the season or getting over an illness. They'd play those by ear. What they really sought that afternoon were the types of wishes that guaranteed instantaneous results. Things that they could witness right away, firsthand. So they had to be sure each wish was carefully worded.

They heard the wolf whistles before they saw the two teenagers ogling them. Alias and Stefán stopped and waved their wands.

"Hey, boys. Want us to grant you a wish?"

CHAPTER THIRTY-ONE

Julie had invited everyone to her first party, ostensibly to show off her new culinary skills. That's how she billed the dinner, anyway. She'd only learned the one dish Stefán had taught her, but she was so insecure she made it two more times, to give herself enough practice and confidence to serve it to friends.

The impetus behind the dinner party was to celebrate Stefán's idea for the beach festival, which was lifting spirits even before it opened. She scheduled the event to take place the night before it started, because she knew that everyone would be up all hours and crazy busy for the rest of the week and probably too tired to socialize then.

The serendipitous discovery of *Yano* the day before, and Theos' subsequent impromptu announcement of the end of the fairy dust crisis added to the fortuitous timing of the get-together, which suddenly had many more causes for celebration. She was glad Stefán had stopped by to show her how to make the caramel-nut cake, too. The momentous occasion definitely called for dessert.

Christophe had briefed Zoë in advance on the substance of the speech Theos would give, and the news of the dust breakthrough put her in a great mood. She had told Julie she didn't want to lose it by sitting in a crowd of upbeat fairies hearing how they'd soon be flitting about the boardwalk granting wishes. Until Alias was convinced of the next step in her treatment, she was still a fairy without magic or wings.

Instead of attending the otherwise mandatory meeting, she chose to help Julie with the dinner. She snickered as she arranged Julie's place settings on the long dining table.

"This is kind of fun. But it sure feels weird. In the palace, I never lifted a finger." She adjusted a fork to look just right. "Except to do magic."

Julie wiped her hands on her apron and brought the large salad bowl to the table. "Welcome to the world of humans."

"Don't get me wrong," said Zoë. "It's fun helping you with this. It's just that doing any kind of work by hand without using magic feels so foreign." She set down the eleventh plate and turned to Julie, who'd gone back to the kitchen. "It was kind of you to let me invite Briar to a dinner with royals, given that they're an Outlier and all."

"Well, as the only human in our little pack, I guess I'm the one who really qualifies as an Outlier. Anyway, happy to have them."

"Christophe messaged me that the Outliers took the brunt of the animus at the assembly," said Zoë. "He said the crowd got ugly. He didn't give me many details, but I'm sure Theos and the others will tell us all about it soon enough."

Julie wiped the counter with the dish towel that usually hung off the front of the stove. She was new to kingdom politics, and despite its ugliness, it was beginning to intrigue her. She understood that Stefán had always considered himself part of Theos' kingdom. He'd told her that he'd even sworn allegiance to Theos' father, though he hadn't elaborated on what that meant.

"Did Christophe mention how Stefán fared at the meeting?" She didn't add her reason for asking.

"What do you mean? Why would he have to take any heat?"

"No particular reason. It's just that as the manager, he's said that he often finds himself in the middle of controversies, and I guess he's had to settle a few. When you're in that position, there's always someone who's not happy with you."

"Oh, I thought you were maybe going in a different direction," said Zoë. "You know, this morning he came by the palace. Like you, he'd expressed an interest in learning fairy history, and he asked to see the book I showed you. Specifically, he wanted to see the photograph of that Lord Steffon."

Julie sighed. "Yes, he told me he came by and that he saw the resemblance. I hope I can trust you, Zoë. I think he is starting to believe that his family was Outliers. I can't imagine what the reaction would be among the fairies if they caught wind of that."

She took a breath. "Listen, Stefán is so well-liked, that in my opinion, it would take a lot for them to turn against him. Besides, as I understand it, most of the ugliness has been coming from that one rabble-rouser. That Belos character."

"Oh, yeah! He was the one we ran into on the beach yesterday, the guy who accused Alias of being a liar. You wouldn't believe the hard time he gave him."

"I'm embarrassed to say that Belos is from our kingdom." Zoë looked down. "Funny. Neither Christophe nor I can place him. But, you know, considering both our memories have gone to crap, well—"

"Hopefully things will start to cool down soon," said Julie. "Stefán told me that all the Outliers were moving out of The Fairy Kingdom tonight to a new location in one of Magda's buildings somewhere. What a stroke of luck that he met her. She and her two friends have been super helpful."

They continued to chitchat on easier topics while they finished getting ready. Theos, Lily, Zsombor, Greta, and Christophe arrived at Julie's together several minutes later.

"We're sorry for being a little late," said Lily. "We were going to stick around after the meeting for a while to field a few questions, but we ended up being punching bags for Belos' insults and had to stay longer. We came here straight from The Fairy Kingdom."

Theos filled Zoë and Julie in on what happened at the meeting, and how they were appalled by the vitriol directed at the Outliers. He also reiterated that Belos had caused most of the trouble.

"The good news is that they should all be moved out by the end of the night. It's sad, because I was hoping that once they all got to Myers Beach we could come together.

Maybe we still can." He sighed. "In the meantime, keeping all the kingdoms separate is probably a good idea for a while."

"I don't get the sense that many of the fairies feel animosity toward them, deep down," said Zsombor. "It's just a few that are stirring up trouble and making the others think they feel the same way." He and Greta walked into the kitchen, and he leaned over the saucepan. "Mmm. Smells delicious," he said. "Nothing makes me happier than a nice vegetarian pasta."

Julie poked him in the stomach. "Not entirely vegetarian, your highness. An authentic puttanesca requires anchovies."

He waved away her concern. "I can work around it," he said. He kissed Greta's cheek. "I've been told that I've become very flexible. Besides, anchovies are little, anyway."

The clanging of Notre Dame's bells in surround sound got everyone's attention.

"The door's open," she shouted over the clanging.

Alias and Stefán bounded in. "I knew it was," said Alias. "I just like ringing the bell."

"The *bell*? More like twenty," said Julie.

"Alias and I came straight from the boardwalk. Man, did we have fun," said Stefán. He regaled the group with a description of their outfits and how they'd intended to grant a bunch of wishes, but because they got started late, they ended up only doing one. "It was a good one to try the dust on, though, because it was an easy wish. They were kids, and kids always want to fall into some money."

"By the way, you are all going to love the wishing well. Stefán did a bang-up job," said Alias. "I can tell it's going to be very popular. In my experience, most humans claim that they don't believe in magic, but they can't seem to resist asking for wishes. I'm thinking we might want to staff up."

Stefán pulled Theos off to a quiet corner and whispered, "I'd like to suggest that we consider letting Julie run it for at least part of the time. I think she'd be perfect, and let's face it, humans won't be expecting to find real fairies, anyway."

"No, I suppose not," Theos whispered back.

"She wants to do her part and be part of our group. And pitching in would help make her feel like less of an outsider," Stefán added.

"And why not?" asked Greta, who'd been standing close enough to hear the exchange. "Lil and I can get her all decked up like a fairy princess." She called to Julie who was still in the kitchen, "Everyone wants you to run the wishing well booth. What do you think? I personally know you'd be great."

Julie smiled and called back. "I'd love to. I mean, that would be every little girl's dream, wouldn't it?" She hung up her apron. "Dinner is served!"

Following the traditional seating protocols she'd learned from her family, she sat at the end of the table closest to the kitchen. She directed Stefán to take the seat at the other end, the head of the table, which for those who weren't certain, was a telltale signal that their relationship had moved to the couple stage. She told the others to sit wherever they wanted to, and after everyone got settled, Theos raised his glass and asked everyone to join him in a toast to Julie.

Greta held up her hand. "Wait. What about these two empty seats? Who are we missing?"

Zoë pointed to the chair next to her. "This one is for Briar, the person I'm seeing. They just messaged me. Something came up to delay them, but they're on their way."

"And the other is for Dame Gabor," said Julie. "And honestly, I don't know where she is. She said she was coming."

"The last time I saw her was at the pool," said Stefán. "I brought her, Lydia, and Emili to the compound for a swim. I had to leave before they did, and I told them to let themselves out."

"Who's Emili?" asked Lily.

"Joe's new business partner," said Greta. "I haven't met her yet." She looked around the table. "Has anyone else, besides Alias and Stefán?" Her question was met with blank faces.

"Come to think of it, I didn't see Lydia at the meeting, either," added Zsombor. "At the time, I didn't think anything of it. I just assumed she was in the lab."

"Gee, I hope everything is okay," said Lily. "We didn't bother to stop at home first. Maybe one of us should go there now to check."

"Christophe and I'll go," said Alias. "We'll be back in two seconds."

When they opened Julie's door to leave, they found Dame Gabor poised to push the doorbell. She looked like Catwoman in a skin-tight black leather outfit. A large bouquet of flowers was clutched in her other hand.

"My goodness," she said. "Are you coming or going?" As

she side-stepped the guys and squeezed around to go through the door, she grazed against Alias.

"We're staying, now that you're here." He pulled her into a hug and kept his arm around her as he and Christophe ushered her inside the apartment.

"We were leaving to look for you," said Christophe. "Nobody saw you at the meeting, and because people were afraid that something happened to you at the pool, we were on our way to check."

She turned her head and spoke inches from Alias' ear. "What could possibly have happened?" They approached the table, and she gave it a once-over. "Where are you sitting, Alias?" she asked. He pointed and she took the empty chair next to him.

Before she sat, she snapped her fingers and conjured a vase. Then she let go of her flowers which floated in the air above the guests.

"The truth is, I am a little embarrassed. Nobody abhors lateness more than I." She flicked a finger at the flowers and each stem landed in the vase and arranged themselves into a spectacular centerpiece. "I hope this was all right, Julie. I wasn't sure what to bring."

"Thanks. It's perfect, because I had forgotten to buy some," said Julie. "Anyway, we're all glad you made it."

"Well, there was certainly nothing to worry about. Dr. Anderson, Emili, and I simply fell asleep on our lounge chairs. It must have been the sun. Anyway, we only woke up a short time ago." She licked her lips. "Julie, do you mind if I make myself a martini?"

"I thought you gave those up?" asked Alias.

"Come on, Alias," said Stefán, adding a wink to Dame Gabor. "You know how resolutions go."

She flicked a finger, and the moment it appeared, she took a sip and looked around the table. "Did I miss anything?" She was met with a table full of astonished faces.

"Where do we start?" asked Theos.

He was about to explain everything all over again when they heard a knock. Zoë ran to open the door before the Notre Dame bells started up again. Briar leaned forward and gave her a peck on the cheek, and then brought out the bouquet from behind their back.

She shoved her nose into the flowers and took an exaggerated inhalation. "Delicious! Thank you, Sweetie. This is my partner, Briar, everyone." She took their hand and led them to the table, where there was a mix of reactions.

Theos, Lily, Greta, and Zsombor hadn't met Briar before, and their expressions conveyed more than approval of the preppy-looking person with curly hair and a million-dollar smile.

Stefán, on the other hand, burst out laughing. "I hardly recognized you, Briar. You clean up nicely."

"What does he mean by that?" asked Lily.

Briar gave a slight bow to the kings and queens and then took the last empty seat which Zoë had saved next to her.

"Oh, I like to switch things up, like most of us Outliers," they said. "I've never had dinner with a king or queen before, so I chose this look out of respect. I hope I got it right."

"You did, and I approve," added Zsombor. "When Greta

and I were starting to see each other, I confused her all the time, because one day I'd be looking like an outdoorsman in flannel, and the next evening she'd see me in tailored Zegna."

"Yes," said Greta. "Keep people guessing. It makes life much more fun."

"Thanks for your approval. Anyway, sorry for being late. You probably heard about the ruckus at the other end of the boardwalk." Their comment was met with blank faces. "No? Well, when I left High Tide—say hello to the new Ludo champion by the way—the cops were all over the place. Something about kids getting robbed. Anyway, I hung around a few minutes to see what was going on."

Alias jerked his head toward Stefán, whose eyes conveyed a sense of dread. "What did the kids look like?"

"I couldn't really tell. They were on one of the benches facing the other way, you know, and surrounded by policemen. From their backs, they looked like teenagers."

"Just curious. Did you see how many there were?"

"No, I didn't. Three, maybe?"

Alias shot Stefán another glance. This time their faces reflected relief.

"Are you thinking they're the same guys you and Alias granted the wish to?" asked Julie.

Alias waved away her question. "No. Why would they be? They got robbed. They didn't fall into money."

She continued. "I just ask because I was thinking about my job working the wishing well, and how it's actually quite a responsibility to be sure the wishes are worded correctly. There's a website called 'Wishes gone bad,' or something like that, where people end up with completely unexpected outcomes of things they wished for incorrectly."

Stefán interceded. "I understand," he said. "Alias and I have granted millions of wishes, and we were very careful to help them word theirs. There would have been no way that their wish to get money could have been misconstrued as being robbed, so I'm sure those two events are unrelated."

"Well, that's good," said Julie. She held up her fork. "Let's eat."

Soon the group was eating and chatting away in multiple conversations from the topic of the upcoming Dust Up, to the inevitable recap of some of the uglier parts of the meeting.

"Since I'm so new at this, I wondered if any of you could help me out," said Julie. "A little while ago, Zoë mentioned something about a Fourth Kingdom. Obviously, it doesn't exist today, but apparently, back in the day it really thrived. Anyway, I think it's fascinating, and I wondered if anyone here had any personal anecdotes about it they could tell me." Without thinking, everyone turned to Dame Gabor.

"Why is everyone looking at me?" she said with a laugh. "Are you trying to remind me how old I am?"

"No," said Julie. "And I certainly don't mean any disrespect, but I've always been impressed with your encyclopedic knowledge of everything. I mean you seem to have met everyone and been everywhere."

Dame Gabor laughed again and took a sip of her martini. "Well, I don't quite remember everything...which is probably a good thing."

Stefán laughed. "You don't look a day over thirty, Dame Gabor."

She elbowed him and laughed. "Don't you get any ideas, Buster. You're too young for me." Then she pressed her knee against Alias. "You, on the other hand, are just the right age."

CHAPTER THIRTY-TWO

"Go Home, Outlier Scum!!"

Lily's mouth hung open as she stared at the bright pink letters scrawled over the front of the storefront. In all her years residing in Myers Beach, this hateful graffiti was the first she'd ever seen on the boardwalk. Being intimate with the target of the slur made the message's hatred sting all the more.

Theos would be headlining the Dust Up's opening show later that afternoon with a repeat of the razzle-dazzle program that won him the title of Kitesurfing Champion of the World, and she'd come down to the boardwalk to watch him practice.

Several of their fairies had egged her on to perform with him, and so as a special treat, she and Theos were going to put on their tandem kitesurfing routine. When he was finished practicing his, she was planning to go up with him to rehearse.

She looked both ways to see if anyone was looking, and after the last few sunbathers walked past, she pointed at the slur and snapped her fingers to make the graffiti disappear. When nothing happened, she tried again.

As a queen, her power was unmatched by any other fairy besides the kings, and since she hadn't been able to make it go away, she wondered if the graffiti artist's magic was stronger than hers, or was it something about her technique that didn't work?

She was eager to have it removed before the hordes of festival goers flooded the boardwalk, and she planned to tell Theos about it and ask what she'd done wrong.

Since the beginning, they'd taken great pains to keep what went on in the upper levels of The Fairy Kingdom from the public. That was why they kept the teahouse and lounge on the first floor open to the public. All the fairies who worked there were skilled at passing as humans, so to any patron, the establishment looked like a classy restaurant and cabaret.

Nor was there a reason to suspect that an entire kingdom of fairies inhabited the building with the traditional indie bookstore on the ground floor. Even the entrance to the upper levels that housed the palace and living quarters was through an obscure door to the right of the bookstore, and Julie's nameplate gave the impression that it was nothing more than the door to her apartment.

Equal care had gone into safeguarding the Outliers' presence in Magda's building, so only other fairies would have known they occupied that space. And since only fairies would be familiar with the term "Outlier," doing the math was easy. One of their own had defaced the building with the hateful message.

Identifying and sanctioning the culprit was within the

queens' jurisdictions, and she would work with Greta as soon as she could. The quarantine wouldn't be lifted until the following day, so since the fairies hadn't been allowed to leave, it would be easy to trace those few who had permission.

Belos or one of his cronies was the likely suspect. Being of the Third Kingdom, his punishment would involve Christophe or Alias, and she felt confident they would not hesitate. Lily messaged Stefán about the problem first. She hoped he could figure out a way to remove the slur before humans noticed and investigated it as a hate crime. The last thing they needed was the police asking questions.

Stefán had been as eager as the Outliers to get them out of The Fairy Kingdom, and as soon as the kings and queens had signed off on the concept, he had begun the process of renovating their building.

With fewer Outlier fairies to accommodate than the other kingdoms, fewer apartments needed to be built, and the result was a luxury apartment complex with spacious apartments and amenities not seen in the other kingdoms —a small consolation for the bigotry and persecution they'd experienced.

A couple of the skilled Outliers pitched in, and thanks to the fairy dust Alias gave him, the group put in an extra-long night and finished the project on time. Magda took charge of the move-in, which, with the help of Eye Patch Man and Cropped Hair Guy, took place while Stefán was enjoying dinner at Julie's.

He'd gone to bed with Julie feeling lighter, knowing that the Outliers would finally have some peace. All that changed when Lily contacted him about the graffiti, and soon he and Magda stood gaping at the desecration. Minutes later he concluded that it had not been Lily's lack of experience that kept her from erasing the writing. His magic didn't work either.

"It must be enchanted," said Magda. "We might have to remove it the old-fashioned way, with a potion my ancestors used to combat magic." She brought out a couple of pails, gloves, and mineral spirits, and then added a strange liquid to the soapy water.

"Let me take care of this," said Stefán. "I feel responsible." He rolled up the sleeves of his white Theory button-down and grabbed a scrub brush.

"Why?" asked Magda. "You did nothing wrong. You've done everything you could to help us." She pushed the sleeves of her Gucci blouse to the elbows and joined him, and together they were able to remove the worst of it.

"Not personally, I know," he said, finally breaking the silence as they stood back from the wall and surveyed their handiwork. "But if it hadn't been for us moving to Myers Beach in the first place, you'd still be living your peaceful lives."

Magda sighed and shook her head. "Maybe, but seeing my fellow Outliers together again has given me a new outlook. I've been selfish for too long, and now I have the opportunity and resources to help them fight back."

"Well, I'm disappointed in the other fairies. I always believed we were above all those petty emotions we always ascribed to humans."

She crossed her arms and leaned a shoulder against the opposite wall of the alley. "I've seen a lot of crazy things in my day, and believe me, this isn't the first time a marginalized group got blamed for the problems of the majority." She gave him a once-over before shaking his hand. "Thank you for stepping up and being part of the solution. We appreciate that you're looking out for us more than you know."

"Anytime," he said, taking her hand. He sighed and looked at his watch. "I should get going. The festival isn't going to run itself." He snapped his fingers and sent the cleaning supplies back inside.

"Yes. I want to commend you for putting that together, too. Now, don't give this episode another minute of thought. We've got this. You'd be surprised what we Outlier fairies are capable of when we're backed into an impossible situation. Besides, I'm convinced someone else is behind this." She waved him off.

When Stefán arrived at the main stage, Greta and Zsombor had taken their marks and Dame Gabor was doing a sound check. He sat in the back row to listen to them run through their numbers, and when he caught their eyes, he gave them a thumbs up. Then he looked out toward the ocean and saw Theos and Lily practicing a series of loops for their kitesurfing exhibition. Things were shaping up well with the headliners, and he was thrilled he'd taken Dame Gabor up on her request to stage manage.

With everything in her capable hands, he decided to go back to Julie's to rest for a while before the big pre-opening night extravaganza.

The bleachers were full and spectators crowded on either side to catch a glimpse of The Greta and Zsombor show. Well before they arrived on stage, a giant screen blasted their names and showcased a montage of photos that played in a continuous loop. At seven p.m., the outside lights dimmed, the footlights flooded the stage, and as the band started playing a few measures of *Let The Good Times Roll,* the duo walked on stage dressed like Sonny and Cher to great applause.

The music quickly segued to *I Got You Babe,* the first in their greatest hit sets, and the crowd went wild. Then Zsombor stood back while Greta took her turn at one of her signature solos, *Gypsies, Tramps, and Thieves.* Julie put her head against Zsombor's shoulder and whispered how proud she was of him.

The audience was clapping along to *And the Beat Goes On,* when suddenly in the middle of the song, the screen behind Greta and Zsombor projected a gigantic photo of Theos and Lily. The floodlights flickered, the sound system went off, and when giant spotlights pointing to the sky illuminated the couple soaring through the air and waving to the crowd, everyone in the bleachers looked up, stood up, and cheered.

Stefán gulped. He knew the two acts were meant to follow each other, not compete, and he grabbed Julie and ran backstage to demand an explanation from Dame Gabor. In the meantime, Theos and Lily continued their dazzling routine, and with each death-defying loop and roll the crowd stomped their feet and roared. Suddenly, in the middle of a particularly difficult stunt, someone killed their spotlights.

Unaware that Theos and Lily were pictured on the screen behind them and upstaging them in the air above them and oblivious to the technical glitches, Greta and Zsombor had kept singing. But with the spotlights on Theos and Lily now out, the audience sat back down and turned their attention to the stage again.

Greta and Zsombor were in the middle of singing a quiet duet when Theos and Lily's blinding spotlights came back on, and the crowd returned to stomping their feet again at the sight of them streaking across the sky.

Stefán had been unsuccessful in locating Dame Gabor, but the human technicians responded with hunched shoulders.

"We have no idea what's going on," said the heads of lighting and sound. They pointed to their control boards. "None of this should be happening." When he asked them where Dame Gabor was, they threw up their hands. "Good question. She never showed up."

By then, the cheers from the audience had turned to boos at all the confusion, and Stefán made the executive decision to kill both acts.

Greta and Zsombor had already stopped singing when they got the signal from a stagehand, and they were already steamed when they saw the picture of Theos and Lily projected behind them. Stefán was the first person they saw when they walked off stage.

"What the hell, Stefán! Theos and Lily weren't supposed to go on until we finished."

"I know," he stammered. "We're trying to figure out

what went wrong. Dame Gabor was in charge of that, and I can't find her anywhere."

Theos and Lily stormed backstage. "We've been practicing for days!" Lily said. "I even risked my pregnancy to do this."

Greta glared back. "Well, Zsombor and I haven't exactly been sitting on our butts, either. We've been rehearsing like mad. I can't believe you upstaged us."

"We weren't trying to upstage anyone," said Theos. "We were given the cue to start."

"Well, so were we," said Zsombor. "Where the hell was Stefán during all this?"

CHAPTER THIRTY-THREE

Despite the disaster that marked the pre-opening evening's entertainment, the events the following day were taking place without a hitch. Joe's Java Joint had secured the attention of the local news, and the Endowment's media muscle pulled in tourists from neighboring beaches who'd begun to clog the streets and the boardwalk.

Stefán walked from the Hersey Lighthouse to the jetty, amused by the constant mechanical sounds from popup rides, ring tosses, other games of chance, and the cheers of people who'd won prizes.

The beach from one end to the other was awash in sweet and savory smells from hotdogs, funnel cakes, and sixteen other types of food and drink, and everywhere he turned, he saw groups of people swimming through the crowds like schools of happy fish, laughing loud and feeding off the good, summer vibes of the event he'd spent so long creating.

Theos had been right. The Endowment for Oceanic Solutions' giant pink tent was a major draw. People could participate in hands-on demonstrations that illustrated some of the amazing initiatives that their scientists and volunteers were accomplishing in all seven seas to help combat climate change and pollution. From the looks of it, people were also donating freely.

But it was the participation of the fairies that most interested him. He'd created the festival for them, and he was pleased that they seemed to be thriving in their new atmosphere of freedom. Furthermore, the fairies blended in so well, at times he was unable to distinguish them from humans, and he made a mental note to ensure that Dame Gabor received the credit she was due.

Julie beckoned people to the wishing well wearing a flowing light-blue dress with bright purple wings hooked to her back with clear straps. Greta had even made her a special wand. Stefán enlisted Cropped Hair Guy and Eye Patch Man to give her a makeover. They'd even managed to weave a flower crown through her short hair, and when Stefán circled back around to see the finished product, he was overwhelmed at how pretty she looked.

She had insisted that another fairy work side by side with her, to be sure that the more grandiose of people's wishes got properly reshaped into smaller, more manageable ones, and Stefán noted that every customer left with a smile. Zoë was one of them who helped. Since she didn't have any magic of her own, she got satisfaction from playing around with the dust.

He was about to make another check on the vendors when Magda found him and pulled him aside.

"I'd like to borrow you, for a few minutes, if you wouldn't mind," she said.

Stefán nodded and he followed her into her home. When they climbed the stairs to the familiar seating area that overlooked the boardwalk, he found Cropped Hair Guy and Eye Patch waiting for them. Magda took the seat between them and gestured to the single chair across from the table facing them for Stefán.

"Why, exactly am I here?" he asked. "I feel like I'm at some sort of tribunal and you're the judges."

She laughed and shuffled some papers before glancing up.

"We've been spitballing around," she began, wringing her hands in a rare show of anxiety. "We're wondering how we could live in better harmony here and maybe find a way of not being under such heavy scrutiny or discrimination."

Stefán nodded and uncrossed his legs. "I agree that your situation has gotten ugly. How can I help?"

"We feel if we had a nominal leader, someone who could be our spokesperson and advocate for us, maybe we could change the hearts and minds of those who seem to dislike us."

He nodded again. "That's not a half-bad idea."

"To make the position work, we'd have to fill it with someone the rest of the royals were familiar with, trusted, you know. Someone who could put them more at ease and one with whom they might be willing to negotiate." As if on cue, they turned to him. "You."

His throat went dry. "I—I'm honored to be considered."

"You've been in our corner from the beginning. You're the only one willing to hear us out, and you know what it's like to be one of us. *And* they know you well and obviously trust you."

Eye Patch Man spoke next. "It's not as easy as the three of us selecting you. As you can imagine, we'll have to put it to a vote. Suffice it to say, though, that our recommendation will go a long way to tip the scales." He picked up a sheet of paper from Magda's stack. "We were given a few questions to ask you, so they could determine if you're the right fairy for the job."

"Okay. Shoot," said Stefán. "I'm an open book."

For the next few minutes, they discussed his views on inter-kingdom relations and his thoughts about the implications of the baby boom on the community as a whole. After each answer, Magda wrote notes in her notebook. Cropped Hair Guy asked the final question.

"What are your thoughts about us Outliers getting a fair share of the new fairy dust? Most of them had little experience with it, and they were dazzled with how it transformed our building so quickly. Frankly, it reminded some of the older ones about the good old days when they went around granting wishes. Anyway, we thought it would be nice to have some of our own."

Stefán didn't need to think. He knew his answer. "I think all fairies should be entitled to fairy dust. It's our right. No exceptions."

"That's what they wanted to hear," said Magda. She checked off the final box. "And so, based on your answers, we've been authorized to offer you the post."

Stefán bowed his head. "You can't possibly know how I feel."

Magda looked at the other two. "But we do know, don't we?" They nodded, walked around their table, and one by one held open their palms. Stefán responded by placing his over theirs," she continued. "We always knew you were one of us."

"Yes," said Cropped Hair Guy. "When I made that birth certificate and those other documents for you, did you think I just pulled the surname 'Lord' out of thin air, Lord Stefán?"

When he returned to her booth, Julie could see his enormous grin. "What did that woman want?" she asked.

He'd bought sandwiches and chips from The Belly Deli and grabbed some tea from The Fairy Kingdom kitchens so they could have a small picnic lunch before getting back to work. They sat across from each other in the outdoor seating of The Fairy Kingdom.

"You're not going to believe what happened. She's one of the Outliers, and I understood that she wanted to ask my advice on something," he admitted. "We went to her place and talked for a while, and then she surprised me by saying that the Outliers took a vote to make me their leader. I'm still in shock."

Just as Julie was giving him a congratulatory hug, Dame Gabor wandered past in watermelon-colored Bermuda shorts and a white tank top. "Kudos, Stefán. Your festival is a huge hit."

"Thanks, Dame Gabor. It was a lot of work, but I think people are really enjoying themselves, especially the fairies. So, are we still on for rehearsal this afternoon? I'm finally off-book."

Her brows furrowed. "Rehearsal?"

"Yeah. For the play."

She gave him a blank stare for a moment and then coughed. "Ah, yes. The play. Right. Yes. The rehearsal for—"

"*Peter Pan?*" Julie supplied.

"Right. *Peter Pan.* At?"

"Four o'clock, I believe you said."

Dame Gabor's face relaxed and she nodded toward the tea house. "We said to meet there, didn't we?"

Stefán nodded and as Dame Gabor disappeared into the crowd, Julie shook her head. "I think somebody needs Alias' new fairy dust ASAP. Poor Dame Gabor has gotten so scatterbrained."

Stefán shook his head. "I don't think it's that. I think it's something else, though I don't know what. She's been acting strange for a while now."

Julie nodded. "I hope it's not some sort of regressive issue."

He finished his sandwich and shrugged. "I'm going to keep an eye on her. I know how much she means to us all." He stood and threw their trash away. When he came back to the table, Julie was standing on her tiptoes expectantly, so he leaned down and placed a quick kiss on her lips. "I'm headed over to the jump rope tournament," Stefán said. "Should be fun. Joe sponsored it, so there's gonna be a lot of people hyped up on caffeine."

CHAPTER THIRTY-FOUR

As night fell, many of the fairies who had given in to over-exuberance at being free to go outside, welcomed the cooler breezes which swept through the beach and took the edge off their sunburns.

Stefán scheduled an invitation-only giant bonfire on the beach as a way for them to celebrate the first full day of the festival, and when he determined that the time was right, he gave the signal and flames shot into the air. As expected, most of the fairies clustered in their own groups, partly because each kingdom had organized separate cele-brations which aligned with their own cultural customs.

Theos' and Lily's fairies were putting on a water dance to bring large swells for the following days' surfing exhibi-tion and contests. Zsombor's and Greta's enjoyed roasting vegetables on skewers and singing campfire songs. Fairies from the Third Kingdom had changed into designer beachwear and were enjoying the cocktail party atmosphere. The Outliers seemed the happiest, and within the greater community, they broke into smaller circles.

They were on their own and free to do what they liked to do best, gymnastics.

Tensions had cooled, and more than a few crossed over and joined in the festivities from other kingdoms. Theos' people taught a few Outliers the water dance. Several Third Kingdom fairies had joined the fire to sing the campfire songs. And the Outliers had even managed to rope several younger fairies from all the kingdoms into setting up an impromptu cheer competition, complete with judges and scorecards.

Since the festival had been a group effort, the plan was to end the evening with a speech from each of the kings. As High King, Theos went first, and his brilliant white teeth caught the reflection of the bonfire flames to create a blinding smile.

"When we were mining *Yano*, the last element, we discovered a whole new enormous space deep in the cliff." He paused for dramatic effect. "And we've decided to convert that area into living quarters for the rest of our kingdom! So, beginning any day now, our fairies will no longer be housed at The Fairy Kingdom. Instead, we will all be together with complete facilities of our own and much more space, up at the compound."

Zsombor and Greta's fairies were as excited by the news as the fairies who'd be moving. It meant no longer living on top of each other and sharing bathrooms and common areas. Finally, they were going to have the room they needed to spread out.

Stefán felt a warmth inside as he watched how politely and respectfully Theos treated his subjects and the other admirers who surrounded him after his speech. When he saw an opportunity to step in, he asked to pull Theos away for a few minutes.

He took a breath. "Listen, I'm just going to come out with it," he said, rushing what he had to say so he wouldn't chicken out. "I've been offered a position as the leader of the coalition of Outliers. I'd like to accept, and more importantly, I'd like your blessing."

Theos put his arm around Stefán's shoulder. "First of all, congratulations! They've obviously recognized the stellar qualities we've seen in you all along. I couldn't be prouder."

"Then you won't be upset if I accept?"

"Of course not. You have my blessing."

"Whew! You can't imagine how relieved that makes me. But there is an important loose end I need to raise," he said. He glanced around and then stepped in closer. "I hate leaving you in a bind, but they'd like me to start as soon as possible, so…"

"Look. Running the teahouse is out of the question, so let's not worry about that now." He stared at Stefán with his deep blue eyes. "If you would permit me, though, I do have one piece of advice."

"Yes, please tell me."

"You've got the rest of the Dust Up to run. Given all the mix-ups of last night's concert and exhibition, which I'm not saying were your fault by the way, I think you'd be better off to focus on those responsibilities for the rest of this week and take on your new position after the festival is over."

"I can't say exactly what happened last night. It was an unfortunate combination of technical snafus and someone jumping the gun to give the four of you the wrong cues." He was careful to accept responsibility and not ascribe blame to Dame Gabor, whom he knew had fallen down on the job. "And I agree with you. My hope was to start after the Day of the Dust celebration on Sunday."

Theos elbowed Stefán and pointed to the conga line. "Don't you just love seeing a good idea come to fruition? Look at what we've done."

Stefán was surprised to see Dame Gabor at the head, weaving the long snake of fairies around the bonfire and cutting directly through the assembled clans. By the time she'd made a full circle, hundreds had joined in behind her. He wondered how she had the temerity to show up at all, and he clenched his teeth thinking how and when he would broach the subject with her. She still had a play to produce.

Theos tapped his chin. "I've been thinking, maybe Dame Gabor. Everyone knows her, and I suspect she's just as well-liked as you."

Just then, she left the conga line and joined a group dancing under a limbo stick. There was a loud cheer from the crowd when she bent backward and made an exaggerated production of holding her breasts in tight so she could squeeze under the pole.

"Before I leave and let you go back to your adoring subjects, I just want to say that I hope I can be as good a leader as you," said Stefán. "You've been my idol since... well, forever."

"That's very kind. Speaking of leadership, what are they planning to call you? Obviously, they're allergic to the concept of a ruler, let alone a king. And not being royal, you couldn't be one, anyway, even if they wanted."

Stefán nodded. "We were kicking around the idea of calling me 'president.' That term is politically prestigious and conveys leadership and representative government, yet it stays away from the concept of a sovereign."

"Nice. I approve, not that I needed to." He left to talk to Alias, and as Stefán panned the crowd for a familiar face, he noticed Christophe trying to get the attention of as many fairies from the bonfire as he could. After conjuring up a drink in every hand, he raised a glass in a toast to his sister.

"To my sister, Princess Zoë," he said. "For being alive and well after the hateful ordeal with Zsa Zsa." Someone started up a chant of "Long live Princess Zoë," which became so loud, that she had to jokingly shush them so that the neighboring humans wouldn't be tipped off that there was royalty partying on the beach.

He couldn't have anticipated what followed the chant. Briar, dressed in cargo shorts and a T-shirt and sporting a bad sunburn across their cheeks, dropped to one knee and proposed to Zoë, and Stefán didn't miss the lovestruck look on their face as they slid the ring onto her finger.

"I've got wings big enough for the both of us," Briar said with a grin, and when Zoë pulled them in for a deep kiss, the crowd cooed and broke into applause at the adorable display of affection.

Julie made her way to stand next to Stefán in the line of fairies who offered congratulations to the happy couple.

"Don't you worry that it's a little…rushed?" she asked.

"Not at all. I think Zoë deserves to be happy, whatever

that entails," he said. He leaned down and kissed the top of her head. "I think everyone deserves a happy ending, by the way. Including us." She blushed and he was about to add more when Christophe, Alias, and Dame Gabor walked over and drew them into a hilarious conversation that somehow turned into a discussion of the new dust.

"You are a national treasure, Alias," said Dame Gabor. She leaned in and gave him a kiss, and when it lasted a little too long, Alias wiggled out of it.

"Thanks," he said, wiping his lips and sliding his arm across Christophe's shoulders. "Starting tomorrow, we'll have an endless supply of the best classic fairy dust we've ever seen."

Magda approached Stefán from behind and asked if he'd gotten the okay from Theos, and seconds after he nodded a group of Outliers lifted him to their shoulders and paraded him around the bonfire and called him their "president" in fairy language.

By the time they'd made a full circle, every fairy from every kingdom learned that he'd been put in charge of the Outliers, and from their expressions, they'd put two and two together and determined that he was an Outlier himself.

CHAPTER THIRTY-FIVE

Stefán was walking the beach, checklist in hand. Organizing and managing a weeklong festival had turned out to be a much larger undertaking than he'd imagined, but he was committed to doing his best. To ensure a quality experience for everyone, he'd made a habit of speaking with each vendor and attraction operator every day to gauge the festival's success.

He was in the middle of receiving very positive feedback from a vendor just outside the bookstore when he heard the blistering comment coming from behind him. Stefán recognized Belos' voice, and he watched the vendor's face tighten.

"I told you all he was one of *them*," shouted the enraged fairy. "He's the Outlier's little leader now, didn't you hear?" Stefán turned to see that Belos was shaking his fist at him. The outrage painted across his face matched the tone in his voice. "I told you all he'd been playing favorites, but none of you wanted to *listen*."

Stefán thanked his lucky stars that Christophe

happened to witness Belos' anger and offered to walk him back to the Third Kingdom. The last thing Stefán needed was a disciplinary issue on top of everything else he had on his plate. He was heading toward the next vendor on his route when he heard more shouts. He followed the raised voices and saw that they were coming from the wishing well booth, where an animated crowd appeared to be giving Julie a hard time.

"Can I be of assistance?" he asked, interrupting a man who was arguing on behalf of his child. "I'm the director of this festival."

"Bah!" said the man. "Why bother? This is such a rip-off." He waved his hand at them and left in a huff.

"I'm so glad you came," said Julie. "Something weird is happening. I'm being very careful about the wording of their wishes, I'm even working with a real fairy to make sure, but it seems that no matter what they wish for, the opposite is happening. It's leaving a bad taste in people's mouths, and I feel bad."

Stefán's face fell when she gave him some examples.

"Are any of the wishes working correctly?"

"No, not really. We've only been open a short time, but we've had a long line and granted a lot of them. I don't know what to do." She pointed to a small hot air balloon that had managed to get stuck in a palm tree with a panicked family trapped in the basket. "That's one of them. I've called the Fire Department, and they're on the way."

Stefán was about to ask what they'd wished for, but after she pointed out a gentleman whose clothes were in tatters and then a child crying to her father he decided the details would be unimportant. Suddenly, he heard horse hooves clopping on the boardwalk, and he had to jump up on the side of the booth to avoid being run over.

"It's the horse that made the child cry," she said. "I feel terrible, but I did everything just like I was told."

"It's not your fault." Stefán put his fingers to his temple to summon Alias, who instantly rode in on his surfboard. Stefán filled him in on the chaos. "From what Julie is telling me, the dust is producing the opposite outcome."

"Damn. It's my fault for not doing enough testing," said Alias.

"So you think the dust was responsible for those boys getting robbed last night, instead of falling into money?"

"Definitely," Alias said. "And one of us should find out who they were from the police and make it right. Did anyone's wish come true the way they wanted?"

"No," said Julie. "And like I told Stefán, I always had another fairy with me, so we were very careful about the wording," Julie said. "What should we do?"

Stefán looked around at the chaos. "First, I better fix things around here. I hope I have enough magic."

"I'll help," said Stefán.

"In the meantime, I don't think we should stay open," said Julie.

"Agreed," said Alias. "No more granting of wishes of any kind until we figure out what went wrong with the dust."

Stefán flicked a finger and *Closed Until Further Notice* signs appeared on all six sides of the booth. Alias pointed to the pail full of fairy dust and sent it flying back to the lab. Then they split up the job of turning things around. With more flicks of their fingers, the woman on the bench who'd been nursing her sprained ankle suddenly smiled and jogged down the steps to rejoin her four-hundred-meter relay team. Handlers from the Myers Beach Zoo arrived and rounded up the loose animals.

It took both of them to jar the balloon loose from the palm tree, and once aloft again, they directed it to float over the stage where the Myers Beach Pops Orchestra was playing a medley of tunes from *Wicked*. The conductor caught sight of it as it floated down to the apron of the stage, and he thought fast and directed the players to jump ahead and play *Defying Gravity*. To be absolutely sure that the family would end up pleased, Alias conjured up a tin man to greet them when they climbed out of the basket.

"What the heck is going on?" asked Theos. "I just saw eight tiny reindeer on Joe's rooftop."

"It's a long story," said Julie. "It had something to do with Christmas, but it wasn't what they wished for, believe me."

"We've got a problem," said Alias. "The dust is faulty. I don't understand why, because we followed the instructions to the letter. Don't worry, though. I'm on it."

"You better be." Theos' tone with Alias was uncharacteristically sharp. "I don't think I have to remind you that we've assured every fairy in Myers Beach that their lives are no longer in danger."

CHAPTER THIRTY-SIX

"Are you sure you said *Fstl Fstl* at the end?" asked Alias. "The instructions were very specific." He knew that the *Yano* wasn't the problem. During the refining stage, all its characteristics fit the book's description perfectly.

He'd called Dr. Anderson to the lab for an emergency session. He explained the problem and emphasized that the pressure on them to fix the formulation before the Day of the Dust was greater than ever.

"Look. I'm as horrified as you, but don't patronize me, Alias. My team and I followed everything to the letter. Oh, and incidentally, you're wrong. You're supposed to say *Fstl* once at the beginning, and then once again at the end."

He rubbed his chin. "That's not the way I remember it at all. We're meant to repeat it at the end."

"I'm not sure what you mean by 'repeating' it," she said. "Do you mean repeating what you say at the beginning, or repeating the word *Fstl* twice at the end, you know, like *Fstl, Fstl.*"

Alias shrugged. "See, the way you just said it makes it

even more ambiguous. Are we supposed to repeat *Fstl, Fstl?* That would mean we'd say it four times. Geesh, now, I'm not sure. In any case, one of us is wrong." He threw his hands in the air. "There's only one way to settle it. Please! Can we see the book?"

She led him to the lab table and cleared a space. Then she waved her hand to make it appear. When nothing happened, she snapped her fingers and waved again. Alias frowned and rubbed his forehead.

"Look, I don't know what's going on," she said. When he saw the corner of her mouth curl in frustration he took her place and snapped and clapped himself. Their eyes grew wide.

"This is not good," he said. "Didn't we make it so that it would come to us from wherever we left it?" When they realized what that meant, she let out a string of expletives and they raced to the vault.

Dr. Anderson waved her hand and the vault door flung open. When the book wasn't immediately in view, Alias' heart thumped as he watched her rummage through the contents. Her face was set in hard, grim lines when she turned around empty-handed. They ran back to the lab and messaged Theos, who came instantly.

"I don't know how to put this to make it sound okay, because it's not," said Alias. "The Dust Keeper's Manual is missing."

"Again? How's that possible?" Theos raised his voice. "You assured me that you kept it in a vault under the utmost security."

"It was...of course, Theos." Alias rolled his eyes and

restrained himself from adding sarcasm to his words. "You know that."

Theos wrung his hands and paced the room. "Then it must be around here somewhere in the lab. Lydia, could you have brought it out of the vault and then forgotten to return it?"

She shook her head. "Impossible. We haven't used it since the day we added the *Yano*."

"So, then what? Someone stole it?"

"It has to be," said Alias. "I can't imagine how, but it's the only explanation." He grabbed a pad of paper and began to write names. "Besides you and Lily and Christophe and me, and Lydia and her team, let's figure out who else has been up here since we used it last."

Lydia spoke first. "Well, yesterday, Stefán brought Dame Gabor here. And then there was that Emili woman, you know, Joe's new business partner."

"Why the heck did he bring her up here?" asked Theos.

"Look, Theos. She's Dame Gabor's friend," Alias said. "She sponsored part of the festival, and it was hot, and everyone wanted to swim. Besides, she never left the pool." He turned to Lydia. "She didn't, did she?"

Lydia hunched her shoulders. "Honestly, I wasn't paying attention. It was my day off, and I was dozing on a chaise."

"Okay, then we'll need to start an old-fashioned investigation," Theos said. "Let's meet at The Fairy Kingdom in ten. I'll round up some of the others. I can't tell you how disappointed I am, Alias. Never mind the egg I'll have on my face if we don't fix the dust ASAP."

CHAPTER THIRTY-SEVEN

After everyone had assembled, Theos identified Stefán and Zsombor as his picks to head this investigation. Stefán, he claimed, would be the most impartial, and Zsombor, because he'd led successful interrogations before. Alias proposed they eliminate Lydia Anderson as a suspect. She had been a trusted member of the Endowment team since the beginning, and he couldn't imagine a motive.

"She said she fell asleep at the pool yesterday when Stefán took her, and the others," he added. "Dame Gabor already admitted that she fell asleep, too. Remember, she came late to Julie's dinner party. Oh, and you all should know that she did follow Lydia and me down to the area of the vault, though I should also add that we were careful not to let her get too close."

"Guilty!" shouted Dame Gabor from across the room. "Not that I needed you to bring up that embarrassment again. Hey! While we're all cogitating, why don't I make us some of my world-famous lemonade?" She clapped her hands and pitchers, glasses, and ice buckets appeared in front of everyone.

"I think you read our minds, Dame Gabor," said Theos. "Thank you. Now back to the vote on Lydia."

By a unanimous vote, he drew a line through her name. As he was reading aloud the rest of the names, a fairy attendant brought him a slip of paper, which he explained that he'd found moments earlier on the front steps. Theos smiled when he read the note.

"It appears that we don't need to worry about these names anymore." He set the list on a table. "According to this note, the Dust Keeper's Manual is in the Outliers' building, apparently in plain sight."

Stefán's heart sank as every face registered shock at the startling news.

"That can't be," he protested. "I know the Outliers, and they would never steal a sacred book."

"With all due respect, Stefán," interjected Theos. "You've been their leader for what, twenty-four hours? Less? I'm not sure we can trust your knee-jerk assessment of their character."

Julie slammed her glass of lemonade on the table in front of her. "That's uncalled for, Theos. Apologize."

"I will not," shouted Theos.

"Well, I think we should go search their place right now," shouted Zsombor.

Stefán was stunned at their behavior, and he glared at all three of them.

"Listen. There's no need to raise our voices. First of all, I'm not technically their leader for a few more days, but come on. Everyone knows that Outliers have survived for hundreds of years without fairy dust. So why would they want to steal a book that tells them how to make it? I'm sorry, but it just doesn't make sense."

"I'd love you to be wrong," said Theos. "But the book didn't just grow legs and walk out of the vault by itself. This tip is our only lead so far, so I agree with Zsombor that we should go there now." He turned a stony glare on Stefán. "Besides, you heard Magda the other night. She admitted she'd love to get her hands on some. And the same goes for those other two guys who are always with her."

"Okay. Have it your way, but understand that I just renovated the building and I've personally been over every square inch of it. I think this tip is more likely somebody's idea of a cruel joke."

"Let's all go, then," said Christophe. "And make quick work of it."

The idea of all the kings descending on Stefán's community to conduct a search was humiliating. When they walked in, he saw Magda's face pulled into hard lines.

She looked directly at Theos. "We don't have your book," she said with sad eyes that came from his lack of trust. "If that's why you're here. For the record, I'm insulted that you think we do. Stealing isn't in an Outlier's DNA."

"Yes, yes. So Stefán has told us. By the way, you look the same as the last time I was here. You told us that you Outliers changed your appearance every day."

"That's not what I said. When we're home, we don't bother. It's only when we go out in public that we switch things up."

"Whatever," said Theos. "Since you're so sure that you

don't have our book, then I can't imagine that you would mind if we looked around, would you? I mean, we did get a tip that it was here." He wagged his finger at the inside.

While they talked, she kept an eye on Stefán who stood silently behind them. His downcast expression caught her gaze for a second, and he gave her a slight nod.

"I don't mind," she said, but as they started to go in, she held up her hand. "But I'm not the one in charge here. Stefán is." He elbowed his way to the front and faced the kings.

"By all means, your majesties," he said. "It's actually a good time. Everyone is out at the Dust Up. Have at it."

He stepped aside, but while the kings spread out to search the floors one by one, Stefán stayed behind.

"Is it possible they could find it here?" he asked in a quiet voice. "I mean, of course I believe you, but I swore up and down to them that it isn't here, so my butt is really on the line."

She took his hand. "Don't worry. There's zero percent chance that it is. And listen, as much as I hate this charade, I really can't blame them. It would be irresponsible not to search." She squeezed her lips. "But I'm furious that someone sent that false tip. Any idea who might be behind it?"

"Not yet, but I'm going to find out."

Magda sighed and put a hand on one of Stefán's crossed arms, "You should know that I've seen Dame Gabor acting strange. We were in the lounge the other night listening to her sing. You know how she usually ends the evening by cracking a joke or pulling a funny line from one of her movies? Always something light. Well, lately, she's been signing off with something oddly academic. 'Chance favors the prepared mind.' I recognize it from my chemistry class at UC Berkeley. Anyway, I thought maybe it would be grist for the mill."

"That does sound oddly familiar," Stefán said, scratching his chin. "I think maybe I've heard Alias mention it. I'll ask him when we get this whole mess sorted."

"Stefán. I'd like to see you up here." Theos' commanding voice boomed down through the open stairway and echoed in the high-ceilinged lobby where he stood with Magda. The message sent a chill down his spine.

He took a breath and collected himself. As the head of a community of fairies of his own, he was no longer going to be commanded by anyone and treated like an underling, and instead of racing up the stairs as he would likely have done a few days earlier, he walked up at a dignified pace.

Theos held two bags of fairy dust. "Would you like to explain why I found these lying on the floor in a corner?"

Judging from the stern look and his uncharacteristic short temper, Stefán wagered that Theos wouldn't be receptive to any explanation, so he called for Alias to back him up.

"I was trying to get the Outliers out of The Fairy Kingdom as soon as possible before the festival began," he explained.

"Yes, and since they have limited magic, I offered some of our dust to speed up the project," added Alias.

"I see." Theos crossed his arms. "Correct me if I'm wrong, but I don't remember authorizing dust for that purpose."

Alias jerked back his head. "Um, since when do I have to go through you on an issue as mundane as that?"

"I wouldn't call finding bags and bags of fairy dust sitting around out in the open a mundane issue," said Theos.

"Oh come on. What's gotten into you, Theos? You do realize this is the old stuff, don't you, and that we've got tons more back at the compound?"

"Considering there isn't *new stuff*, as you casually call life-giving fairy dust, because you've failed at getting the formula right, I'd say what I'm holding here constitutes an extravagance. I'm bringing them back."

Alias sighed. "Fine. The building is finished, anyway." He peered into the pouches. "And as you can see, they're practically full, so obviously the Outliers haven't exactly been throwing it around and wasting it."

The three of them went back down to the front hall, and after searching their designated sections, Christophe and Zsombor returned. To Stefán's relief, both were empty-handed.

Theos opened the front door to leave. "Sorry to have bothered you, Magda, but just because we didn't find it, doesn't mean it's not here."

"It isn't, Theos. I'm sorry you don't trust us. I hope you will someday soon."

Christophe apologized for Theos and thanked her again for making the building available.

"I'm glad that Stefán met you," he said. "You and your colleagues have been an enormous help to all of us. And you certainly have made a beautiful place here for the Outlier fairies."

"Yes," Zsombor said with a raised eyebrow and a bitter tone. "Quite lavish."

Alias shook his head when they got to the boardwalk. "I knew they didn't have it. What a waste of time."

Theos held up the two small bags of dust. "Oh, I wouldn't say so. Anyway, thank you, Stefán, for organizing this little search mission. Even if we didn't find the manual, finding these was very informative."

"We've still got to get to the bottom of the theft," said Zsombor. "Why don't we meet up at the compound in thirty minutes to debrief and plan our next move."

"Very well," said Stefán. "You all go on ahead. I'll join you up there in a few."

CHAPTER THIRTY-EIGHT

When they reunited in the compound's spacious living room, Theos had put together a larger group. Along with Stefán and the queens, he'd asked Julie and Zoë to join them, to see if they could shed any light on the problem.

"As you can see Dame Gabor is sitting in again. She always has her ear to the ground, and I'm hoping she'll pass on any street gossip she may have picked up. Incidentally, now is as good a time as any to announce that I've put her in charge of the teahouse…Stefán's old job."

The room gave her rousing applause, and after she made a slight curtsey, she held up her hand.

"Thanks for that," she said. "But I'd like to take a quick moment to show you my latest prop for the play. As Tinkerbell, I'm supposed to sprinkle fairy dust all over the place, and since we can't have the humans see me doing it with magic, I made this wand. It's got two buttons. One shoots it out over the audience. Watch!"

She waved it in the air and silver dust filled the room and filtered down over everyone.

"Brava!" Said Greta. "I love good props."

"The other button just sends it straight up and spills down on me like a fountain." She waved a hand in the air. "But I think we've got enough dust around here already, so I won't bother to demonstrate."

Theos clapped. "You know, every time I turn around, I'm grateful for your service, Dame Gabor," he said. He looked at the wall clock and frowned. "Unlike some people. Judging by Stefán's lateness to this crucial meeting, I think we can all be glad you have his job and he's not working at The Fairy Kingdom anymore."

Julie slammed her fist on the table in front of her. "What?"

Theos gave her a snarky smile. "Oh, Julie. None so blind as those who will not see."

"And what's that supposed to mean?" She looked around the room but found no sympathetic faces.

"It's an old English proverb, in case you were wondering," Theos added. He suggested that while they waited for Stefán, they save time by sharing their takeaways from the search.

"I can tee it up." Zsombor leaned back on the sofa. "For being a pack of bohemian fairies, those Outliers sure do have swanky digs. Here I thought we were doing them a huge favor by inviting them to Myers Beach. I didn't realize they would end up in more sumptuous quarters than our own. I'm glad you weren't there, Greta. The smallest apartment in the whole building makes ours look downright shabby."

"Do tell," said Dame Gabor. "I've never been inside."

Zsombor and Theos regaled them with vivid descriptions of the recreation facilities, the massive indoor pool, and the other spacious common areas of the floors they'd inspected.

Zsombor added a swipe at the end. "A bit over-the-top, in my opinion. It was almost as outlandish as the palace of the Third King."

Christophe laughed. "Just because you and your fairies prefer to live like peasants in the woods, there's no need to be snarky, Zsombor. The decor of the Third Kingdom has a rich history of preserving art and literature, as you well know." He then added an element of sanity by arguing that since there were fewer of them occupying the same size building, it was only logical that there would be more space.

Suddenly, the two massive floor-to-ceiling glass sections of the living room door slid open and Stefán strode in, holding the Dust Keeper's Manual over his head like a trophy.

"I've got it!" he shouted. "We're safe!" He gazed around the room and puffed out his chest at the rehabilitation of his character he knew its discovery would bring. "Great, huh?" He tossed the book to Alias who carried it to the large easy chair on the other side of the room and immediately started flipping through the pages.

"So I guess it was in the Outlier building after all, huh?" asked Lily. "And the tip was right?"

"I knew they had it," said Theos with an eye roll. "I wonder how we missed it. Which floor was it on?"

Stefán scrunched his face. "As a matter of fact, that's not where it was. I found it in the Third Kingdom."

"What?" Christophe jumped up from his seat at the other end of the sofa. "Where?"

"Your Throne Room, sorry to say."

"That's impossible," he said. "Where exactly?"

Stefán raised his eyebrows. "On your throne, actually."

Dame Gabor gasped and covered her mouth. "Holy Moly," she interjected. "I would never have suspected the Third King was a thief."

Christophe gave her a dirty look. "Are you crazy? Of course I didn't steal it." He glared at Stefán. "What gave you the right to search my palace?"

"Well, I'm glad he did," said Zsombor. "Obviously, you figured your throne room would be the last place we'd look."

Christophe protested. "I have no idea why Stefán would claim that he found it there, but I want to know why, all of a sudden, you believe that I could have anything to do with it?"

"Nobody accused you of anything, sweetie," said Alias. He got up from his chair to sit next to him. "At least they better not."

Christophe glared at the room. "But they just did!"

"No," said Stefán. "I didn't accuse you. I only said that I found it there."

Dame Gabor spoke up. "I was invited here to give my opinion, and I'd just like to say that I think it's rather suspicious that it should end up there, you know, considering that all the evidence pointed toward the Outliers."

Stefán's face turned red with rage. "What evidence? You're talking about one stupid fake tip. I'm telling the truth."

Theos walked slowly around the room, scratching his chin like Sherlock Holmes.

"Well, I'm beginning to wonder if he really did find it in the Third Kingdom. He is the new leader of the Outliers, and he did stick around after we left. It strains credulity to believe that he just happened to suddenly out-of-the-blue put his hands on it across town."

Lily leaned against Theos. "Look, the last thing I am is biased, but I'm all in with Dame Gabor on this. Stefán's own people could have hidden it from you guys. I mean how do we know for sure?"

"You can start by asking Zoë," said Stefán. "She was there when I found it. Jeepers, Lily! How could you suggest such a thing, unless you think she was in on it, too?"

"Don't talk to your queen like that," Theos shouted. "Oh, I forgot. She's not your queen anymore. You deserted us. Moved on from the ones who took care of you for your entire life."

"Theos! You told me I should take the job. "

Julie's face stiffened. "Why are you being so unfair to him? He found the damned last element you guys spent forever looking for and didn't find. And then he found the book that contains the most crucial whatever that fairies need to survive. For god's sake, I'd say he has a better track record than all of you."

"I'd suggest you stay out of this," said Zsombor. "You're not a fairy, and judging from the mess you made of our wishing well, I hope you never become one!"

Stefán took a deep breath to keep from hyperventilating. "Wow. Just wow, Zsombor. I guess Julie and I won't be looking to you to bless our marriage."

When he saw Julie jerk her head, he took her hand. "I was hoping to ask you properly, but he and Theos were being such jerks, it just came out. I'm sorry."

"Thanks, everybody," she shouted. "You just ruined the most important day in my life!" Then she whispered to Stefán. "We'll have to talk about this later, when we're alone."

Alias clapped his hands. "Guys! Stop arguing. I've found the problem with the dust." He got up and plopped the book on Theos' lap and pointed to the page. "I told you I was right! See? *Fstl, Fstl.* We needed to repeat it twice. I had a feeling that was where we got it wrong."

Theos drew his brows into a visibly irritated wrinkle and handed him back the book without looking at it.

"I'm sure none of us has any idea of what you're talking about," he said. "We're all glad you finally figured it out, but if you were so sure, why didn't you get it right the first time...or even the second?"

"Or third," added Zsombor from his seat on the sofa.

Alias stood up. "Hey! That's uncalled for!"

"Oh, come on," said Zsombor. "I know you consider yourself the only genius around here, but speaking of track records, yours on the dust project has been sketchy at best."

Christophe jumped in. "What are you talking about? What he made has improved the lives of all the fairies and saved countless others, including yours."

Zsombor took Greta's hand. "We know several thousand fairies who would beg to differ." She looked to the floor instead of directly at Alias, but he saw her nod in agreement.

Christophe pointed a finger. "That's not fair!" he

shouted. "Since the pandemic, Alias has devoted every ounce of his body and soul to figuring this out. What have you done that could possibly compare to that?"

"Listen, pal. Don't talk to me about taking responsibility," replied Zsombor. "While you've been playing around on your skateboard, Greta and I have been ruling a kingdom."

"And don't you talk to him like that!" said Alias. "I don't know why everyone here is suddenly at each other's throats, but as soon as this meeting is over I'm going to the lab to make some fairy dust for you ingrates."

"And I'll go with you," said Christophe.

Julie slumped down into the sofa. "Good. There are still a few wishes that went wrong that haven't gotten fixed, so when it's ready, I'd like some."

Theos held up his hand. "I don't think so, Julie. Saving the lives of our fairies is going to take priority over your bungled wish granting."

"You leave her alone!" said Stefán. "You know darn well that the dust was responsible, not her."

As Alias was leaving, Zsombor raised an eyebrow. "I hope you're not planning to go to the lab alone!"

Alias blanched. "And why not? Are you saying you don't trust me?"

"Well, since you asked your husband to go with you, and he appears to have stolen the book, I'd say that someone definitely needs to be in the lab with you...probably from now on."

"For the last time, I didn't steal the damn book!" shouted Christophe.

"And Zsombor, how dare you accuse my brother of being dishonest!" said Theos.

Zsombor crossed his arms. "Oh, I'm so sorry, *High King*." He spun around to the others. "You know I believe it's time we did away with that whole title nonsense. I think the High King crap has outlived its usefulness."

When Theos raised his fist, Dame Gabor leaped to her feet and put herself between them. "Stop it, you three. What's happened to everyone?"

Christophe raged, "You stay out of this. This is between the kings."

"I'd watch it if I were you, *Third* King," Zsombor said. "You don't really have any ground to stand on right now."

Alias spun around. "I heard that, Zsombor, and I'm sick of you treating Christophe like he's less than you. Being the Third King doesn't mean he's in third place."

"Why don't we all break for lunch and get some air?" suggested Lily. "We've set it out on the deck."

"Great idea," said Zsombor. "But only after we take a vote on my request to abolish the High King title!"

Christophe stood. "I agree. I think letting Theos make decisions for the rest of us has proved to be a dumb idea. I'm in favor."

"That makes two of us," said Zsombor. "What do Alias and the queens say?"

While Lily opposed the idea, Greta looked her in the eye and voted to remove him. It was three against two when Stefán added his vote against Theos.

"I'm sorry, Christophe," said Alias. "But as much as I disapprove of his horrendous attitude lately, I'm going to side with my brother."

Theos threw up his arms. "Okay. As you wish, but this charade hasn't brought us any closer to finding the culprit."

"At least the fairies don't know about the theft, as far as we know," said Dame Gabor. "God forbid they find out. All hell would break loose.."

"Yeah, like it is in here!" said Stefán. He felt Julie squeeze his hand and he wondered if she'd done it in solidarity with him, or if she was trying to encourage him to stop adding fuel to the fire.

At Lily's suggestion, some of them walked out to the pool for the fresh air. Theos dove into the pool, and after swimming a few laps he walked to the cabana, where Dame Gabor passed him a towel.

"I think what they did to you was shameful," she said, giving him a slight bow. "I hate to see my king so humiliated."

Theos nodded but didn't speak, and as he toweled his hair he walked to the far end of the pool deck and plopped down on a chaise.

"I don't understand what got into him," said Stefán. He and Julie were resting their elbows on the metal railing of the platformed outlook and gazing out at the ocean. "I've never seen him lose his temper."

Julie sighed and snuggled closer. "Well, I can kind of understand where he's coming from, can't you? I mean you have to admit…this whole situation…it's just fishy." She ruffled the short strands of hair at the back of her head.

"What's fishy about it?"

"First of all, I find it impossible that Christophe had anything to do with it. I mean, come on."

"I don't disagree," said Stefán. "But that's where I found it. What we need to focus on is who put it there."

She pulled on his ear lobe. "Listen, you know I'm one hundred percent behind you. We're going to get married, after all. By the way, I accept." She laughed and then lowered her voice. "But really, did you find it there, or are you just saying it to protect the Outliers?" He snapped his head away and took a step to put some distance between them.

"I can't believe you said that!"

"Okay, okay. So you did. But do you think maybe one of them helped?"

"I hope you're not still talking about the Outliers," he said. He pursed his lips which hardened the rest of his face. She reached for his arm, but he pulled it away.

"It wouldn't be the first infraction we've seen from them, would it? From what I heard they were behind some of the worst fights in The Fairy Kingdom when they lived there, and caused all kinds of trouble."

"Those were rumors!" His nostrils flared. "Who the hell has been feeding you full of these lies? You can't really believe all that, can you? They didn't steal it."

"Listen, don't go crazy on me. I don't want to believe it but put yourself in my place. All of a sudden, the book that can save all my best friends' lives goes missing. I know it can't be any of them, so who else can it be?" She tried to touch him again. "I just think maybe you're trying too hard to defend them."

Stefán pushed her finger away. "Because I believe someone else stole it, someone we haven't considered, and because I'm willing to give the Outliers the benefit of the doubt. I think it's horrible that you're not willing to do the same."

Julie turned away. "If I'm so horrible, why are we even together?"

"Good question!" He regretted those two words the moment they came out of his mouth, and the hurt that flashed across Julie's face nearly killed him. "Julie, I—"

"Save it." She ripped the pendant from her throat and tossed it at him. "This brought us together, and look where that got me. You're the one who really needs help, and I hope it works for you. But don't come crying to me if things fall apart."

CHAPTER THIRTY-NINE

GYÖRFI

I wish I had a nickel for every time I overestimated the intelligence of the fairy royalty. My mission in Myers Beach so far has been child's play.

Of course, I was prepared. I can't help that. "Chance favors the prepared mind" has been my mantra forever. God knows I drilled it into the boys plenty of times when I was their tutor. I wonder if it ever sank in with them.

This time, I'm probably over-prepared. Thanks to Zsa Zsa, when I took over her body, I walked away not only with the magic she learned from her mother but with the princess power she stole from Zoë. That's not counting her magic pendant and the box of Arbara rocks. Then, of course, there's the magic I got from taking over Dame Gabor, which by now amounts to overkill. I have so much at my disposal now that I'm not certain whose I'm accessing.

Hard to believe, too, that once I coveted the fairies' wings, and now here I sit with two pairs, Zsa Zsa's gorgeous black and red ones and Dame Gabor's smaller set, which I really don't need. I definitely did the right thing by taking over her body, though. As much as I loved strutting around in Chet's buff body, impersonating her made getting an entrée into their inner circle a breeze. I certainly was lucky to be in The Fairy Kingdom Lounge that night, where she spilled the beans about being close to the kings.

In a way, I feel like a kid in a candy store. There are so many sweet opportunities all around that are mine for the taking, like the Dust Keeper's Manual. With one flick of my finger, I knocked Lydia and that other woman out like lights, and all I had to do was command the vault door to open. I was expecting at least to have to pick the lock.

The book itself was disappointing. I thought I'd find instructions on how to make super dust, but I combed through the whole thing and didn't come across any. It wasn't a complete waste, though, because planting it on Christophe's throne added to the chaos and dissension in the ranks. Sending them that little note about the book being in the Outlier may have been my greatest stroke of genius yet.

With all my power, it's been hard to resist taking over the whole bunch of them. And since I heard about the tough time they had removing my graffiti from their building, I know I've got the chops to do it. God knows they've included me in plenty of gatherings and I've had opportunities. Fortunately, every time I thought I might try, Zsa Zsa's face flashed in front of me and reminded me not to act impulsively the way she always did.

I've got my mother to thank for teaching me that anger spell I threw over them. Twice. Once, when I spiked the lemonade, which they conveniently gulped down, and then when I sprinkled them using the stupid fake wand. Now that they're at each other's throats, I've made them sitting ducks for my takeover. Zsa Zsa would be proud of me, I'm sure.

Right now I'm trying to focus on the bigger prize, my beautiful Alias. Christophe is almost out of my way, so I'm close. At this point, though, I can't afford a misstep. The timing has to be just right. Now that I know that he's made super dust, I have to be careful. I'm not sure how he did it, but once I get my hands on it, it'll be game over.

CHAPTER FORTY

After their cooling-off break and lunch during which the kings gave each other the silent treatment and Lily and Greta avoided eye contact, Zsombor managed to reconvene the group. Out of deference to Stefán, his co-head of the investigation team, he suggested they go through the list of suspects again before going their separate ways.

"We should discuss the last name on the list—Emili. I'll start by admitting that I've never set eyes on her. Someone invited her to the pool, so I assume at least one of you knows her, am I right?" He went around the room, and her name was met with mostly blank faces.

Stefán and Alias admitted that aside from meeting her briefly at Joe's when she agreed to sponsor Jumping Joe's Jump Rope World Cup, she was a wild card and that neither had further contact with her.

"In retrospect, it was a bit suspicious that she was so eager to come to the pool, considering that she'd just met us," Alias said.

"Yes, I suppose it was, but I'm not so sure I'd characterize her as being *eager*," said Stefán. "Actually, I recall that she asked if *we'd* invited *her* to 'butter her up,' as she put it, to fork over sponsorship money."

"And then there's her ring," said Alias. Zsombor asked for clarification and Alias told him about the ruby-red stone that resembled Zsa Zsa's.

"Good lord. You don't think Emili is really Zsa Zsa, do you, and that she stole the book to make dust of her own?" asked Greta. "I couldn't bear it if she was back in Myers Beach."

Dame Gabor rolled her eyes. "Good lord. We've already been over this. Just having jewelry with red stones doesn't make every woman an evil witch." She pulled out her ruby. "Hello! I've got one, too. You all gonna arrest me?"

They agreed that Zsombor and Stefán should pay Emili an unscheduled visit, and the two left right away. When they popped into Joe's Java Joint, she was standing behind the counter poring over paperwork, and when she heard the witch cackle doorbell, she looked up and smiled.

"Need a table, gents?"

Zsombor took the lead and introduced himself. "Not necessary. Stefán and I are simply here to ask you a few questions."

"About the Dust Up? Joe and I are so thrilled that we agreed to be sponsors. We've had more customers this week than we've had in ages."

"I'm so glad it's working out for you," said Stefán. "I have to say I've been surprised at how exciting that jump rope competition has been. I honestly wasn't aware of how complicated their routines could get. The championship should be awesome to watch."

"Yes, and I've been meaning to tell you that we're going to have live-streaming coverage, and there are logistics involved that we should discuss."

"We've got something else to ask you about, first, but I'd be happy to stick around afterward."

Zsombor cut to the chase. "Were you by any chance at the compound swimming pool at the top of the cliff yesterday?"

She gave him a puzzled look. "Well, yes. Stefán, you know I was. You invited me. Brought me up there, too. Why?"

"We were wondering if you noticed anything strange or out of the ordinary while you were there?"

"No, other than it was the most fantastic house, pool, location, and view on the planet."

"So, what happened?" asked Zsombor.

"Nothing much, which was the point. We were there to relax. Dame Gabor, I think that was her name, fixed everyone martinis. I declined because I had to get back here for the afternoon shift." Zsombor pressed for more details. "Well, whenever I find myself in a pool, I generally try to swim a mile or so, which I did. The water was glorious. Then I laid out on one of the most comfortable lounge chairs I've ever been on and fell asleep."

"Did you see anyone enter the house?" he continued.

"Only when the others went in to run some sort of errand. I believe that's what they said they were doing."

"She's right. That's exactly how it went," Stefán confirmed.

Zsombor turned back to Emili. "And did you see them return?"

She laughed and shook her head. "No. I didn't see any of them come back. Like I said, I was dead asleep. I almost didn't wake up in time to get to work."

"One more question," said Zsombor. "Tell us about your ring."

She scrunched her face and spun the ring around her middle finger. "This?" She laughed again. "What's there to tell? I took my goddaughter to Disneyland when she was a kid, and she won it in one of those kiosks with the pincher thing that drops down. Cost me about a buck fifty in quarters." She scrunched her face. "Your questions seem random, and frankly they're confusing me. Mind telling me what this is about?"

"Sorry about being a bit opaque. Something was stolen from the house, and we believe it might have happened during the swimming party."

"Well, I'm sorry I can't help you, fellas. Now, Stefán, did you say that you could stay? It won't take long."

"I'll wait outside," said Zsombor.

He was sitting on a bench when Stefán joined him a few minutes later. After a quick debrief, they agreed to scratch her from the list. Since they'd already eliminated Dr. Anderson, that left Dame Gabor and Julie.

"And you," said Zsombor. "We already know you took bags of dust from the lab. You could've easily taken the book at the same time."

"Easily? Are you out of your mind? Yes, I walked past the vault, but it's super secure, and it isn't programmed for my biometric. And you don't need to rub it in that my magic is inferior to yours."

"But Lydia's biometrics *are* programmed, and you could have overpowered her and made her open it."

"Yes, I supposed I could have, but I didn't. If you don't believe me, ask her. She's working today, I understand." He shook his head. "I suppose you want to go after Dame Gabor next. And why wouldn't you? You seem to like picking on people weaker than you."

Zsombor ignored his slur with a huff. "What about Julie?"

Stefán slammed his fist on the bench. "As a suspect? Now, that's going too far. She wasn't even there."

"Does she have an alibi?"

"For what? You're being ridiculous, but you'll have to interrogate her yourself. We're not speaking."

The rehearsal for *Peter Pan* later that day did not go well. People were giving each other the silent treatment, and since they stood as far apart from each other as possible, nobody took their correct marks. Dame Gabor had enlisted the Myers Beach Players to fill in some of the parts with their own actors, and during their initial discussions, she admitted that she was too old to handle the huge production, and she paid their manager out of her own pocket to direct the show.

Bystanders at the run-through noticed the chilly atmosphere on the stage, and rumors about the falling out among the royals quickly grew among the fairies. Theos seemed particularly snippy at the rehearsal, and Stefán wondered if it was because he was still smarting from being demoted as High King, or because he only had a bit part in the play.

Stefán noticed that the rest of the world around them was having fun. The Dust Up Beach Festival was in full swing and had proceeded without any further incidents. He had given Julie space after their fight, too, and though he was still bitter about her remarks, he hoped they'd reconcile.

He looked at his watch. The tea house wouldn't open for another hour, and since he was still insecure about the state of his acting chops and because the rehearsal had been a bust, he hoped he could snag Dame Gabor for a coaching session before she started work. Despite her earlier offer to help and the schedule they set up, she always had a reason to cancel, and so they'd never managed to get together.

"I'm sorry," she said. "Since the scuffle yesterday, the kings have given me a new job, on top of running this place, if you can believe it." She brought him to a corner table where she flicked a finger and presented him with a frappuccino.

"Mmm. This is good. Tastes pretty much like my own," he said. He wiped the foam from his lips. "Mine's a little sweeter."

She waved her hand over his glass, and the liquid churned itself. "Now try it."

He took another sip and nodded. "You've got it on the nose."

"I found the recipe posted on a wall down in the kitchen, so I put it on the menu," she said. "I've made a lot of changes around here, and actually they've given me a really cool new job."

"What are they having you do?"

"It's actually simple, but quite delicate, to say the least. Since none of the kings are speaking to each other, they've tasked me with passing messages between them."

"Kind of a go-between, huh?"

"I prefer the term Kings' Emissary. At least that's the title I ran past them. By the way, you'll be on my circuit" She conjured a martini.

Stefán's eyes popped. "Wow, and they let you drink on the job?"

She took a gulp. "Listen, I figure I'm doing them a favor."

"Man, they must really trust you. As the president of my group, I can imagine the kinds of sensitive information they're asking you to deliver."

"A lot of it has been sniping back and forth, but I pass along lots of important intel, too. Alias, for example, has me keep them all up to date with his dust production, and by the way, he's already made a bunch. I mean the show must go on, right?"

Stefán shifted in his chair. "I haven't spoken to anyone since the blowout, so I'm out of the loop on anything that doesn't involve the Dust Up Festival or the Outliers. So, I guess that means they solved the problem with the formula's magic words."

"Yes. And apparently, it wasn't easy. Turns out the instructions on how to say them were open to interpretation. Something about repeating the words *Fstl Fstl* the right number of times." She held her hand up to prevent anyone from listening. "It's four, by the way. You have to repeat both words twice."

"Wow. Alias told you that? I understood it was top secret."

She tossed her hair. "Funny you should mention it. To be honest, Alias and I have become quite close. He asks me to hang with him all the time, which I do whenever I can get time off work. And he basically shares everything with me."

"Holy smokes! I'm impressed." Stefán lowered his voice. "Then I suppose you know about the other dust he's made, right?"

She jerked her head. "Probably. Which one's that?"

"If I recall correctly, the code name is super dust. He says it's going to be like nothing the fairies have ever seen. More powerful than the magic of all the kings combined. Can you imagine how dangerous it would be for the kings if it got in the wrong hands?"

"I'm a little surprised he hasn't mentioned it. I thought that the whole thing was a myth."

"Oh, no. It's far from fiction. He gave me a demonstration. Mind-boggling!" He leaned in. "Ask him to show you. He keeps it on him all the time now in a little pink pouch around his waist."

"Oh, I'm sure he will." She touched his wrist and laughed. "Can you keep a secret?" Stefán nodded. "Alias says after the Dust Up Beach Festival is over and everything gets settled down, he wants me to quit this menial job here and come work for him as his personal assistant."

Stefán threw his head back. "Wow, Dame Gabor. Look

at you! Talk about moving up. How is Christophe taking all this? You can't really be making him jealous, can you?"

"Get this. Alias told me in total confidence that being around me was starting to make him think twice about being gay." Her eyes sparkled. "And of course it's no secret that the bloom is off the rose in their relationship anyway. That contentious vote to take away Theos' High King title started it." She wiggled her eyebrows. "So, stay tuned."

CHAPTER FORTY-ONE

Stefán returned to his office at the Outlier building, which they agreed to start calling The Clubhouse, and he called for Magda.

"I want to apologize again for the kings' rudeness. I've never seen any of them behave that way." He led her to the large adjacent sitting room and sank into the sofa. "You won't believe how they criticized these rooms," he said, gesturing to the carpets and artwork.

"Envious, maybe?" Magda turned up the corner of her mouth.

"I don't know. Before yesterday, I wouldn't have thought so, but after what I saw, I'll believe anything. Tea?"

"Let me," she said, and she held her palms over the coffee table and manifested a large pink ceramic pot with matching cups. "There are a few tricks I can still do." They sipped tea silently for a few minutes, and then Magda broke the ice.

"When you first showed up at the door yesterday, I was worried."

"Me, too. If the book had been here, we'd all have been toast."

"No. I was worried about you."

Stefán set down his cup. "Let me explain. Something happened earlier that ruffled everybody's feathers and put them all in a bad mood. How that happened is still a mystery, but I wasn't the only one who felt the sting. You should have heard them when everyone got back to Theos' house and lobbed bombs at each other. It was crazy."

"Well, I was proud of you when you did take charge." She poured another cup. "Want to know what I believe? I think they were under a spell."

"Hmm. I hadn't thought of that. Who could have done it? Or have the power to do it."

"I think that's something that you are going to have to find out. I believe it's your mission. And if you want my advice, you can start by changing your own attitude."

"Magda, I—"

"I'm not done. What I mean by that is that you are the head of a great group of fairies. As such, you shouldn't let Theos, or Christophe, or Zsombor push you around. You are their equal now."

"You're right. Politically, I am. When it comes to blood-lines, though, I know I don't measure up. Funny. I never cared that my family wasn't part of a kingdom before, but now that I've got this position, I'm suddenly aware of it."

"And does it bother you now?"

"A little, to be honest. I know you were joking when you guys called me Lord Stefán, but it's the difference between their fairy magic and mine that puts me at a disadvantage, you know, not being a real royal with king power and all, like them."

"We may not call ourselves a kingdom anymore, but most of us came from one. Oddly, history books call it the Fourth Kingdom, which doesn't make sense, because when I grew up, my ancestors always referred to it as the First."

"Funny you should bring that up. Zoë shared a book with Julie and me. There's a section in it, and I've been meaning to go back to their palace library to read it."

"Big leather-bound book? The ultimate authority? Weighs a ton?"

"Yes. So you've heard of it."

"As a child, I read it cover to cover. Since it updates itself, though, one must constantly keep consulting it."

"Well, there's a photo of someone named Lord Steffon, who apparently I resemble. Maybe you've seen it."

"Ah, yes. Lord Steffon. My mother said he was quite the looker."

He laughed. "Yes, Dame Gabor used to date him, I think she said."

"I'm not surprised," said Magda. "She was quite the diva."

"Since you know so much about him, maybe you'd come with me to look through the book together. I'd be happy to show it to you sometime. We'd have to go to their library, though. It's a one-of-a-kind, and Zoë says they don't permit it to leave the palace."

"Is that what she told you?"

She poured them each another cup of tea and gestured for him to take his with him and follow her. She led him into the hallway and down a few feet where they stopped at a gigantic ornate floor-length mirror. She waved her hand, and the mirror vanished, revealing a passageway that connected the club to her private home next door.

"How did I not know about this?" Stefán asked.

"Honestly, we added it after the renovation. I didn't think you'd mind, and I was planning to tell you. I'm old, and it's just easier for me to go back and forth." She took him down the spiral staircase to the first floor and into the grand sitting room off the front lobby.

"This is where I keep all my memorabilia," she explained. "You may remember my telling Lily when you all visited that I had all her fairy figurines. I keep them here, too." She pointed to a wall of statues and carvings and bronzes. Then she asked him to sit in one of the large leather chairs by the fireplace. Getting there took him past a long library table, and he stopped when he noticed the large book. He looked back at her, and she gave him a devilish smile.

"Look familiar? It should. It's identical."

He thumbed through the pages. "How is this possible?"

"Truth is, this one is the original. I can't blame Zoë for not knowing about it. After the overthrow of the Fourth Kingdom, it was like someone put a black curtain over the whole incident. Expunged everything from textbooks, too, so nobody would ever learn about it." As she watched him flip to the chapter on the Fourth Kingdom, she continued.

"The reason I have this one is because my mom was the head librarian, and she gave it to me for safekeeping. That and the clothes on my back were the only things I took when I fled."

"Good lord. This is fascinating." His fingers went to the photo. "Here he is, Lord Steffon." He swung the book around to show Magda.

"Yes, the one and only," she said. "And your great-grandfather."

CHAPTER FORTY-TWO

"So does this make me a lord?"

"Yep. My family were academics, part of the intelligentsia, but you're definitely a direct descendant of one of the high mucky mucks."

Stefán closed the cover. "You know, Theos' father took such good care of me. Why do you suppose he kept that particular fact from me?"

"Look, he was a good man. Always was. At first he probably kept quiet because you were too young and he feared for your safety. Then after your parents were assassinated, he may have kept you hidden so that the royalists who wanted to reorganize wouldn't try to talk you into agreeing to be their lord. Because by then, you would have been the next in line."

"To what? I would still only be a lord."

"Yes, but the Fourth Kingdom never had a king. I know it's odd to call it a kingdom if there isn't one, but that's another story. Our kingdom was always ruled by a lord."

He drank another sip of tea. "And so you knew about me all along?"

"Yup. I try to keep up." She flipped to the back. "I can prove it, too. Look. It says so right there in black and white. S-T-E-F-F-O-N." She pointed to his name and snickered. "Actually in sepia."

"This really isn't proof, though. None of the kings would believe it. My name is spelled differently, as you know."

"Read on. You'll see that Theos' father changed it. Again, probably to protect you."

"So, now what? I'm head of a group of free spirits, and I've got a title I can never use."

"Let's not count that out," she said. "I've noticed how happy they've become now that they're together. Also, I've seen the way they've been drooling over the magic the other fairies have. Not saying it's a bad thing, by the way. These are good people."

He shifted in his chair. "I'd like to ask you something else that's been troubling me."

"And that is?"

"I think the same person who leaked the information about the dust shortage is the one who stole the book, and probably also responsible for stirring up the chaos among the royals. *Entre nous*, I have a very strong suspicion that Zsa Zsa Hajdu is behind it. I believe you said you'd heard of her."

"Yes, poor Zsa Zsa. I'm guessing you didn't know that she was your cousin. Not blood, of course. She was the child of two humans. Once her human father died, her mother had a whirlwind romance with your uncle, and they married quickly."

"Was? As in deceased?"

"Yes. Hasn't been gone all that long, either." Magda thumbed through the pages of the more recent history. "It's all written right here, and what a sad story it was."

"Then if it's not Zsa Zsa, I don't know who we're up against." He signed and dropped his head into his hands. "I haven't even told Julie any of my suspicions. And since we're not speaking, I don't know when or even if I'll be able to."

"Then let me give you another unsolicited piece of advice. First and foremost, pay attention to your relation-ship with her. Once that's solid, there's nothing you can't do."

Stefán got up to leave. "I'm going to her place now. My head and heart are both bursting to tell her everything I've learned. And I need her to know I love her."

Suddenly Magda cocked her head to the side. "What's that sticking out of your pocket?"

Confused, Stefán pulled out the pendant Julie had thrown at him. "This thing?" He held it up to the light. "Just some chunk of cheap jewelry all the kings and queens believe gives you good luck. Julie believes it too. She threw it at me before storming away from our argument." He shook his head. "I've been carrying it around since. I'm not really sure what to do with it, but I didn't want to throw it out."

Magda gently plucked the necklace out of his hand and gave the stone a good rub.

"It's a powerful artifact. I could feel its magic from across the room," she said. Then she clasped it around his neck. "I think you should wear it. It may come in handy when you least expect it."

CHAPTER FORTY-THREE

Stefán went over to Julie's to try apologizing for not taking her concerns about her friends seriously and for losing his temper. But when she didn't answer the bell, his heart sank, and he set out to find her.

First, he tried her usual haunts: the bookstore, The Fairy Kingdom, the Tiki Hut, and even Joe's Java Joint. When he didn't find her in any of those places, he swung by the Third Kingdom to ask for Zoë, but when the attendant who answered the door told him she was out, he found himself back at square one.

He flopped onto the nearest bench and was staring into the middle distance when the sound of laughter broke him out of his reverie.

"King me!" said an elderly man at the public checkerboard table next to him. Stefán turned his head to watch his elderly female opponent slap a checker on top of his.

"High time," she said with a snicker. "I was getting tired of winning."

Stefán stood up abruptly and thanked them for their

help, and they gave him a curious look when he raced down the boardwalk.

Zoë and Briar, bent over a hexagonal board game with lots of little blocks and cards around it at their usual window table at the High Tide Tavern, saw him enter first. They murmured something, and Julie's head shot up with panicked eyes. Stefán froze in his path to their table, and after a slight hesitation, Julie gave a slight nod and Zoë waved him over.

"Briar and I are gonna go get some lunch," Zoë said, eyeing both Julie and Stefán like they were bound to break into a fight at any minute.

"You have my number, if you need anything," he heard Briar say. They left, and despite the awkwardness, Stefán was glad Julie had managed to befriend someone so loyal. After a quiet moment or two, they spoke at the same time.

"I just wanted—"

"I'm totally—"

Julie shot Stefán a sheepish smile and he let out a small laugh, sliding into the chair opposite hers.

"You go first," she said, as she picked up one of the blocks from the game and fidgeted with it.

"I wanted to apologize," he began. "I understand now that your concerns were valid, and I'm sorry for not hearing you out. The Outliers have been facing a lot of discrimination for things they had nothing to do with, and I guess I was just being defensive."

Julie leaned her head against the window. "I'm not a fairy, and I don't know anything about fairy politics, so I should have kept my mouth shut. It was wrong of me to blame them for anything, especially now since they've been facing so much." She reached for his hand and he squeezed it back. "And for some reason I got really angry. Just so you know, I'm never like that."

"Neither am I," he said.

She blushed and looked away. "Does that mean we can still get married? I do love you, you know."

"And I love you more." He stood. "Let's get out of here, so I can show you how much."

<hr>

They were catching their breaths from hours of lovemaking when Julie leaned over to give him a peck on the cheek. At her touch, he gently opened his eyelids.

"Your—your eyes!" she said, clutching the sheet to her heart like a set of pearls. "Your eyes—they're *gold!*" She handed him her phone from the nightstand and adjusted the camera app so he could see for himself.

He stared into the camera and the set of deep gold eyes that reminded him of Magda's. Then he blinked and brought his hand to his chest.

"Wow! The pendant stone changed, too. It's funny, Magda told me to wear it," he said, as he fingered the smooth stone.

He was still staring into the screen when Julie settled in next to him. "I can't imagine how weird it must feel, but in case you were wondering, I think the new color is sexy as hell." She took the phone out of his hands and pulled him close. "Before we got distracted this morning with, um, you know, you said you had some things you wanted to tell me. Does it have anything to do with Magda?"

"It does," he said, and he proceeded to summarize the revelations he'd learned about his lineage and the news about his cousin Zsa Zsa's death. "I think it's time you met her and see where I've been calling home...at least during the day."

Like the other buildings that had been adapted to accommodate six-inch fairies, there were only two floors that she could visit. They passed several Outliers milling about in the halls and he made a point to acknowledge each one and introduce them to her. He learned that she was excellent at remembering names and faces, and later when they were alone in his office, he was impressed that she could rattle off what she'd learned and had made associations with everyone she'd met.

Confident that she was ready to meet Magda and her crew, he steered her next door to Magda's private quarters. On the way, he explained that even though the Outliers had been known for eschewing the concept of an actual kingdom or royalty, Magda and her friends would be the closest thing to a ruling class, if they had one.

"I'm so nervous," she said. "I imagine it's like meeting your in-laws for the first time."

Magda made her feel comfortable. To Stefán's surprise, it turned out that she had known who Julie was for a long time. As a longtime customer of The Fairy Kingdom, they had interacted together many, many times, without Julie realizing it. Stefán leaned back and listened to them talk about Lily's struggles with the store and the unfortunate and premature death of her landlord Mrs. Coffey, which had thrown the store and their lives into turmoil. And

Magda shared her personal thrill when Lily met Theos and struck it rich.

Magda regaled them with stories about her early time in Myers Beach and the funny things she'd seen as it had grown into the town it had become. Soon she and Julie swapped stories about the characters they knew in common: the fearsome banker, Katherine Needham, and of course Joe and his ever-changing hair color.

"Since I change mine every day, I didn't object to the concept," said Magda. "What cracked me up about him was the crappy job he did."

"Right?" said Julie. "He never quite got the back done right. It seemed there was always some leftover color from the last dye job."

"This was marvelous," Magda said when they finished the last of the tea and pastries. "I just know we're going to be good friends. Has Stefán shown you his suite? When we had it constructed, we made sure it was big enough for two...with a lot of room to grow. Have you thought of having kids?"

"That is the plan," Julie said. "After we get married, of course. Thanks for the lovely chat."

Magda pulled Stefán aside and he waved Julie on, with a promise that he'd meet her outside.

"Have you come any closer to figuring out who you're up against?"

Stefán shook his head. "Since you told me that Zsa Zsa was dead, all Alias and I have is that Dame Gabor Theas been acting weird. I'm off to meet him now. But, in the meantime, can we be realistic about what I can do? I've got my love life nailed down like you suggested, but I still feel the threat against the fairies is bigger than any of us can handle."

"Then, Lord Steffon. I will let you leave with one more tidbit that you may find useful." She opened the front door and took both his hands. Her eyes sparkled. "You may have inherited the title of lord...but it came with fairy king power. You've had it since your folks died, and you just didn't realize it."

Stefán felt his knees weaken and he leaned against the door frame to steady himself. Magda offered her hand, and he took it and snickered.

"Feeling faint is probably not the reaction a normal fairy would expect after learning they'd joined the ranks of the world's most powerful ones. I guess after believing I was average for so long, I never tried to push myself beyond the limits of a normal fairy."

"Don't beat yourself up. Seize it now. You've got your whole life ahead to take advantage of it and do some good," said Magda. "Can you stay for one more minute?" He looked out at Julie, and when he saw her chatting away on her phone, he nodded.

"Yes, and I feel fine, now."

"The Outliers have decided they'd like being in a community after all, and after seeing how the other fairies have benefited, they've been talking about maybe forming a kingdom again. No king, of course, but they've already taken a shine to you, and they would like to experiment by making you their lord. Only if you'd be okay with that."

It was Saturday, and since both the beach and the boardwalk were super crowded, the director of the *Peter Pan* play made the decision to schedule the final run-through at eleven in the evening, after most people had left. Crews quickly threw up extra ranks of Klieg lights to illuminate the giant replica Jolly Roger anchored just offshore that Stefán had managed to conjure up at the last minute.

The air was still chilly between the royals, but Stefán guessed that the director was pleased that at least relations had thawed enough for the cast members to get into their roles. As Wendy, Julie made an effort to warm up to Theos and Alias, who were playing the part of her younger brothers. Lily and Greta seemed to take pleasure in acting brash and rude to each other and everyone else in their respective roles of Captain Hook and Smee.

Christophe had volunteered for the role of Tiger Lily and was having a blast getting her character as historically accurate as possible within the bounds of the play, while his sister Zoë, who had no ax to grind, had fun goofing off with Briar in their respective roles as Nana and the Crocodile. Even Zsombor had loosened up and gotten into the narration.

"You guys have really pulled it out," the director said. "I think we've got a hit on our hands."

Stefán was about to call it a night, too, and he was heading home with Alias and Christophe when they heard a small group chanting, "Dust, Dust, Where's the Dust!" They turned and saw Belos with three older fairies holding signs and raising their fists.

"Where the hell is all this fairy dust you promised?" said

Belos. "This beach party is fun and everything, but it isn't worth a hill of beans if we're all going to die in a week." He turned to Stefán with bloodshot eyes and a cruel smirk twisting his mouth. "Or did you just give it to the Outliers? I knew you were one of those nomad freaks from the beginning."

Stefán pulled away from Christophe and Alias and stormed over to the protestors. He fumed and flicked his finger at Belos and the others which shrank them into tiny dung beetles. Then he conjured a jar and scooped them up.

"Sorry about this," he said to his friends. "But that man exhausts me, and I'm tired of letting him spew hate toward my people. I'll let them sit in there for a couple days. Maybe by then, they'll have settled down some."

"Nice trick," said Christophe. "I'm impressed."

CHAPTER FORTY-FOUR

Alias had invited Dame Gabor up to the compound, and she'd jumped at the chance to hang out by the pool with the gorgeous Alias the day before the big play. Alias greeted her in nothing but tight swim shorts and a blinding smile, and inside her body, Györfi mentally squealed at how well his plan was working out.

"Glad you could make it, Rita." Alias pulled her into a tight hug and let her graze his butt with her hand.

They'd settled on the lounge chairs and Alias sat so that she could rub sunscreen onto his back when the door to the guest tower banged open and Christophe burst out. His mouth was pressed into a thin line.

"Well, I'm all packed."

Dame Gabor faked a shock, "Packed for what?"

Christophe shrugged and shot daggers at Alias. "He didn't bother to tell you? Alias and I are taking a break. I'm moving back to my palace."

This time, her reaction was real. "Really?"

Christophe sneered. "I would've thought you already knew, since—"

"That's enough," Alias said. "If you're going to go, go."

"Fine. Like I wanna be here any longer, anyway." He twirled his finger and sent his bags off in a funnel cloud. Then he flipped Alias and Dame Gabor the bird, popped out his wings, and flew off.

"Great," said Alias. "With him gone, there's more time for you and me, Rita." He leaned back so they could cuddle.

She stroked a hand through his hair and sighed. "This is perfect."

"Even more perfect is that I finally finished making that super dust," Alias murmured.

"Isn't that something?" she cooed.

At five in the afternoon, Stefán took the stage in his Peter Pan costume. As he gazed up at the full bleachers and the crowds of spectators standing on both sides, he used every bit of his new king power to keep from shaking. It wasn't from stage fright. What scared him was what would follow the play. He took a breath and spoke into the microphone.

"Ladies, gentlemen, and all you children in the audience. What you are about to see this afternoon is perhaps the greatest play about eternal youth, adventure, evil, motherhood, and family the world has ever known. Without further ado, as the culmination of the Myers Beach Dust Up Festival we present for you, *Peter Pan*."

The lights went out. When they came on again an instant later, the set had changed to the bedroom scene of the Darling children. Peter was crouching on the window ledge, and the play began when he lifted open the window and woke Wendy and her two brothers, Michael and John.

To keep the Never Never Land island vibe, the director moved much of the action to the beach directly behind the stage. Staging the flying sequences both required an intricate network of wires strung high above the stage and beach, and while Julie was thrilled by the tech, she couldn't help but suppress a giggle at Stefán, Alias, and Christophe who she caught rolling their eyes at the idiocy of having to wear harnesses to fly.

As expected, Dame Gabor stole the show and worked her wand flawlessly to dispense fairy dust at every opportunity.

The director had gotten innovative and even used Hersey Lighthouse as the tree Peter and his Lost Boys used to enter their home. During a scene where the boys were sleeping and the stage lighting was dim, Dame Gabor crept on the floor over to Michael, played by Alias, and so carefully untied the pink pouch of super dust that he wore around his waist, that he didn't notice. She then stuffed it into her tutu.

The play eventually moved from the beach to the Jolly Roger for the scenes with Captain Hook and Smee. Blasts from the ship's cannons kept children and grownups alike engaged and continued to thrill, excite, and frighten the audience all the way to the final act, which concluded as it began, back on the stage in the set of the children's bedroom.

At the conclusion of the play, the lights went dark, and when they came back on again, the cast returned to the stage one by one for their curtain calls to great applause. The co-stars Peter Pan and Tinkerbell came out last, and as they walked forward to the center stage, Stefán noticed that Dame Gabor was clutching the pink pouch. He gave the signal to Alias.

Stefán backed away and the cast formed a circle around the star, Dame Gabor. The audience continued to cheer and shout as she raised her hands and twirled around at the adulation. Then she stopped.

"Ladies and gentlemen. You have no idea what this moment means to me. I have waited decades for this opportunity to show my appreciation to my close friends who have formed this circle of friendship around me. And I'd like to return their kindness with a special gift of my own."

With a menacing grin, she dipped her wand into the pink pouch and held it over her head.

"This is not just the end of the play, it's the end of you. With this super dust, I am now invincible." As it rained down over her, she bared her teeth and pointed at the royals. "Bow down." One by one, they fell to their knees. Alias was lowering himself to the floor when she stopped him.

"All, but you, my love." She walked over to him and caressed his cheek. "You, I'm going to spare, because I will become your queen."

He raised his head and laughed. "Like hell, you will!

There's no such thing as super dust, Mr. Györfi!"

Stefán tore open his costume to bare his chest and expose the pendant. "Now!" he shouted.

With that all the royals stood and snapped their fingers in unison, blasting blue, green, and bronze-colored bolts of magic directly at the gold stone. Stefán tilted it toward Dame Gabor, sending the combined power of five fairy kings, two fairy queens, and a fairy princess directly at her. Her body convulsed, she flailed her arms, and she dropped her wand.

"Fortune truly does favor the prepared mind," said Alias. Stefán held out his palms and then clapped them together. Dame Gabor convulsed so violently that Györfi's body came flying out across the stage where it landed in a heap. Chet's body flew out, too, as well as Zsa Zsa's. Sparks of gold, silver, and red blew out in all directions, some landing on Zoë, whose body reacted immediately by sprouting new wings.

When the dust settled, Stefán gave Zoë a nod, and she stepped forward, twirled her finger, and enveloped the bodies of Györfi, Zsa Zsa, and Chet in funnel clouds.

"Be careful of summer cyclones," she said. She snapped her fingers and sent them flying out over the ocean.

Meanwhile, audience members were screaming and stampeding in all directions to get away from what some were calling the Apocalypse.

"Okay, everyone. It's time," said Alias. "Take out the good stuff."

Then, on cue, the royals popped their wings and took to the air to sprinkle the entirety of Myers Beach with Alias' newest high-test fairy dust.

CHAPTER FORTY-FIVE

The outdoor seating area in front of The Fairy Kingdom was still Greta's favorite place to sit. It wasn't just for the fragrance that continuously wafted from the proliferation of roses that completely covered the overhang and both sides, but because the entire construction had been a gift to her from Zsombor. She remembered how astonished she'd been when it happened. She simply mentioned late one night that it might make good business sense for him to expand out onto the boardwalk, and by morning he'd erected the whole thing.

As she sipped her tea with Lily and Julie, she giggled at how blind she'd been to Zsombor's magic. In less than two weeks he'd completed a massive renovation of the entire building, which included adding an enormous greenhouse stocked with mature plants and trees and even a swimming pool on the roof.

"I was so gaga for him that I lost all sense of logic. He defied the laws of physics over and over in front of my eyes, and I fell for his lame explanations every time."

She patted her tummy and looked up at the glass front of their vast apartment. The latest version included a nursery, and as she put her teacup down, she dreamed of the day she'd give birth and be able to drink coffee again.

With Lily and Theos' fairies now comfortably ensconced in their new digs beneath the compound, Greta and Zsombor had immediately renovated The Fairy Kingdom to create spacious new accommodations for their fairy subjects. They knocked down a few walls to open up the teahouse and lounge floor plan and give it a more contemporary vibe, too, but she had put her foot down on any changes to the front.

They'd offered to host Julie and Stefán's wedding and reception in their apartment earlier in the week. The recent makeover had made it more gorgeous than before, and the couple jumped at Greta's offer. There would be two weddings that week. Zoë was going to marry Briar there in another day or two.

"Don't talk to me about defying physics. I think I take the cake on that," said Lily. "I was so nuts about Theos that I let myself believe that it was the wind that kept us floating in the sky for several hours in that kitesurfing harness. If I'd had any brains, I'd have looked behind me and noticed he was a fairy flapping his wings."

"But why would you have?" asked Julie. "Back then, the only fairies we knew were the statues you made." She pushed her cup and saucer to the side. "Does anyone know if Dame Gabor is joining us for dinner?"

"Alias was hopeful that she'd be strong enough," said Greta. "What a wild ride she took. I'd love to hear her side of things."

Stefán snuck up behind her. "Are you ready? We've got just enough time to make our reservation."

Theos and Zsombor were with him, and they took their wives' hands and strolled across the boardwalk to the Tiki Hut, where Alias and Christophe were waiting with huge grins.

"Close your eyes and hold hands, everyone. Christophe is going to lead you to the table."

"Why the mystery? Can't we sit at our regular one?" asked Lily, as she groped her way through the line behind Theos. "I can't imagine sitting anywhere else."

"Don't worry, I don't think you'll be disappointed," he said. He stopped them when he got to the center palapa.

"Christophe and I decided that the queens' table needed an upgrade," said Alias. "So we talked the management into putting in a larger one and adding a few more of those chairs you liked."

"You can open them now," said Christophe. "Ta-dah! Now we can all sit on bamboo thrones."

The first thing they saw was Dame Gabor sitting on one of them.

"I hope you won't mind if I don't stand up for your highnesses," she said. "I'm not quite at a hundred percent." They immediately crowded around to give her hugs and express their excitement at her miraculous recovery. "Sit, sit," she said. "Now that I've got my own throne, I'm going to give the orders for a change. And I've got a lot to say." She was still laughing when they took their seats.

Alias had already ordered the prosecco, and when Eric the waiter finished pouring, she raised her glass.

"To all of you for the roles you played in what turned

out to be the most important show of my life. Cecil B. DeMille would have been jealous as hell. I wish I'd had my marbles and been able to watch it, and I'm not talking about the *Peter Pan* play. I'm talking about how you saved my life and fairydom, for that matter. The staging, the script, and the acting must have been genius from beginning to end."

"Hmm. I wouldn't go that far," said Stefán. "Many of us noticed your weird behavior. We just didn't know what it meant."

"Honestly, Dame Gabor, my jaw dropped when I watched you flying through the air over the jetty toward us in your sequined floor-length gown," said Julie. "I didn't know whether to laugh or cry."

"Alias and I sat up late some nights worrying that you'd slipped into dementia," said Christophe. "You were forgetting things left and right."

"There were dozens of other things, too," said Stefán. "Like when you started making cute little curtsies instead of those deep diva bows you always made. By the time we figured out that something serious was going on, we assumed that somehow Zsa Zsa was back and behind it."

"Yeah," said Alias. "Never in a gazillion years would I have guessed that it was Györfi instead. We all thought Zsa Zsa had killed him, not the other way around."

"Until we started linking all the little clues, like seeing you drinking martinis with a vengeance after swearing them off," said Stefán.

"And of course, Christophe and I knew a martini was Györfi's drink of choice," said Alias.

"But once he and Stefán did figure it out, we all went right to work to save you," added Theos. "I should say we started as soon as those anger spells you threw over us wore off and we stopped fighting with each other."

"Wow. That's a first," said Dame Gabor. "I didn't know I could do that."

"Stefán and Christophe and I agreed to start watching you more closely," Alias said. "We caught what you were doing in time to immunize the three of us. We figured that the only reason to do something that drastic was so we would turn on each other, and to make you think you were succeeding, we let your spell reach everyone else."

"It was so weird being forced to yell at people we loved," said Theos. "It was even harder to keep pretending we were still mad when it wore off."

"So if you all knew what was happening, why didn't you clue me in on the plan?" asked Julie.

Stefán pulled her into a hug. "We love you, Julie, but we agreed you were just way too nice to be able to pull off being mad, and that would've cost us the whole charade. To help us sell it, we needed you to be as genuinely angry as they were."

"So what was Györfi's goal in all this?" asked Dame Gabor.

"I'll answer that," said Alias. "Ever since he set foot in the palace of the Third King to be our tutor, he was envious of our magic. You could see him drooling over our wings."

"Talk about drooling," said Christophe. "That was nothing compared to the way he lusted over Alias." He touched Alias' chin. "I warned this guy from the beginning that he was the teacher's pet, but he didn't believe me."

"And then he actually came on to me. I lost my head and retaliated pretty hard. Then, of course, we all know the story of how Christophe's aunt banished him. I guess he'd held a serious grudge and wanted to get back at us ever since. Then when he took over Zsa Zsa, he picked up her animosity against all the fairies, too."

"Györfi was too smart for Zsa Zsa, which is saying a lot," said Greta. She rolled her eyes. "And I know a bit about her. No offense to your cousin, Stefán, but good riddance, is all I can say. Does anyone know what made her so evil?"

"I do," said Dame Gabor. "At least I know the story. Something about a jealous uncle that got mad and split the family up. Sent her alone as a little child off in a funnel cloud. I'd have been pretty sore about it, too."

"When Alias finally realized you were really Györfi, he was able to predict your behavior, and he told us what to look for. That's why, when you were cozying up to him, he went along and pretended to be turned on by you, even going so far as to fake a split with Christophe."

Dame Gabor shot Alias a wry smile. "Pretended to be? Harrumph."

Alias pecked her on the cheek. "Don't worry, Dame Gabor, you've still got it. But it did allow me to fill your lovestruck head with the ruse about super dust."

"Then we trusted that Györfi's oversized ego would help us finish you off during the curtain call," said Stefán. "Although with all the magic you'd accumulated, we knew it wouldn't be easy."

"Thanks to the addition of Stefán's king power, you did," said Julie.

"Duh. Which I apparently had all along," Stefán said.

"And which is why we weren't ever sure you *were* an Outlier," said Theos. "You always had more magic than they did, and then, of course, back then your eyes were blue, not gold." He raised his glass. "Anyway, here's to Stefán, Lord of the Fourth Kingdom."

As the rest of them cheered, Stefán interrupted. "Not to put too fine a point on it, but we're calling ourselves the First Kingdom, now. That's what Magda said it was originally called." He reached under the table and pulled out the ancestry tome he'd brought from the Outlier building. "Speaking of Magda, she said I could bring it here to show you the updates."

He flipped open to the pages at the end that chronicled the past weeks, including his and Julie's wedding.

"Can I take a look?" asked Greta. Julie swiveled the book around and watched Greta smile while reading about her romance with Zsombor. "You should see these pictures, honey," she said. "We both look pretty fabulous."

Then she flipped forward and back a couple of times until she stopped in frustration. "I don't see where it's written that Zsa Zsa died. This latest entry states that she's living on the island of St. Martin."

"Impossible," said Stefán. "Julie and I both read that she'd been found dead on the floor of her club in New York."

Dame Gabor clapped her hands. "Well, that will have to be a problem for another day. I'm not going to let her spoil this occasion. We've got too much to celebrate." She raised her glass. "To us and to magical Myers Beach where, as the new billboard says, *'All your wishes come true.'*"

THE END

AUTHOR NOTES

AUGUST 21, 2023

I can't describe the mixed emotions that came from finishing the <u>Magic at Myers Beach</u> fantasy series. I've lived with Theos, and Alias, and Lily, and Greta, and Julie, and Stefán, and Zsa Zsa, and Györfi, and Christophe day in and day out for well, as long as it took to write four books, and I felt guilty about leaving them behind. I'm bold to say that I've already taken up with a new cast, however, and by the time you read these notes, I'll have finished Book One in my new thriller series, which I hope you'll check out, too, wherever books are sold.

Let me start my discussion of *Book Four, Summer Cyclone,* by admitting that <u>pasta puttanesca</u> is one of those dishes that I enjoy at home every couple of weeks. I'm notorious among my friends for not cooking much, and because that particular pasta is one of the few things I can whip up successfully every time, I used the book's hero, Stefán to share that proud fact by teaching the recipe to his girlfriend, Julie. Fun fact: When I'm in Italy, I eat much more often– daily, though I likely alternate it with my other favorite, <u>ravioli funghi porcini</u>. (Another fun fact: the recipe in the link happens to be from a guy named Stefan... no relation.)

And as long as I'm coming clean, I might as well go one step further and admit that despite my reputation as having highbrow musical tastes, I'm a big <u>Michael Bublé</u> fan. Since Alexa knows this too and has his *Sway* ready to play at all times, I thought his Cha Cha only fitting to be the tune behind Julie and Stefán's first dance.

I can't tell you how many characters in a novel are too many; I just know, because I stop reading and set the book aside. And since keeping track of them in other people's novels annoys me, I put an unspecific but smallish cap on the cast in my own. On the other hand, I have an endless supply of descriptions in my imagination that need to come out somehow, so in *Summer Cyclone* I created Magda, Eye Patch Man, and Cropped Hair Guy. To avoid being recognized, these three fairies change their looks every time they leave their houses, which gives me the opportunity to let my imagination run wild yet keep my cast at a minimum.

Speaking of characters, I believe that chief scientist Lydia Anderson is the only one in the entire series, or in any of my books for that matter, with a first and last name. In her case she bears the maiden name of my maternal grandmother, and I trust that revealing it here will not encourage my readers to attempt to use it for one of my password recovery clues.

My Saudi Arabian prince friend introduced me to the online version of <u>Ludo</u> two years ago. It's a horribly addictive game that's popular in the Middle East. I'm well aware that it's absolutely rigged against me, but the app lets me win just often enough to keep me playing and losing at least once a day to other addicts.

One doesn't have to be too perceptive to observe that all my male characters have great hair. Once upon a time I did, too. So, there, I said it.

For those of you who've read all four books in this series: I really intended to kill off Zsa Zsa. She'd been a most glamorous, wicked, and hilarious villain, and when Györfi took over her body in the middle of the book, I thought that would be the end of her. If you paid attention to the ancestral fairy book that updates itself constantly, though, you would have noticed that she wormed her way out. Whether or not her new incarnation leads to another sequel, I know for certain that I'll need to look over my shoulder for her on my next trip to <u>Orient Bay in St. Martin.</u>

I hope you'll let me know your thoughts on *Magic at Myers Beach*. I always enjoy chatting with my readers, and I hope you won't be shy in approaching me. I'm on most of the social media platforms, and you can find my contact information somewhere in this book. Reviews are always welcomed, too, of course. Authors live and die by them, so remember not to be too cruel.

Look for my new thriller series, due to debut in January 2024.

ACKNOWLEDGMENTS

To Lawrence, for not complaining too much about the time he had to spend alone while I wrote these seventy-two thousand words. To Gabrielle Hersey, my even more indefatigable assistant. And especially to Robin Cutler, my publisher, for believing that I could actually finish the series I started.

CONNECT WITH ALAN

Website: http://alanbgibson.com/

Instagram: https://www.instagram.com/alanbgibson/

Twitter: https://twitter.com/abgibson1

Facebook: https://www.facebook.com/alan.gibson1/

IMBD: https://www.imdb.com/name/nm6561512/

YouTube: https://www.youtube.com/channel/
UCYkZ6C1sv3Ha_bSfViw7Tzw

Amazon author page: https://www.amazon.com/stores/
author/B018UG2AS0

Summer Thunder, Magic at Myers Beach, Book 1

They call him Theos, the King, the handsome and charismatic reigning kite-surfing Champion of the World. But he keeps his real identity and his other title a secret... Crown Prince of a fairy kingdom.

While at a competition in Myers Beach he learns from his father that in an act of revenge, someone contaminated the kingdom's fairy dust supply and set off a pandemic. His father gives him the monumental task of making new dust, which includes finding new sources of its nine elements.

Lily makes and sells fairy figurines in her shop on the Boardwalk called The Fairy Kingdom. Though every day she assures her customers that, "Fairies sweep away bad dreams, make worries disappear, and grant wishes," she doesn't believe in fairies herself. Theos seems an unlikely customer for a fairy figurine, but when he buys one, he takes on a second mission—to convince her that they do.

She gives him a good luck pendant, which sets in motions a series of magical happenings that bring them together and reveal that the small California beach holds the keys to the fairies' survival.

Summer Storm, Magic at Myers Beach, Book 2

The clock is ticking as Theos' kingdom suffers increasing casualties from the contaminated fairy dust and the quest to find the additional ingredients to make a new supply becomes more urgent.

Greta the Witch, the shopkeeper next door to the Fairy Kingdom, longs for fame and fortune and a fairytale romance like her best friend Lily. She meets Dos, an attractive man who is not the royalty she was seeking, but his kindness and a mystical quality in his voice win her over.

But Zsa Zsa Hadju, a rival witch with look-a-like features complicates her budding love relationship and skyrocketing popularity.

Summer Lightning, Magic at Myers Beach Book 3

Theos's brother, Alias, the stunningly handsome surfer once mistaken as a heterosexual beach ne'er do well, turns out to be a brilliant scientist with quirky, mysterious powers and a boyfriend.

As they find additional elements to make fairy dust, Alias' incomplete formula goes haywire with side effects that complicates his effort to save all three fairy kingdoms which now have only two months of fairy dust left.

Alias confronts his past with the Third King and discovers that he is holds a key to solving their kingdom-wide catastrophe.

Summer Cyclone, Magic at Myers Beach, Book 4

With only one month of fairy dust remaining and one more ingredient left to find, Theos, Lily, Zsombor, Greta, Alias, and Christophe must join forces to fight the ones who sabotaged their fairy dust and who continues to threaten the fairies who have relocated to Myers Beach.

Will the fairy dust Alias finally creates from all the elements be strong enough to succeed, or will it take a force even greater?

Previously published under the pen name A. B. GIBSON

The Dead of Winter

Four young professionals pick the wrong weekend to overnight at a family-friendly pumpkin patch B&B. When a scary moonlight hayride spirals into twenty-four hours of deception, they must escape the farm's mayhem to avoid becoming unwilling participants in a horrific family ritual.

High Voltage

When an unassuming hiker fresh off the Appalachian Trail needs extra cash, a curio shop owner in Harpers Ferry, WV, suggests day work at Winters Farm. What seems to be a lucky break leads to a series of unexplained disappearances of fellow hikers, including his own fiancée. After stumbling onto the dark truth about the farm, his frantic search requires a desperate escape from Ma, the farm's kooky owner. But a foreboding electric fence stymies his chance for freedom.

Tracked to Kill

A handsome young billionaire tech superstar goes

missing on the 2100-mile Appalachian Trail. High tech and low tech collide, and the rescue becomes complicated when his uncle's counter-terrorist group learns that a notorious assassin is out to get him first.

No one is who they seem in this intricate and fast-paced plot of global intrigue, revenge, and a ragtag group of colorful hikers with cryptic trail name aliases. Scenic Harpers Ferry, West Virginia, provides the stunning and dramatic backdrop for the unpredictable ending.

OTHER FLORID ROMANCE BOOKS

To be notified of new releases and special promotions from Florid Romance, please join our email list:

https://floridromance.lmbpn.com/about/sign-up-for-our-newsletter/

For a complete list of books published by Florid Romance please visit our website:

https://floridromance.lmbpn.com/

9 798888 786147